Little Man Gone

PHYLLIS LYNN

"......But the truth of it is that the amount of love you feel for someone and the impact they have on you as a person, is in no way relative to the amount of time you have known them."

Ranata

Chapter One

ROD

"Are you ready for me?"

I asked this of the beautiful woman laying beneath me. I inhaled her tantalizing scent as I moved my lips along her cheek line cruising down her neck then further to her full firm breasts.

"Are you wet for me baby?"

She moaned as she moved her hips trying to make contact with my hardness.

"Are you?"

I asked insistently, raising my body, positioning myself to slide effortlessly into her as soon as she gave me the answer I wanted. I was so anxious to be thrusting into her hot pussy, I could feel her eagerness and impatience growing. I liked that, I wanted her so hot for me that surrendering her body to me....

"I, I want to be, but it's been so long for me," she whispered.

"How long baby? You have to tell me how long."

She moaned as she continued to move her hips anxiously against mine.

"Five...five..."

"Five months since..."

"No," she whispered, "five years."

Five years! God that made it almost virginal for her! I needed to be careful, I didn't want to have this be a bad experience for her. I touched her moist swollen lips with my fingertips, she was dripping with desire for me!

"Yes," I whispered, "you are very ready for me."

I raised slightly then looked down to watch as I guided my body inside her. Whoa, that was a rush! She came up to meet me, I pushed deeply into her. As I pulled back, my dick glistened with her wetness.

"Oh, oh," she moaned softly.

"Oh what? Tell me if you like this."

"Yes, you feel so good, I like the way you're, you're....."

"Fucking you? You like the way I'm fucking you?"

"O yes, yes."

She moved her hips in cadence with mine as she grabbed hold of my ass cheeks pulling me deeper inside her, I loved her responsiveness, her hips were like magic!

"Do **you** like this?" she asked as I felt her need to come rising in her! Her breathing was getting faster and deeper, her movements almost desperate.

I kissed her deeply, whispering in her ear.

"I like you. You are beautiful. Your body could be a sculpture. You are perfect from your rounded hips, to your waist that fits between my hands. I want to bury my face in your breasts. I want to see how much hotter you can get!"

I captured her nipple, tugging and sucking on it. I drove deep into her, that was what she needed to go over the edge!

She yelled out my name as she bite my shoulder sending a jolt thru me. I was in bed with a wildcat! I slowed so she could catch her breathe. If the pulsations from her were an indication of the intensity of her orgasm this was definitely a win-win for her.

"Are you good," I asked?

I couldn't keep my lips from her body. I kissed her face, her neck, nibbling on her ear. There was something about her, fucking her was different than any woman I'd been with in a long time, or maybe ever.

"Oh yes, so so good, but you're not." She raised her head, her eyes were full of concern.

"I'm going to be, it's been a long time for you."

She giggled slightly, "But so worth waiting for!"

"Really? I'm that good, huh?" I chided her!

"Yes."

I started to move slowly again, she sighed and nudged my hips.

"I want to be good for you," she smiled shyly, "Can I?"

She didn't have to ask me to fuck her, I was so ready. I drove my dick deep inside her, I moaned, her pussy was still so wet and swollen. I was so anxious for her body as I rolled, she was on top of me, uttering a surprised gasp!

"Ride me baby, if you want to be good for me, ride me."

She blushed, "I've never done it this way." Her voice was breathy, husky, almost whispering.

Her shyness was a mega turn on.

"Put your knees on the bed, place your hands on my shoulders, now raise your hips."

She was as apt a student in bed as she was in my ER as she immediately did as I asked. The first time she brought her hips down to mine I could tell she was going to ace this as she did everything else. She bit her lower lip moaning a deep moan, then she threw her head back and rode me like she had been doing it forever! God. She was beautiful! Her breast bounced as she rode me, as she leaned down to kiss me I caught her nipple, I was almost savage with it. That was what we both needed and wanted.

"Yes, yes, yes." she hissed as she rode me faster and harder. "Oh Rod, I'm going to come, I'm going to come again."

"That's it baby, come with me, come on!"

She did, I did, it was incredible! I yelled out, I couldn't hold it back. Damn! Where had this woman been? Wow!

She collapsed on me. I loved the way her tits were smushed against my chest, we were both wet with the sweat that lovers share.

"Here, lay beside me," I encouraged her.

I helped her to my side. I put my arm around her, kissing her sweet lips. I nipped at the bottom one. She made a noise, teeming with satisfaction as she nuzzled my neck. We laid quietly for a short while, she broke the silence.

"I have to pee, where's your bathroom."

I sat up and pointed to the half open door.

"Switch is on the left."

She got up and walked naked into the bathroom. She had an ass that was fucking perfect, those tits! Best I'd seen and had my hands on in a long time.

I rolled over and looked at the clock. Four AM! We'd been at it for a long time. I know she said she wanted to sleep until 1:00 PM but that wasn't happening at my place. Today was my day with Emmy and she'd be over bright and early brightening my day with her enigmatic smile and endless energy. I hated to end this so quickly but I didn't want to have a woman sleeping in my bed when my daughter was here. If McKenna went home now it would avoid a lot of hassle later this morning. She could sleep all day in her own bed. Emmy and I could have our day together. That was the plan. I went to the kitchen to get a bottle of water when I returned she was sitting up in bed with her legs tucked, half covered by a sheet. I could see the mounds of her ample breast, it made me want to have another go at it but I didn't really have time for that right now. I'd follow up with her later, after all I saw her every single shift I worked.

"Would you like a drink of water?"

I held out my bottle of water to her.

"Drink?"

"No thank you. I don't drink after anyone."

I looked at her in disbelief! That woman had her tongue all over my mouth. Inside it, outside it and practically gave my neck and my right ear a bath and she wouldn't drink after me!

That's thoroughly asinine. Calling a cab for her wasn't going to be as hard as I thought. Geeze, what is her problem?

She started to lay back down.

"Would you like me to call you a cab?"

She sat bolt upright, obviously shocked!

"What?"

"Would you like me to call you a cab?" I repeated slowly.

She looked at me for what seemed like an hour, not blinking an eye then I saw tears begin to fall down her cheeks. Feeling badly for maybe being too abrupt with her I sat down on the bed beside her. As I reached over to touch her, she pushed me away!

"What kind of man are you? You want to call me a cab? Boy was your ex-wife ever right about you! You are a prick! Your semen is still dripping out of me and you want to call me a cab!"

"Now McKenna," I made the mistake of actually touching her and she hit me! She started crying.

"I knew I shouldn't trust you! Leave me alone! I'm not one of your musical bed floozies! I don't sleep around! I'm not like that! I haven't slept with anyone for five years I told you that! I was stupid I made the mistake of thinking you were a nice guy. A good guy. You are a womanizer, you only brought me here for the thrill of the chase! You should be ashamed of yourself!"

She pommeled me with her fists until I finally caught her and tried to calm her down. She pushed me away, she was in a rage! Wow! Can you say 'short fuse' or 'crazy woman'? I stood and looked at her as she yelled at me.

"You got me drunk and took advantage of me! How does that make you feel? Proud of yourself?"

I was getting piqued now!

"Come on McKenna don't make yourself out to be such a naive little lamb! You knew what was going to happen all night!"

"You got me drunk! You plied me with alcohol to skew my judgment!"

"Oh come on! You rubbed your tits against me like it was

your job!"

"Get out! Get out of here! I can't stand the sight of you!"

She boohooed, God she was still some what drunk. I didn't realize that before. She was drunk and out of control!

"There's only a slight problem with me leaving, this is my apartment," now I was yelling while I poked my finger in my own chest to let her know how crazy she sounded.

That only made her cry harder, she was a mess!

"Okay, okay! You stay here and I'll go across the hall and sleep."

I grabbed my pants and dress shirt putting them on quickly not even bothering to put on my shoes as I went across the hall. Not having a key I had to knock on the door. After some wait thank God Helen answered the door.

"What's your problem?" she asked as her calculating eyes gave me the once over.

"I need to sleep here for tonight."

"Like I asked, what's your problem? And it's not actually night."

"I've got a hysterical woman in my bed so I need to sleep here. Is Viv at home?"

"No and you ought to be glad she isn't! What's the hysteria about?"

I knew Helen wouldn't let me in without an explanation, she never gave me a break, so I had to come clean.

"Just a little misunderstanding, she's also a little drunk."

She stood there eyeing me skeptically with her arms folded over her chest in a very closed stance.

"I can guess why she was in your bed to start with, but why did she get hysterical?"

"Because I asked her if she wanted me to call her a cab?"

"How'd she get to your apartment? Just wander in off the street?"

Helen could be such a wise ass!

"Ha ha! No I brought her home with me from a party."

"So she's drunk, she comes home with you, you do your thing and then you want to toss her out!"

"It's not like that Helen. We were both a little drunk."

"How old is this woman?'

"I think she's twenty-seven. She's my resident."

Her eyebrows shot up at that piece of information.

"I think I'd be a little hysterical too if I just had sex with my boss and he tried to show me the door."

"Okay, okay, I'll apologize in the morning. I need to get her up and out of there before Emmy comes home."

She stepped back and let me in the foyer.

"Same room as always. You want me to call you?"

"I got it covered. See you in the morning."

When I said that, I realized I didn't have it covered! I hadn't not worn a condom since the last night I had sex with Viv. Maybe that's why it was so much better tonight, something sure made it different and better. Maybe not better... just more intense. Maybe not more intense just...just. I didn't have the words I needed to describe what had happened between us, I just knew I wanted to experience it again!

CHAPTER TWO

MCKENNA

I never witnessed that sweet side of him until then. I saw him immediately when I walked into the Chief's party room. To say I was impressed by this entire party deal was putting it mildly! Impressed? No. Awed and intimidated? Yes!! Who has so much money you can afford one room in your house that's only used for parties? I wanted to turn right around and go home but Nanette would not let me. Nan was the senior charge nurse on our team. She had welcomed me with open arms when I arrived here at the University of Birmingham six months ago to start my residency. She has continued to nurture me both in and outside the ED. I only came to this party because she wouldn't let me out of coming.

"Nanette I can't stay here, I'm not like the rest of these people. I don't have money, I don't come from some society family and I don't want to hob nob with snobs, that's not me!"

"Stop it. You think Ralph and I come from money? Are we snobbish? Puleese! We are the furthest thing from that. We're here to have a good time, we all work together saving lives, most of the time we don't find things to even smile about, so let your hair down a little. You are a real knock out once you get out of those baggy scrubs! I even had to elbow Ralph when he saw you tonight! Girl you are dynamite!"

She grabbed a drink off a tray as a waiter walked by passing it to me.

"Here sip on this! You look like you need some liquid courage."

I looked down in my drink trying to decide if it was champagne, when Nan started talking to me out of the side of her mouth, like she didn't want anyone to know her lips were moving. That was a laugh 'cause anyone who knew Nan knew if her eyes were open her lips were moving.

"Oh God, here comes the welcoming committee! It's Dr. Curry with that killer smile! Don't look up but I think he's headed straight for us. No straight for you!"

He came up behind me shocking me when he put his warm hand on my elbow.

"Dr. Tipton!"

He said my name as if we were great friends who hadn't seen each other in a long time.

I turned just in time to see him staring at my boobs! God I hated when a man did that. I didn't have gigantic ones but to say I had been blessed in that department was some what of an understatement! That is precisely why I wear baggy scrubs all the time.

"Ralph,"   he   nodded.
He removed his hand from my elbow to shake hands with Nanette's husband.

Leaning down he kissed Nan's cheek. Crap! Crap! Crap! If he did that to me I would pee my pants on the spot! As if they weren't wet enough already with that smile and hand on my elbow deal! He laughed while speaking to Nan, I didn't even hear what was being said, I had to tune back in.

"Thank goodness the life of the party is here! Why don't you come with me and let Ralph take Dr. Tipton to the bar for a decent drink."

He started to walk away when Nan said, "Oh I don't know about that idea, I've already had to give him the stink eye once for ogling her. Maybe you better take McKenna to the bar. I'll keep Ralph here with me -nice and safe."

She smiled at me, her smile saying. 'gotcha'!

I know I was probably already pink when Nan said that but when he looked at me and winked I turned the color of a boiled shrimp!

"You know you're right. That's why you're a hell of an ER nurse, you always think ahead. Come on McKenna let's go to the bar."

And just like that I was no longer Dr. Tipton, I was McKenna! He placed his hand against my bare back to guide me to the bar. I was speechless, not to mention all quivery inside!

"We'll get you a drink then I'll introduce you to Vivian and Dr. Giovenetti. I know you know Viv but I want to brag on you a bit because you've just taken off and made my job as your mentor very easy. What do you want to drink?"

"I'd like a Long Island Iced Tea."

He raised his brow in surprise as he studied me intensely.

"Really? I didn't take you for that kind of girl."

Wow! That was insult if I ever heard one, 'that kind of girl' just because I wanted a Long Island Iced Tea. We weren't in the ED so I didn't have to "yes sir" everything he said. He just insulted me for no reason. I don't know why that bothered me but it did. So I straightened my back and snapped. "And what kind of GIRL would that be Dr. Curry?"

He laughed at me.

"It's Rod and don't get your panties in a wad, unless of course you intend to throw them in my direction." He said smugly.

I couldn't help it, I gasped! He leaned in close whispering, "In case you haven't noticed McKenna we're at a god damned office party which in itself is very boring, so let's lighten this place up."

He straightened up and asked the bartender for my drink.

I was so turned on and embarrassed, I couldn't look at

him, that hand on my elbow again!

"Really McKenna, I'm sorry if I've offended you with my familiarity but we work side by side every day being so professional. Tonight we're here to have a good time, so can you let that fun side of you out of it's box? I know you have one because I've seen it at work with other people. What do you say?"

What he said made perfect sense. I hadn't spent over two hundred bucks of my hard earned dollars on a dress to come here and be in work mode so I gave him my best smile.

"You're right I'm sorry. I've just have been in serious mode for so long with med school then this residency, it's hard to step away from it."

"You're not a doctor tonight, you are a beautiful young woman here to enjoy yourself.

Here's your drink, now let's go meet the powers that be."

He took my hand leading me to the other side of the room.

"Dr. Giovenetti I want you to meet my protege', Dr. McKenna Tipton. McKenna this is our illustrious leader and his assistant Dr. Curry."

It was like he got special delight in introducing her as Dr. *Curry, maybe being a little snide.*

"Dr. Giovenetti it's a pleasure to meet you and you as well Dr. Curry."

Dr. Giovenettii's smile was warm as he offered me his hand. Dr. Curry's smile- not so warm!

She looked for all the world like she was jealous but she certainly had nothing to be jealous of on my part. First of all her "man" wasn't interested the least bit in me, and secondly as I heard it she was the one who divorced him, it was over six or seven years ago, so pull the claws in honey, I am not a threat.

"Dr. Tipton, Dr. Curry." She nodded at both of us, nothing friendly or congenial in her greeting!

She had to be pushing fifty, still drop dead gorgeous, with

a killer figure. I found myself wondering if she had work done!

"Viv, I have to thank you for this one," he continued on after introducing me, "She is top of the line. Six months and hardly needs mentoring at all. Spot on with her diagnoses, knows her procedures, she even talked another doc, not a resident I might add, thru putting in an art line! Did a damn good job! And beautiful on top of all that! I think we need to work on recruiting her when her she finishes up next year."

Dr. Curry, "VIV" laughed, "Rod you always were one to jump to conclusions on very little evidence/! Never taking time to form a solid opinion. Judging everyone and everything by what's on the surface only."

His eyebrow shot up! I looked at Dr. Giovenetti who looked a bit embarrassed, I could feel the color leave my face. That was a low blow! She didn't even know me. The day I interviewed with her she barely looked at me, all she looked at were the scores of my boards.

"I apologize Vivian, I forget that it is always your opinion in ALL things that holds the most weight. Dr. Tipton, forgive me. I misspoke. My opinion holds no value in any affairs involving Dr. Curry." He nodded his head curtly at "Viv", turning he smiled, "Dr. Giovenetti we'll move on, sorry to have interrupted your conversation."

"No need to hurry on Rod. We were just chit chatting, nothing of any importance."

Dr. Giovenetti's smile was genuine.

"Nah, catch you later Lou," He nodded in Viv's direction again, "Dr. Curry."

He put his arm around my waist as he led me away.

"Shall we get you another drink?"

I hadn't realized it but my glass was empty, I must have stood there guzzling down that entire drink.

Crap! Dr. G probably thinks I'm a sot!

"Uh, sure. I need to go to the ladies room."

"Down this hall, second door on the left. Why don't you

meet me on the veranda?"

Veranda? Again, such posh! Who has a porch big enough to be called a veranda. Man, I really was out of my league here! I found the bathroom easily, it looked like it was straight out of some 40's movie set, again very POSH. Just as I was washing my hands guess who waltzes into the bathroom? None other than good ole VIV!

She glanced into the mirror as she got out her lipstick, pausing to look at me before she started to apply it.

"He's a player you know."

I had just about had it up to here with Queen Vivian! Dr. Curry was right, this was a social gathering and there was no reason to bow and scrape before her. That alcohol was making me brave!

"And why would that be of importance to me?"

"Because I saw what he was doing." Her tone was so denigrating.

"Really, I thought he was introducing me to the host of this party and my big boss."

When I said "big boss" I hoped she got the inference that more than her opinion counted when it came to my staying or leaving at the end of my residency.

"On the surface that's what it appeared to be, but he's just trying to get you to go to bed with him."

"Why are you so sure about that?"

"Because that's who he is, he can fool anyone!"

"Anyone as in who?"

I was out for blood! How dare she insinuate I was some bimbo who slept my way thru med school and intended to do the same with this residency.

"As in who," I repeated.

She still didn't answer.

"You mean anyone as in you? Especially you?"

I think I shocked her.

She still didn't answer me.

"Dr. Curry, I have no interest in your husband.."

"My ex-husband."

She corrected me at warp speed!

"Really because you act like he's still your husband. As I was saying, I have no interest in Dr. Curry except as my mentor. I knew exactly nothing about him except his reputation as the guru of emergency medicine when I applied for this residency, my only interest was in getting the most from someone who is tops in his field. After working with him for six months I know I made the right decision and it's not based on his looks or his pick up lines. I can learn so much from this man, things they don't teach in books. That is why I came here and that is why I go to work every shift anxious to learn something they didn't teach me in books."

"You're just his type you know," she persisted.

"No I don't know, and even if I did I wouldn't let a lapse in judgment think it was okay to go to bed with my boss which is something he apparently didn't understand."

That was so mean of me to say, not only mean but vicious and I was not that kind of person. Again I could only blame it on alcohol! I really did feel badly because she acted like I had slapped her in the face! I was ashamed but I wasn't going to apologize so I turned around and walked out.

The first person I saw was Nan. She had a worried look on her face.

"What went on in there? I saw her follow you in."

I could feel the tears come as the anger fell away from me. I swallowed hard.

"I'm fine, I'll tell you about it later."

I went to the veranda, I needed that drink Dr. Curry had promised me. He greeted me with a big smile.

"I thought maybe you changed your mind after that little display of rudeness by Vivian."

"No, I'm, I'm fine."

"Really because I'm certain I see one lonely tear drop right here."

Reaching over he used his little finger to brush away the tear on my left cheek.

"I'm really sorry about that. I don't know what precipitated her actions."

"Maybe she was jealous."

He threw back his head and laughed like I'd never heard him do before!

"Well she had a strange way of showing it. She played a number on me. She wanted the divorce, not me. She wasn't through playing around as she put it. But that's enough of that, that ship sailed a long time ago, the heartache was well worth it, I have a beautiful seven year old daughter who keeps ole dad on the straight and narrow."

"Not too straight and narrow if what the nurses say is true."

He laughed again, "So I'm a legend in my own time?"

"According to ER 101 you are." I quipped.

"You know you're quite funny when you turn off that serious dial."

"I go to work to learn, that's why I'm there. That's all I'm interested in right now, that's all I have time for."

"So you don't have an interest in knowing why I study you and what you do all the time?"

"That's your job as my mentor."

"I agree, but only 50% of my interest is in being your mentor. The other 50% is personal."

"What do you want to know Dr. Curry? I'm not a very deep person. Pretty much what you see is what you get."

"Oh but I think you are- deep and interesting. Maybe mysterious is a better word."

It was my turn to laugh!

"Not so. I am from the hills of West Virginia, I got a scholarship to West Virginia University, graduated summe cum laude and went on to Johns Hopkins Medical School, worked my tail off there to be at the head of my class so I could be first pick for an ER residency."

"You're right that isn't mysterious, I can read CVs, but what about you? What interests you besides ER medicine? Who do you live with here or do you live by yourself? What hobbies do you have? If you couldn't be a doctor what else would you have chosen for your life's work?"

God this guy is deep. At least he wants to get to know me before he tries to get in my pants, that is if what "Viv" says is true.

"Well if I couldn't be in emergency medicine, theater would have been my second choice. And don't wrinkle your nose, it too is an honorable profession. Who do I live with? It's just my sister and me. Our parents have been gone a long time, we were raised by an uncle who was drunk most of the time. Don't you dare even think about feeling sorry for me because I came out all right and so did my sister. We share an apartment here. She's an investment banker, has her MBA from Harvard. And yes, she went on scholarship just like I did."

"Why would you think I would feel sorry for you?"

"Because your kind always does."

"I'm not sure what my kind is." He sounded a bit piqued!

"You rich kids or as the professors used to say, "students with means" always sat in groups, walked in groups, talked in groups, ate in groups and pretty much looked askance at us poor kids like we might steal your wallet if you totally ignored us."

"Well I can assure you Miss Johns Hopkins that I wasn't one of those kids. My parents, my mother especially made me work at an after school job all thru high school and college. She cut me some slack my last year of undergrad before I started to medical school, and it was probably a good thing she did or I would have flunked out. I was one of those kids who couldn't sit still long enough to read the things I needed to know and do in med school and hold down a job. My mom realized that, she is a special woman,"

"She was raised poor?"

"Oh no, no! My mother is or was one of Richmond's elite, she just doesn't live there anymore, but my grandmother, her mother still does and believe me she is the snobbiest of the snobs. Old money. That doesn't impress me. Even though I'm my Gran's favorite she's still embarrassed to mention my name in some circles!"

"What does your mom do?"

"She and my dad are retired."

"What did she do?"

"She was a surgeon and my father was an ENT."

"Wow! Talk about credentials!" I scoffed!

"Listen to me McKenna Tipton I don't believe in legacy in anything. I think each person should succeed or fail on his or her own merits."

He started to walk away. Dang! I just insulted my boss!

"I'm sorry," I said quickly.

"Sorry doesn't cut it sometimes Tipton."

He walked thru the door and disappeared!

"He went out of here like a bat out of hell didn't he," Ralph was laughing as he stepped from the shadows.

"What are you doing out here?"

"Nan sent me out here to see if you were okay. She said you were crying. I needed a smoke break anyway."

"Why are rich people so touchy, always getting their feelings hurt? I'm poor and you could tell me a lot of societal traits that go along with being poor but if I'm not that way, I wouldn't get mad at you and walk away."

"Hey, I refilled your drink."

Rod reappeared handing me another Long Island Iced Tea, he noticed Ralph and turned to go. Ralph beat him to the punch.

"I gotta go back inside McKenna. I don't smell too much like cigarette smoke do I?"

I had to laugh at Ralph as he leaned toward me.

"To any one who smokes you're fine, to anyone who doesn't smoke you're bearable."

"Thanks girl, see you later," he kissed my cheek and winked before leaving.

I stood by the railing actually sipping my drink this time. I didn't know what to say, I figured he'd leave with Ralph but he didn't.

"Can you leave your drink here and come walk with me down to the lake? This is a sweet place, you'll love it."

"I'd love to but I can't in these stilettos, I don't want to ruin them."

"Set your drink down, now raise your arms up."

When I set my drink down and raised my arms up above my head he picked me up flinging me over his shoulder. What was wrong with this man?

"Hey put me down you dumb galoot!"

"I would put you down if I knew what a galoot is."

"It's a man who has more brawn than brains!"

He howled with laughter!

"Now babe, you know that is not true, because I do have a lot of brains and a reasonable amount of brawn, however I'll put you down because we have reached our destination."

He set me down and turned me around. I know my mouth dropped open in awe!

"Oh Dr. Curry this is so breathtaking."

I was so touched by what I saw. It looked like a scene from a Thomas Kincaide painting. We stood by a lake that was so quiet and serene, made more picturesque by the slight haze drooping over it. The darkness hung over us like a canopy, not a star in the sky. You could hear the soft wailing of loons in the distance.

He turned me to face him, placing his hands on my shoulders, looking directly into my eyes. God he is so hot!

"My name is Rod. If you call me Dr. Curry one more time I'm going to give you a hickey on your neck in a very noticeable place!"

I couldn't help it, I snickered! I was high enough on alcohol to be losing some my inhibitions.

"Oh," was my best response.

"You've been warned McKenna. Got it?"

"Yes ROD I've got it!" I snickered again.

"Damn girl, I bet you are a lot of fun when you really loosen up."

"I don't know ROD, why don't you try and see." I snickered again! My snickers were definitely alcohol induced.

"Well enough seen down here, time to get you back to the alcohol."

He picked me up and threw me over his shoulder again then smacked me on my rear end!

I giggled and started singing "Row Row Row Your Boat" the best I could, flung over his shoulder like that. Why I did that I'll never know. When we got close to the house he smacked my ass again!

"Enough singing!"

He set me down, I didn't have good footing after walking in those stilettos so I fell right into him. I couldn't help it I had wet panties in a second! I looked up at him not saying a word.

"Oh McKenna, I want to kiss you so badly but there are too many people watching."

"If your ex-wife is watching, please do."

I was still slightly annoyed at her. Only annoyed and not angry due to the effects of alcohol.

"No believe me, that's the last person you want to see me doing that to your beautiful lips."

He opened the door as we walked in, no one seemed to notice we'd been gone.

"Let me get you another drink,"

"Let's dance first."

There was a band playing swing music and if there was one thing I could do well besides being a doctor it was dancing!

We were dirt poor but drunk Uncle Abe always saved enough for us to have dancing lessons. He'd come watch us at our recitals like it was best thing we'd ever done. We never had the right costumes and if we did they probably weren't clean but we were there and on that stage dancing! He was proud of us.

Rod was a good dancer, easy to follow. I was a little inhibited because my skirt was short and straight but he seemed to enjoy it. I started to walk way when the song ended. He caught my hand, pulling me back toward him, enclosing me in his arms.

"My turn to ask you to dance."

Wow, he pulled my hips tight against his, there was no doubt that dancing wasn't the only thing on his mind! I don't know what possessed me to do it but I ground my breasts into his chest and laid my head against him then I suddenly realized where I was and who I was dancing with. My boss for god's sake!

After that dance we went back to the bar where I practically chugged down another Long Island Iced Tea thinking about how I had acted with him. We danced some more, it seemed where ever I was he was there too. At one point when we were slow dancing he asked what my plans were after this party was over.

"I'm going home, get into my ratty PJs and sleep until one o'clock tomorrow."

"You're going home by yourself?"

"That's what I usually do."

"How about I go home with you?'

I wanted to slap him!

"I am not your kind of girl, and even if I was you're my boss and we both could get into trouble."

"What kind of girl is 'my kind'?

"The kind who plays musical beds! I'm not like that. I've only been to bed with two guys and it was a mistake both times, even though they were both long term relationships."

"Just because I date those kind doesn't necessarily mean that's what I'm looking for McKenna."

"Please. I'm going to forget this conversation."

He must have agreed, he didn't say anything else about it the rest of the night.

I continued to drink Long Island Iced Teas, and he continued to flirt with me. We began to talk more, he seemed very sweet at least that's what my alcohol addled brain told me. When it came midnight he was there to welcome the new year in and give me a kiss that made my toes curl, and wrecked my panties for the second time!

Shortly after that kiss Nanette and Ralph came offering to see me home safely since I had been drinking.

"I'll see she gets home. I have to get a cab I've been drinking too much, I don't want to wind up in an ER somewhere, I might see someone I know!"

We all laughed.

"I'd like to go now, I'll just go with Nan."

"Yeah you can spend the night with us. We've got plenty of room." she encouraged me.

"Why don't you let me see she gets home. She already told me she has a hot date with some ratty PJs!"

I should have been embarrassed by the referral to my 'ratty PJs' but with my friend alcohol sticking with me I wasn't.

"Yeah, he can get a cab for me. I'll be fine. I'll call you tomorrow." A definite lapse in my judgment.

Nan raised her eyebrows at me, "OK if you insist." She hesitated giving me the opportunity to change my mind.

They walked reluctantly away.

"Do you have a wrap?"

"No".

I almost followed it with I spent all my money on this dress so I left my ratty sweater at home tucked away with my ratty PJs!

"Let's go." He took my hand.

As we stood waiting for a cab he put his hand on my bare back gently making circles barely touching my skin with his fingertips!

He looked down at me. I know he wanted to see if it was affecting me. IT was, big time, but I wasn't about to let him know that. Getting no response he reached down kissing my shoulder, I shivered, I couldn't help it!

He put his arm around my waist pulling me to him, his hand came to rest on the side of my breast. God! He was killing me! Mr. Alcohol was doing all my thinking, so I didn't even resist.

After helping me in the cab he got in beside me, he didn't even ask for my address, he gave the cabby his, and turned to me.

"Please, may I kiss you again."

I didn't answer I couldn't, I just turned my face to his. If I thought the first kiss was a panty wetter, this far exceeded it. I was goner and I knew it. I had enough alcohol to justify what we were doing. It had been a long time since I had been with a man, a very long time and he seemed just like the one to end my drought! I was very enamored by him. It also had been a long time since I had a serious 'crush' and he was it! When he sauntered into the ER that first day and introduced himself I wondered what he looked like without clothes on, wanting me! I heard all the nurses talk about him, how good he was in bed and it crossed my mind multiple times in the six months I'd been here that I was seriously attracted to him. He never even so much as looked sideways at me, at least I didn't think he had until he said he did tonight. I had to be truthful to myself I wanted him now and I knew he wanted me. Maybe he wasn't such a player after all, maybe he did want a 'some one special'.

By the time we got out of that cab going up to his apartment in the elevator we were practically tearing each others clothes off. Well not practically, we were. He unzipped my dress and I let it fall as I stepped out of it right inside the door of his apartment! When I turned around he unfastened my strapless bra dropping it to the floor! I grabbed hold of the buttons on his tux shirt and ripped everyone off in one jerk.

"Damn girl! Working trauma has taught you some tricks!"

He laughed as he put his hands on my breast, slowly rubbing my nipples between his thumb and index finger. He leaned over, put his mouth on my nipple sucking on it. I was about to come it had been so long! He pushed my panties down and when I stepped out of them he put them to his nose and inhaled. I could tell he liked my scent!

I had to touch him! He was big and hard! I placed my hand over the tip gently fingering it, he moaned. Then I leaned over kissing the tip.

"McKenna if you do that I'm going to erupt like a volcano. I want you on the bed."

I think I practically ran to his bed, when I laid down he smiled at me, "You are so so fucking beautiful, looking at and touching your breast alone makes me get hard."

He practically worshiped my boobs as he kissed and sucked on them. My breast were my 'on' switch! I couldn't lay still, I was on fire! He kissed down my belly threading his fingers into me to feel my wetness. He laid between my legs, the head just touching me, he was poised to enter me, then he asked me if I was ready! I had to tell him it had been so long. I wanted him to know that so if I wasn't totally ready maybe he would understand. He kissed me again and again, talking with me, being really patient. When he finally entered me I was so ready! The chemistry between us was like firecrackers on the fourth of July! That's how hot it was! His thrusts were deep and powerful then he rolled over putting me on top! I had never been on top before but judging from his reaction at the time it was a win win for both of us! I felt great, I was so satisfied! There was such a feeling of tenderness from him after he was satisfied. I truly felt like he had made love to me, not just "fucked" me. Even thinking about the word 'fuck' made me uncomfortable. Laying beside him was perfect, just perfect until he asked, "Do you want me to call a cab?" His semen was still leaking out of me and he wanted to call a cab! God! What kind of man was this? His ex-wife knew what she was talking about! *I* was so angry at him, I wanted to hit him and I did. I don't know what came over me, well yes I do. I was embarrassed, disappointed in me and him too. I don't know why I thought he was any different than any other man just because he was great in ER medicine. Now here I lay, bawling my eyes out at four o'clock in the morning and to make matters worse he left me here. Of course he could go Viv's! They were probably still involved and that's why she was so jealous. Here I sat, arms around my knees rocking back and forth clueless as to what to do. This was bad but the very worst part is I either had to call Nan or wait until he got back in the morning to borrow money for a cab because I left my purse in the cab last night. It didn't have any ID or credit cards only forty dollars and my phone. Since I couldn't cry any more I decided I needed to lay down and sleep. What else can I do?

CHAPTER THREE

ROD

I woke up with a slight headache but pushed it aside as I let myself out of Viv's quietly and tip-toed into my apartment in case she was still there. Whoo- no clothes on the floor! You're the man Curry! I fisted my hand in the air in victory! Yep she was gone.

I needed a cup of coffee so I headed for the kitchen almost stepping on Poseidon.

"God dog, what are you doing laying in the middle of the floor? Take that thing and go to your bed and chew on it."

Dutifully he got up to go to his bed to finish destroying whatever he had in this mouth.

Something shiny caught my eyes, God it looked like metal.

"What have you gotten into boy, you could kill yourself chewing on metal. Here give it to me."

As I reached for it, he dropped it on the floor. When I saw what it was I just wished I could go back and change the last 48 hours of my life no matter how good it was to fuck that woman! It was a black strapless bra, rather it used to be a black strapless bra! It was mauled, holey, and wet as could be. I scolded Posey who tried look as contrite as a Great Dane could, telling him he didn't chew on human things. What bothered me is why she would leave without her bra. It would have been pretty noticeable in that dress she wore if she didn't have one on. The top was black see thru lace, her nipples would have shown thru, she didn't even have a jacket to cover herself.

Suddenly I realized she didn't leave without her bra! I walked to Posey's bed and found her panties, pantyhose, and her dress. Her dress didn't look too bad, but that dog enjoyed that woman's pussy as much as I had judging by what was left of her panties. Well at least he got the juicy part! Her pantyhose were shredded, and one shoe was completely wrecked, the other was pretty much intact except the heel was gone. I picked up the second shoe and almost pissed myself! God-these were Jimmy Choo's! He had just destroyed a pair of Jimmy Choos! That was an expensive chew toy, probably $800 shoes! Well I would have to replace those, although I don't think she would want me to buy her a bra and panties. If we parted on better terms I might have offered to replace them if she agreed to model them for me. Umm! That woman had a body under those baggy scrubs, those tits! Um,um. The best I'd ever seen or tasted. I'm going to have to fight off thoughts of that body. I wasn't sure I could look at her in those scrubs and not remember the real thing.

I knew I was wasting time, I had to face the music sometime. I put what was left of her clothes in a bag and went to my laundry room for a clean T shirt and sweat pants.

I took a big breathe and knocked on the door, she didn't answer. I knocked a little louder, still no answer so I opened the door and walked in, JUST as SHE walked out of the bathroom naked!! She didn't see me, she bent over to get back in bed, God what a view and I almost missed it. I started to get hard imagining myself standing behind her...stop stop, quit acting like a teen-age boy who just got his first piece last night. I had to salvage this situation.

"Ahem" I cleared my throat.

She screamed then realized it was me. Her scream brought Posey roaring into the room.

He ran right to her, jumped on the bed and sat beside her.

I expected her to scream again but she didn't.

"Aw, you have a dog," she cooed, at which point he laid down beside her.

"You are so handsome, what is your name." An editorial question but I answered any way.

"Poseidon."

"Well that's a big name for a big guy!" She gushed at that dog and hardly even looked at me. Damn.

She made over that dog and he loved it. He laid down on his back so she could rub his belly. He barely did that for me, but I guess he felt they were well acquainted since he chewed her panties, especially the crotch part!

"Gee, if I knew you loved dogs so much I would have had him ask you about the cab."

I thought I was being funny, her only reaction was, "Ha, ha. He's about the only redeeming quality you have."

I chose to ignore that remark.

"Listen McKenna there's a couple of things we need to deal with."

"A couple?" She gave me a look of pure disgust.

"Just please listen to what I have to say about this situation then we'll talk about today's situation."

"We don't have a situation today. I just need to call my sister! Shit, my phone was in my bag."

"What bag?"

"I left my evening bag in the cab."

"What!"

"I didn't have any thing of value, just my phone and $40."

"Don't you need to stop your phone service or something? Is your phone locked?"

"Yes and it's a flip phone that I've had for fifteen years. I need a new one. I don't have anything stored in there not even phone numbers, I keep them all in my head."

"Good. Now to get back to last night. I'm sorry if I came across the wrong way."

"And what wrong way would that be?" She really was snappish!

I scratched the side of my neck, knowing what I wanted to say was not what was the truth and not what she wanted to hear!

""Well?"

"McKenna I am a player. I know I tried to pass myself off as something else and that was dishonest and immature of me."

"Now you develop a conscience?"

"Let me finish! See, you've been this itch I couldn't scratch since about the second or third time I worked with you. I am used to women throwing themselves at me, well not throwing themselves but they are always the one to make the first move."

"And do you want to know why you let them make the first move?"

"I'm lazy."

"That's part of it, but then you don't have to feel guilty when you don't call them again because after all you didn't initiate it."

God this woman was smart! A lot smarter than me. I had never thought about why I did it but that made perfect sense. Also because the last woman I pursued let me catch her then worked me over like a farmer plowing a field!

"You might be right about that..'

"And your ex-wife was right about you."

"What did wonderful Vivian have to say about me and when did she say it?"

"Last night after you introduced me to her and Dr. Giovenetti, she followed me into the bathroom."

"Wow, that's pretty low, even for Viv. So what did she say?"

"She just said I was your type and you were a player."

"How did you respond to that?"

"It really doesn't matter how I responded, you... are a

player and you were playing me like a fiddle just like she said and for being as smart as I am I didn't even see it.."

Damn! She started to cry again, not sobbing mad like, more like a child does when it's hurt. Curry is there no end to your bad habits? I started toward her.

"Don't. Don't you dare take another step toward me. I'm fine. I'm more angry than anything else."

"Angry at me?"

"No angry at myself. I've avoided men like you for five years and a moment of poor judgment caused me to be stupid."

"I just feel bad about how this has turned out."

"Well probably not bad enough to not do it again," she snapped!

"You're right. The next time I'll just make sure it's someone not as..as... as fragile as you."

"Fragile? Is that your way of saying crazy?"

I had to laugh at her. We had worked side by side for six months and never really had a conversation. She was pretty damn cute even when she wasn't drunk!

"No not crazy at all McKenna, just a wee bit more particular about who you let between your sheets then most women!"

"I think the word is screw or fuck!"

"Okay, call it what you want, carnal relations, shagging, I don't know... the wild thing?"

"Doesn't it make you sad to know that whoever you decide to marry or just live with..."

"Doesn't it make me sad what?"

"I don't know. I put a different value on sex than other women. To me sex is not casual, I'm giving away a part of myself that I'll never get back again. It's like when you fall in love with someone you give them a piece of your heart and no matter if you live together happily for fifty years or break up the next month, you never ever get that part of yourself back."

"I guess if you put it that way it is sad but..."

"But let me guess, you've never given a part of yourself, it's pleasure for a moment and that's all you want. That gratification that lasts how long? Until you get out of bed, until you fall asleep, or in my case until the cab is called."

I sat there and stared at her, she was deep!

"Don't worry Dr. Curry, you'll never be anything to me but Dr. Curry, my mentor who not only taught me about ER medicine but that life is not always the way it appears to be. I'm not a kiss and tell person, even if I was I'd be too embarrassed to tell anyone I slept with you. No one will ever know what went on between us. Is this a solution to today's situation?" Her tone was catty at best!

I sat looking at her. She just handed me the worst compliment a woman could ever give a man, she was embarrassed to admit she had sex with me! Even after ending five years without sex it still wasn't good enough to talk about!

"Well for what it's worth I thought that sex with you was pretty great. You are a very responsive woman even though you try to deny your sexuality. Why I'm not sure, because I'm certain there are plenty of men....."

"Please, you can't be as dense as you act! I just sat here and told you why I don't have casual sex and you act like you think I'm some freak of nature denying my sexuality. Recognizing my sexuality and having sex are at opposite ends of the spectrum. So maybe I'm stuck at one end, but admit it Curry you're stuck at the other. I like going to bed knowing I can control my appetite for sex, not like a mongrel dog in heat."

"Now wait a minute! You better not be comparing me to a dog."

"I'm not, you are! This is the end of this discussion. Again, what is the situation for today?"

I didn't even know how to broach this huge faux pas!

"Ah,....the situation is in this bag. Here,"

I handed her the bag which she dumped out on the bed. She picked up each piece and looked at it, she gasped when she came to the shoes!

I expected her to lose it, but she didn't, another major difference between her and the other women I had in my bed.

"I know those shoes cost a lot so I'll replace them and I'll have your dress dry cleaned if you leave it here. I can replace the other stuff if you want me to but I think buying something intimate for you would cause a rift in your conscience."

"It's fine. You don't need to replace anything, You didn't drag me here I came on my own, it's the price I pay for being indiscriminate."

I was mad now! Red hot mad!

"Good lord McKenna don't you ever give yourself a fucking break! Indiscriminate my ass! You were a guest in my house and my animal which I'm supposed to have under my control destroyed some very valuable property that belongs to you. I will replace those shoes and I don't want to hear another word about it."

She sat looking at me, rather thru me.

"Yes Dr. Curry what ever you say. May I borrow some of your clothes to wear home and money for a cab? I'll pay you back on our next work day."

"McKenna don't, please. I feel bad enough, don't act like you're a freaking slave. Look me in the eye when you talk to me. And I'm not loaning you money for a cab. I'll take you home."

"I don't think so. That doesn't look very good."

"For god's sake, no one we know will see us. And if they do I'm just giving you a lift because you lost your purse and your wallet. Here is something for you to wear, sorry as much as a **douche as** you think I am I don't have a collection of women's underwear stashed away in case my dog decides to make a meal of my guests under clothing!"

She snickered, then she just laid back on the bed and howled with laughter! God how I wanted her! I wanted to pounce on her turning her laughter into moaning! Suddenly she saw me looking at her, she sat up immediately.

"Sorry." she said, "but you have to admit it's pretty funny!"

"Now you find something to laugh about! Come out when you're ready, I made some coffee."

"Thank you I could use a cup, and do you have some Tylenol?"

"I don't know, might have children's. But I know I do have ibuprofen 400 mg."

"Ibuprofen is fine."

I headed to the kitchen to wait on her.

I heard her come out of the bedroom.

"You drink yours black don't you?"

"Yes."

Poseidon followed her out of the bedroom and sat at her feet. We sat in silence drinking our coffee when my door flies open as Emma comes running thru jumping in my lap!

She kneed me right in the balls, I let out a yelp!

"Oh sorry Daddy did I hit your sore rib again."

"Yes sweetheart." I grunted!

I could barely talk, McKenna snickered! Immediately Emma turned to her.

"Hi."

"Hi yourself." McKenna smiled at her.

"Who is this woman Daddy, is she the cleaning lady?"

McKenna and I both howled at that! That was too good!

"What's so funny? She's dressed in old clothes, isn't she here to clean?"

"No Petals, she works with Daddy and, well.... Posey jumped on her and tore her clothes so I had to lend her some of mine."

"I promise to bring them back," McKenna held up her hand as if to do the Girl Scouts pledge.

"She's not one of those ladies Mommy says I'm not supposed to ask about, is she?" She whispered this loudly.

"I'm not sure why Mommy says you shouldn't ask me about my friends, but no McKenna is not one of those ladies."

"So she's not your friend?"

"Emma my name is McKenna and I'm actually like a student of your dad's. I'm a new doctor and he's teaching me all about emergency medicine. I came all the way from Baltimore, Maryland to study under your daddy. Now can you tell me something about yourself."

Study under me! That was a poor choice of words! I coughed to disguise my laugh.

"I'm Emma but you already know that. Emma Elizabeth, named after my two grandmothers, only one died. Mommy's mommy died when I was a little baby so I never got to go visit her but Grandma Emma lives two hours away so I get to visit her a lot.

That's Daddy's mommy, and when Daddy scolds me she laughs and tells me my daddy was a 'case' when he was growing up. I didn't understand that and great grandma Gran told me that meant he never listened and had to learn everything the hard way. Now I don't know what the hard way means but I don't care because I'm sure it means my daddy wasn't perfect growing up. My mommy says she never got in trouble when she was growing up. She was pretty much perfect. I want to grow up to look just like my mommy and act nice like my daddy. Mommy always gets cross when she's worked hard all day but Daddy doesn't because he says that's why God made doctors so they have to work hard to help people get better. So I just come over to my daddy's when my mommy's cross."

I saw McKenna raise her eyebrows at that little speech, surprised she didn't snicker again!

"Well it's very nice to meet you. I've asked your daddy to take me home because I left my purse in a cab on the way over here."

"Emmy, hop back to Mom's house and I'll take you for ice cream when I get back, you have to eat all your lunch."

Emma got down and almost curtsied, "It was so nice to me you Miss McKenna, I hope we get to talk again. Real soon when you come to see my daddy again."

"Off Emma, I'll be right back."

We started to walk out side when I realized McKenna didn't have any shoes on.

"Gosh, I'm sorry. Let me at least get you some socks. You wait here I'll bring my car from the garage."

I thought it was the least I could do since I didn't have any extra Jimmy Choos laying around.

"It's okay. I can walk."

"No! Stay here I'll be right back."

CHAPTER FOUR

MCKENNA

Dr. Curry sure drove a fancy car, I think it was a Porsche. I would have asked but it was almost like admitting not only had I been poor but I was also dumb!

"Your car smells new."

"That's because I just got it last month. Emma helped me pick the color, I'm not really a pearlized cream person but she liked it. It was a small concession. She's a great kid. I'm so fortunate to be able to live close so she's not one of these kids who lives one week with mommy then the next week with daddy. I know that has to be hard on a kid. Kids thrive on continuity, they love knowing what to expect, even if it's hot dogs and beanie weenies every Friday night, they know what to expect."

I didn't say anything, I didn't know how to respond to that. I was silent all the way to my apartment. When we got there he started to come around and open my door but I was out of the car before he could get there.

"This isn't a date. You don't have to get the door for me."

I didn't want or need his help getting out of a stupid car!

"No this isn't a date! This is a gentleman treating a lady with courtesy."

He was gritting his teeth by this time, "So the next time let me get the fucking door!"

He slammed the passenger door and was in the car so fast

he was gone before I knew it!

I didn't care if he was mad at me! If he wanted to act like a petulant teenager that was his problem. Right now I was tired and needed to sleep since I hadn't slept well the night before despite the alcohol.

I took off his sweat pants but left his T shirt on. Even though it had just been laundered it still smelled of him. All of a sudden I was overcome with a sadness I couldn't identify. I started to cry. Why had I let myself go to his place and let him make love to me. It was the hottest sex I'd ever had. Maybe it was only the hottest because I didn't have much experience! I had fantasized about that man and he was everything I thought he would be, except I was just his toy for the night and then he threw me away. I had given a part of myself to him and he didn't even know it! And if he did he didn't even care!

I woke up about 7 PM when my sister and her boyfriend came in. They were laughing and singing! What was *their* problem?

"Hey guys, there's some people trying to sleep around here! Be courteous," I grouched as I came out of my room.

"Oh McKenna you would have loved the concert! It was jam packed, people upon top of people, everyone singing and having a good time! Birmingham was beautiful at midnight. We had such a great time! Please promise me you'll go the next time. Simon has a friend, you met him at a bar one night, he's hot to go out with you. He really is a nice guy, isn't he Simon?"

"Yeah, Ken, he's super nice. Got a good job, wants a family, but not right now. He thinks you'd be a lot of fun! He said just thinking about going out with a doctor turns him on. Why don't you give him a chance?"

"Okay, okay! I'll think about it. Now that you guys woke me up I'm really hungry. There's not much to eat here, how about we go out for Chinese."

"Sounds good to me. Where's that place you go for lunch?

You always rave about it?" My sister Paige asked Simon.

"Peking House sounds good to me too, it's a little ways across town if you girls can wait I can too,"

"Yeah, let's go. Let me go change clothes."

"Hey whose clothes do you have on?" Paige suddenly noticed the over sized T shirt and sweat pants I had put back on.

"This guy I know! I'll tell you about it later!"

It's a good thing my sister has ADD because it was easy to distract her!

"Ok. We'll meet you in the car."

I broke my previous record of six minutes and was ready to go in four. Simon was right it was a good forty five minutes away. My sister talked all the way there. I was hungry, I was tired and still hadn't gotten over the disappointment of last night so I was ready to tell her to stick a sock in it! Thank goodness when we got there it was not super busy so we were seated right away. I looked up from my menu to see Emma and an older woman come out of the bathroom! If I had any idea of going to the bathroom I squelched it right there. No way was I going in there and have Queen Vivian follow me again and gloat!

We ordered and Paige started quizzing me about the party. I was doing a pretty good job of staying away from the "guy" subject by describing all the excess at Dr. Giovenetti's house, heck it was a mansion, when suddenly Simon and Paige started staring at my left shoulder. I looked down to see if I had dribbled on myself. I hadn't.

"Okay what's wrong? What are you staring at?"

"Who's that?" Paige pointed to me. I turned and almost knocked Emma down! I grabbed her to keep her from falling and sat her on my lap.

"Emma what are you doing here?"

"I came to say 'hi' and Daddy said I musn't interrupt so I had to stand quietly until you stopped talking."

"Well thank you that is very polite of you. Are you enjoying your dinner."

"Yes, I'd like it better if I could use the chop sticks but Daddy said they're too messy. I need to practice at home before I can use them out."

"Well you said so yourself, your daddy had to learn the hard way. He's probably really messy with chop sticks so he speaks from experience. Maybe it's really always best to do what your daddy says."

"Good insight, Dr. Tipton."

God! He was standing right behind me and probably heard every word I said. I could have said a lot more!

Emma giggled, "Did you hear her say you're messy Daddy?"

"No, I said probably messy."

"Probability describes me to a T. I trust you're having a better evening than last Dr. Tipton?"

"Yes! Different company goes a long way to improving my evening."

"Good, glad to hear that. Come on Emma say good night to Dr. Tipton. We have to be going."

To my surprise she hugged me!

"Good night Miss MeKenna. Thank you for talking to me!"

"Good evening Dr. Tipton." He looked directly at me as he nodded curtly.

"Good evening to you also Dr. Curry." I wanted to look away but I couldn't.

Emma took his hand skipping off, but not before asking, "I thought you called her McKenna today. Is she Dr. Tipton cause you're mad at her?"

Too bad I didn't hear his reply. Why did we have to see him? That conversation between us was terse at best. I was just beginning to think I could go into work tomorrow night with no problem. I felt the urge to cry.

"Excuse me, I have to go to the bathroom."

The tears started before I got to the door! I stayed in there until I had gained control. Now I just wanted to go home and go to bed.

"Good are you ready to go," Paige asked as I exited the bathroom.

"Sure I'm ready, did you get a doggie bag?"

"We finished ours. We can get you one at the register."

"Don't bother, I'm not hungry anymore."

As soon as we got home I went straight to bed, cried myself to sleep again. All the next day I dreaded going into work and seeing him. I couldn't cry, whatever happened I couldn't cry.

Fortunately as soon as I hit the door four traumas were wheeled in. Dr. Curry and I worked side by side on two of the traumas. We both knew what to do, if he needed something he asked and I gave it to him, but I tried to anticipate his needs. One of the traumas I intubated was a black male, only two years younger than me. He was all muscle and fighting us with every ounce of strength he had. He was a front seat passenger in a compact car with a beer bottle setting in his lap, the bottle ruptured on impact lacerating his right femoral artery in multiple places. He was bleeding out fast! The entire time I was trying to get the breathing tube in he fought us. He was probably combative from the blood lose leading to decreased oxygen to his brain. I kept talking to him in a calm voice trying to reassure him he was going to be okay. While I was working on that tube, the nurses were trying to get IV lines in so we could give him medication to put him to sleep so we could work on him. In the end the thing that he had going for him to fully recover from this trauma was his demise. His youth and power to fight us made it impossible to save him. The only way was to give him anesthesia by mask. Both anesthetists were in emergency surgery and the on call was still fifteen minutes out. If we had drop ether an old, old anesthesia we might have saved him. Dr. Curry finally called it and gave the time of death as 21:47 (9:47 PM). My hands were shaking when I walked out of the trauma room because we lost a young man who had his whole life ahead of him for such an inane reason. This is something they don't teach in books. This should have been easy: intubation, IV lines, fluids until the blood got here, medication to calm him, pressure on the lacerations to stop the bleeding until he got to OR. Easy peasy! But that wasn't what happened. Apparently the driver of the car he was in looked away, crossing left of center he hit another vehicle head on. That vehicle was a passenger van with a mother and her 18 month old daughter. The woman was already intubated and on her way to the neuro ICU in neurogenic shock from a spinal cord injury. No seat belt! Who knew if she would ever be anything but a human body void of the ability to respond to anything or anyone, but I didn't have time to dwell on that because they brought in the baby, still strapped in her car seat. She had been found about thirty feet away from the car screaming her head off! We checked her over determining other than scrapes and contusions she appeared to have no injuries! A totally intact 18 month old still screaming! She was transferred to the nearest children's trauma hospital. I was so relieved that baby was okay! I don't know if I could have dealt with it right on the heels of the one we lost.

The other young man, the driver had minor injuries. He was very contrite and submitted readily to the blood requested by the officer investigating the accident. It was only around 10:30 and already I was wiped out. Everything was quiet on our side (the trauma side) so I decided to go to the machines down the hall for something to eat. Suddenly I felt an arm around my shoulder, it was Dr. Curry walking with me.

"Are you all right kiddo?" He asked looking down at me. This was the first time he had ever said anything to me after we had worked together on traumas. I couldn't look up at him but I was honest in my response.

"I will be until the families get here."

"Yeah I know. That's the worst part."

I continued on down the hall. He went into the doctor's lounge.

I hadn't even gotten back from my snack run when I heard the commotion and I knew the family or families had arrived. I opened the door to the lounge.

"Dr. Curry they're here."

"I heard. Why don't you go on and do the best you can."

I gasped in shock. This was the first time he hung me out to dry! I stuck my Hershey bar in my pocket and stomped toward the nurse's desk.

"Come on!" I dragged Nan by the arm.

"Where's Cu...."

"He's not coming!"

I entered the room and the deceased's mother was there along with two brothers and the cutest little baby I had ever seen! The baby was happy but the rest of the room was disastrous! I went to the mother who held his baby.

"Come sit down with me." She knew the minute I said that, it was bad. She started to shake and sob. Nan reached out and took the baby.

"I'm so sorry, his injuries were more than his body could handle. I want you to know we did everything possible to save him. I wish it weren't this way but we are human and can only do the best we can, the rest is in God's hands."

I don't know why I said the last part because I wasn't even sure if a God, at least that God existed. Her next move surprised the heck out of me. She grasp me and hung on to me crying so, so hard her shoulders shook.

She kept saying, "My baby, he was my baby. Why, why did he have to go?"

The sons, trying to hold it together came resting their hands on her shoulders.

I tried to answer all their questions as best I could.

"Come on Mama. It's over. We can't do anything else."

Now I had one more step. It was a good thing, something positive could come out of this terrible event.

"Mrs. Garrison your son was a healthy young man and

losing him is a terrible thing. I know you think nothing good can come out of this and for you that is true. Is there anyway you would consider donating any of his organs?"

After more tears she looked at her sons, the older one nodded yes.

"Mama he's gone, we can't bring him back but maybe some family somewhere can be blessed by his leaving this earth."

"Okay, okay," she said.

"Mrs. Garrison you can stay in this room as long as you like, use the phone whatever. Would you like for me to call the clergy?"

"No my boy here is a minister of God's and he can help us."

"Yes please call him. Mama I need some ministering to right now," he admitted without shame thru his tears

"Okay, okay," her replies sounded automated. I know somewhere inside her heart and mind she was still trying to handle the turmoil and sorrow that existed within her.

"I'll call for you. Let me know if there's anything else I can help with. Did you want to see him before we move him?"

They all wanted to see him so I left Nan with them still holding the baby. Curry was standing outside the door and if I expected any understanding from him I didn't get it.

"You didn't ask if he had a wife? She can't give her consent to organ donation if she's not the next of kin," he said as he followed me down the hall.

I had about enough! He had been doing this for at least ten years and he left me holding the bag, now he wanted to criticize what I'd done!

"You SIR can go ask that if you want the answer. I'm done! I'm going to the cafeteria for my supper break!" I walked off leaving him there, as I rounded the corner of the nurse's station I stopped.

"I'm going on my supper break," I snapped!

I didn't know who was at the desk and I didn't care! The long trek to the cafeteria helped to cool me down. I ordered a grilled cheese and tomato soup. Nothing else looked appealing. I stood staring at nothing waiting on my food.

"Hey you did great in there." I didn't even look at Nan as she got in line behind me. My order was ready, I picked it up and sat at an empty table. There were a few other people from the ER there but I wanted to be alone. Nan joined me shortly.

"Say how did it turn out the other night?"

"What night?"

"Come on, New Year's eve night. Did Curry end up at your place?"

"Nope."

"Really because I would have bet my next paycheck on it after his remark about the ratty PJs he would end up there."

"Sorry to disappoint you, he did not end up at my place."

"Oh I'm not disappointed but I'm sure he was."

"Well that's his problem! He can just deal with it."

"I'm proud of you! I was here before Curry came and you are the first and only one to turn him down."

I looked down at my plate the whole time I was talking to her.

"Hey you're not sorry you turned him down are you?"

I looked up at her, "Nope, even though I'm just his type according to Queen Vivian."

"What happened with her?"

"She..."

Curry sat down at the table with his dinner tray.

"Go ahead. Don't let me interrupt your conversation."

"I'm just going."

I picked up my tray and left as Nan's mouth hung open in shock!

CHAPTER FIVE

ROD

That woman was an enigma to me! Loved dogs, loved my daughter, hated my guts! She was on my mind all day. Man when she cut someone off she cut them off! I thought she'd lose it over her shoes, she didn't. I thought meeting my daughter would be uncomfortable to her, it wasn't. I thought opening the car door and being a gentleman was the thing to do, it wasn't. I did not get angry easily but in less than twenty-four hours she managed to push my buttons at least three times!

Whatever last night was, no matter how good I thought it was, and I think she thought it was pretty great too, it was really a bust! Well I learned one thing, we had no future together except as professionals. Dang! She was still an itch I couldn't scratch and just as irritating! I just had to forget her and go on.

That was a good plan except the first thing Emmy talked about when I picked her up for ice cream was "your work friend McKenna." I got her off that subject while we ate our ice cream.

"Are we going home now Daddy?"

"No the stores are all open so I need to shop for some shoes?"

"Okay, can we go to the little girl's department too?"

"Sure Petals."

Once in Neiman Marcus we rode the escalator to the second floor past women's clothing and shoes then onto the third floor to the children's department.

Emmy jumped off the escalator and ran to girl's purses!

"Oh Daddy, look at this!"

She held up a bright yellow purse backpack that was really loud! It was good quality leather, and would piss Vivian off royally! "Oh Roderick (she called me that when she was irritated with me. What she called me when she was really mad at me would make a sailor blush!), that's so gauche!" She'd follow this with a facial expression like she smelled something really vile! Luckily I was immune to all her antics so if pleasing my daughter pissed her off? So be it!

"This is great Petals, let's find something to go with it."

A young sale woman approached us.

"Is there something I could help you and this little lady with?"

She raised her brow and looked at me letting me know she was glad to "help" me.

"I'd like something to go with this backpack."

"What did you have in mind?"

"Sneakers Daddy sneakers!"

"That would be ideal and we have some just the same color! Right this way."

We followed her to the shoes.

"I like these Daddy," Emma picked up a white sneaker with bright yellow polka dots.

"Those are cute. How about these."

I spied a black pair with that same bright yellow piping.

"Yeah, those too!"

"What size does she wear?"

"Why don't you size her foot, it's been a long time since I brought her shoe shopping."

We ended up with jeans and a light weight jacket and a top

to go with her shoes. It was fun! I worked nights, so Emmy and I didn't get to spend time together during the week but she was off for Christmas break so I had been with her several days in a row.

She got her packages and we started down the escalator.

"Oh aren't you going shoe shopping." She reminded me.

"Yeah."

We got off the escalator and I led her to a seating area and sat down with her.

"Emma you know I don't ask you to keep things from Mommy but I am asking you not to tell Mommy what I'm doing today."

"Why?"

I could see the wheels turning in her little head

"Well you know my work friend McKenna?"

She nodded, eyes open in wonder!

"Well Posey ate some very expensive shoes that belonged to her."

She got a frown on her face, "How did he get her shoes?"

"She forgot and left them at my house."

"Oh."

"Those shoes were Jimmy Choos."

"OH MY GOSH," she put her hand over her mouth suppressing a squeal!

"Mommy hates Posey so she would be really mad if she found out Miss McKenna left her shoes at your house and Posey ate them."

"You're right. That's why I don't want you to tell Mommy. If she asks you if I bought Jimmy Choos for Dr. Tipton, don't lie."

"I don't tell fibs Daddy, you know that's a bad thing to do."

"Yes Petals it is." Her innocence was tearing me up!

God leave it up to a seven year old to remind her ole man he's not the most honest person when it came to the place women hold in his life. Suddenly I remembered what

McKenna said about giving a part of herself to me! I wanted to be sick for what I had thoughtlessly done to her.

"Are you okay Daddy?"

"Yeah, I'm fine. Let's go. You can watch as daddy forks out big bucks because Posey likes the smell of feet."

He liked the smell of something else that belonged to her and I couldn't disagree. Why hadn't I eaten her pussy? I wanted to. I loved the scent in her panties! This is a woman that I could have taken a long time to explore but no I had to be in a hurry to get her out of my apartment so I didn't have to deal with a sick hangover and my daughter asking questions. I was getting sloppy in my old age. I was almost forty two, she was a kid, 26 or 27? And hadn't had sex in five years! God it was good! Don't pat yourself on the back Curry, not good enough for her to tell anyone about it! Well that would remain as our secret. In a year or two we both would forget all about it.

"Daddy look at these!" Emmy's voice was filled with wonder!

She picked up a silver colored shoe with rhinestones.

"They're so beautiful! I can hardly wait until I'm old enough to wear shoes like that."

I was looking that shoe over trying to decide what made them worth the thousand bucks they were priced at.

"Daddy, when I'm big I can wear shoes like that, right?"

"Yeah and Daddy will have to get out his shot gun."

"What?" She asked as she turned her head sideways, wondering if she heard me right!

"It's a joke. Daddy's funning you."

"Oh," she said still looking bewildered.

Another sales person approached us. Wow this one had it going on!.I noticed she was checking out my left hand. She was gorgeous but in a plastic way. Lots of make-up, not the natural fresh look McKenna had. Dr. Tipton had very dark hair and eyes but her skin was so fair she had a sprinkling of freckles over the bridge of her nose and cheek bones. Last night was the first time I'd seen her wear make up, mascara, blush, eyeliner. Man that smoky eye shadow gave her eyes a special look. Yes, she was naturally beautiful.

"What can I get for you in the Jimmy Choo line, or would you prefer Louboutins?"

"No, I'm looking for a particular shoe. It's a Jimmy Choo,"

"His dog ate his work friend's shoes," Emma blurted out crossing her arms over her chest.

I thought she was finished, boy was I mistaken!

"She left them at his house. I guess it was overnight because she was there pretty early in the day."

The clerk simpered.

I know I must have turned slightly red.

"Really." The sales person was now smiling outright!

Now my daughter was finished! I opened my mouth....

"And I thought she came to work because she had on work clothes. You know sweat pants and a T shirt. My mommy never wears sweat pants and T shirts cause she says it's low class and no lady looks good when she dresses like that. Right Daddy?"

"Thank you Emma. Yes, Mommy is always right." I gritted my teeth trying to get that out.

The sales person laughed out loud at this, but gave me the courtesy of trying to stay on task.

"Perhaps if you describe the shoe I can find it for you."

"That sounds like the quickest route. It's black suede, a stiletto, with an ankle strap."

"Any thing else? There are a lot of Jimmy Choos like that," she smiled.

I had to think for a minute.

"Oh and it had a rhinestone thing going across the foot from the back to the front." I tried to use my hands to show placement of the rhinestones.

"I think I know the one you're talking about. Let me show you."

She brought the shoe up on her computer screen right away.

"Yes, that's it!"

"What size?"

I knew I'd have to go home and check the size in the destroyed shoe. Luckily she left the bag of what was left of her clothing in my car.

"Can I give you a call with the size? I'll pay for them now and you can send them to my house."

"Unfortunately these shoes have to be ordered from Jimmy Choo's warehouse. They are a 2017 design and are considered almost a collectible."

"That's okay. I have to replace them. When do you think I can expect them?"

"It will probably take about two weeks. I can have them sent directly to you from the warehouse,"

"That will work."

She busied herself getting everything rung up, then looked up at me with a smile.

"Okay with shipping, taxes and insurance, you do want insurance don't you?"

"Yes."

"Okay the total is $2176."

"Two thousand and one hundred and seventy six dollars," I blurted out!

To say I was shocked was putting it lightly. Emma only made it worse!

"Wow Daddy, that's a lot of money."

"Yes I know Petals. Let that be a lesson to you that we have to be responsible pet owners."

"Yes Daddy." She was dancing, ready to go.

I handed my credit card to the sales person.

"Daddy can we go eat Chinese please? Please?'

"We need to check with your mother. I'd like to take you and Helen out for dinner if your mother doesn't have other plans."

I go my credit card back and we started out.

"Thank you very much Dr. Curry."

I nodded and took Emma's hand starting down the escalator.

"Oh Daddy we forgot my packages."

"You stand right here where I can see you and I'll run get them."

I walked briskly to the shoes not letting her out of my sight, I didn't have to look for the packages. The woman who helped me order the shoes was standing with her back turned talking to another clerk.

"Apparently his dog ate all her clothes, even her Jimmy Choos."

"God. Wonder how he explained that to his wife."

"I think he's divorced. Lucky woman. I'd give a pair of Jimmy Choos to spend the night with that hunk."

I couldn't hold back any longer.

"Well she certainly didn't share your sentiment."

The clerk turned around, her face beet red! She was speechless! Good! That statement was living proof that most women didn't think it was a waste to spend the night experiencing wild sex with me.

Emma was especially quiet on the way home. I could tell she was sleepy.

"Why don't you and I take a nap when we get home?'

"Okay." she yawned.

She and I settled in on the couch and as soon as we started watching, "The Secret Life of Pets" we were both gone. I woke up before her. Just looking at my beautiful daughter gave me a feeling that compared to no other. The spitting image of her mother, red hair, green eyes and pale, pale skin. She was a beauty. The only thing she took after me was her lips. Viv had thin lips that showed her displeasure easily, my lips were full. I looked at her still trying to figure out how we got here!

I remember my first day at University Birmingham Hospital. Vivian was introduced as my mentor and it was love at first sight! God, she looked like an angel. Beautiful, beautiful, beautiful! And she let me know from day one she would help me in things other than ER medicine. She was hot in bed! We were a couple immediately and even though she was my mentor and chief doc in the ER it didn't seem to make any difference.

We were married within eight months. She wanted to get pregnant right away because her biological clock was running out of time. She was thirty eight. Ten years older than me, but I didn't care! My mother was very cautious of her in the beginning because she thought our relationship inappropriate since she was technically not only my mentor but my boss. Once we announced our engagement she changed her mind. She really liked Vivian and had the utmost respect for her as an ER physician. It only took me about two months to get her pregnant, we were in love and at it all the time. Vivian's mom was on top of the world! She loved me and was finally getting the grandchild she always wanted. Viv was an only child. Things were great even after Viv's mom came to live with us.

When Emma was about six months old her grandma Elizabeth begin to feel ill. One day she was fine the next day she was jaundiced, weak and failing badly. We took her to the best GI guy there was but he couldn't do one thing for her, she had terminal liver and pancreatic cancer. We cared for her at home, she lasted not quite three months. Emma was nine months old when she died. I tried to console Viv, I encouraged her to take time off work. We didn't need her money to maintain our lifestyle, I was now an employee and not a resident at University Hospital plus I had a trust fund I had never touched. She changed practically overnight. The last time I made sweet, sweet love to her was the night of her mother's funeral. After we made love she turned away from me, even though I insisted on holding her in my arms. She never turned to me again. We celebrated Emma's birthday with my family and Helen, on the surface things seemed perfect.

That night I went to bed early. Emma was fussy so I laid down with her. When I got up Vivian was gone. Some time during the night she came in and sat on the bed.

"Rod, wake up."

"Sure baby. What's the matter?'

I was barely awake but what she said next jerked me into consciousness!

"Rod I want you to move out of this bedroom, find a place of your own as soon as you can. I want a divorce."

What! I knew she was grieving but I thought she just needed time. There was no discussing it, we were done! Finished!

I couldn't figure out how one minute I was sleeping in the bed I shared with my wife, whom I loved very much, the next I was looking for an apartment. Luckily the apartment across the hall was opening up and when I told her I was moving into it she informed me she was moving out. The only way I could get her to consent to staying was to agree to continue to purchase her apartment as well as mine. It was worth whatever I had to do to stay close to Emma.

I worried how it would be to have to work with Vivian once word got out we were no longer together. I didn't have to be concerned long because the next week she had me permanently moved to the night shift! She could do that, she made the schedule.

Well my trip down memory lane was over. I had to get those things out of my car and call the store with the correct shoe size. I shook Emmy softly, and kissed her ear.

"Ewh! Daddy that tickles. Oh we missed the movie!" She said as she stretched before sitting up.

"Here let me start it again. I'll be right back. I need to find out that shoe size. I have to run to my car."

She was watching the movie and eating a jello cup when I got back. I found a size 9 in the shoe and called the store. The person who answered said the 'sales associate' who placed the order was gone so I could give the information to her. Gone my foot! She was probably just too embarrassed to talk to me and rightly so.

I got a jello cup and sat beside Emma to eat it.

"Daddy I know you don't want me to tell Mommy about the shoes but can I tell Helen about it?"

"Maybe when we go out to dinner tonight."

I changed into khakis with a long sleeved button up shirt, and put on a sports jacket with no tie then I went across the hall to get my dates! Helen answered the door.

"Hey is Viv in."

She raised her eyebrows as if to question my question?

"Yes but you don't want to be talking to her now."

"I just wanted to let her know where we're going and that tonight's my night with Emma."

"She knows. You can text her later, that would be your sanest choice!"

"Good, are y'all ready to go?'

"Yep!"

Emma ran toward the door in her new yellow outfit and I got Helen's drift! Vivian couldn't talk Emma out of wearing her new very loud clothes and she was pissed at me!

Worth every penny I paid for those damn clothes!

We sat down and ordered before Emma brought up the Jimmy Choos. I had to explain a few details but Helen could read between the lines. I knew she contained her laughter to try and preserve some of my dignity.

The food was good after I talked Emma out of using her chopsticks.

"Emma, believe me from experience you need to try those chopsticks at home before you use them out in a restaurant."

"Daddy you're no fun!"

She sure was good at giving me the stink eye!

"Really? What do you think your mother would say?'

She rolled her eyes at me, "I guess you're not so bad!"

Helen and I were discussing her coming on a trip to my parents cabin in Tennessee when Emma jumped up and pointed!

"There's Miss MeKenna! Can I go see her? Please Daddy, please please please with pretty please wrapped all around it!"

Emma seemed fascinated by McKenna. I could say I couldn't understand it but I could.

"Emma remember your manners." Helen reminded her.

"Oh sorry, but can I go please?"

"Yes, but walk over there quietly. Don't interrupt when adults are talking that's rude."

"Okay Daddy." She walked off sedately.

"Don't tell me, is that Ms. Million Dollar Shoes?"

"Yep,"

We continued talking. It seemed like Emma should be coming back to our table soon.

"Can you see her? What's she doing?"

"Just standing there."

"Just standing there?"

"Well you told her not to interrupt. Oh, the people with her are pointing to Emma now."

Helen laughed!

"What's so funny?"

"Miss Million Dollar shoe woman almost knocked her down but she caught her and put her in her lap."

"Her lap? Emma never sits in any one's lap but yours and mine."

"I know. Guess she didn't have much choice,"

"What are they doing now?"

"Talking."

"Well that's our cue. She doesn't know when to stop sometimes."

Helen cackled!

"You got that right!"

We slowly approached McKenna's table as she continued her conversation with my daughter.

"You said yourself your daddy learned the hard way, he probably was really messy with chopsticks, so you should always listen to what your daddy says."

"Good insight, Dr. Tipton."

"Did you hear that Daddy? She said you are messy!" Emma giggled!

"I said probably messy." McKenna corrected her.

"Yes probability describes me to a T. I trust you're having a better evening than last?"

"Yes much improved, different company."

"Good. Come on Emma we have to be going. Say good evening to Dr. Tipton."

I took Emma's hand with Helen following, and before I could get away Emma said loudly, "Didn't you call her McKenna today? Are you mad at her? Is that why you called her Dr. Tipton?"

If I could have run I would have. Emma's intent was not to embarrass me, she was simply sensitive to the nuances in mine and McKenna's relationship.

It didn't help any that Helen had to comment, "Humph, she might be worth whatever you had to pay for those shoes."

If I was concerned about the interaction between McKenna and me at work it was a waste. Four major traumas hit the door as we came in the day we returned to work. McKenna did a hell of a job with that young man. I know she was devastated we lost him but we have to get used to it because it's an every day occurrence when you work trauma. Luckily that baby was fine, I'm sure it would have wrecked her for the night if the baby wasn't. I was so proud of her walking out from losing that patient straight to the screaming baby, so when I saw her walking by herself I couldn't resist putting my arm around her shoulder.

"How you doing kiddo?"

She didn't even look at me, she just kept walking!

"Okay until the families get here."

I agreed with her. That's the only response I got from her. Well I guess I got put in my place. I walked into the doctor's lounge and laid down scrolling thru the news on my phone wondering if the accident was reported yet. I heard a quick knock.

"They're here Dr. Curry."

Well she seemed so unscathed by everything that happened I decided I'd let her go solo on this! She didn't object she just left.

I laid there a minute or two then I realized what a jerk I was being, I had brought our personal relationship into work! God, what was wrong with me? I knew better than that!

I had been in her spot and it was not an easy one especially if you had some conscienceless jerk trying to undermine you! I had to make this right. I headed toward the family room, she had already started without me so I stood there and listened to her. She was perfect, simply perfect! Why I jumped on her I don't know, yes I do know. I resented that she didn't need me! I knew she didn't need me outside these walls but I wanted her to need me inside them. I thought I was finished with Dr. McKenna Tipton but I wasn't. I had to fix this.

She snubbed me at dinner then stayed clear of me the rest of the night except when we were working together. I walked past the nurses' station and she sat alone in the corner reading a book.

"Dr. Tipton do you have a minute? I have something to discuss with you?"

I saw her face redden then I realized it sounded like there was something negative in what I had to say.

"You did such a great job with that family this evening I thought maybe it would be a good idea to talk about how that made you feel, since it was your first time solo."

She didn't say a word, just closed her book loudly and walked toward me. I went into the doctors lounge, she followed and stood waiting.

"Please sit down McKenna."

She sat down without even looking at me. She stared at her hands resting in her lap.

"Dr. Tipton, please give me the courtesy of looking at me when I'm speaking to you."

She looked up at me with such, such what? I couldn't figure out what was in her eyes. I sat down and took her hands in mine. She looked down at our hands and I knew she wanted to pull away but she didn't.

"I have to start off by asking your forgiveness for the way I've acted today. You stated very clearly the other morning how you wanted our relationship to be, and I was angry because you rejected me. I brought that anger to work with me tonight. I felt rejected again because you didn't need me here at work either. I put you in a position you should never be in with your mentor, then I criticized you. I apologize. That won't happen again. You did a super job with that family, professional all the way but also letting them see your human side at recognizing their loss. Congratulations! As I've said before, you make my job of mentoring you very easy."

She smiled the first genuine smile I had seen since the beginning of the shift.

"Thank you."

She got up and left.

I got a call from the hospitalist in ICU. He was having problems getting an art line in and asked for my assistance.

"Come on Tipton let's go show that asswipe in ICU how to put in an art line."

She laughed and followed along with me. Once we got to ICU I turned McKenna loose on the ICU 'I Know It All' and I stood back and watched her do her magic! After the line was in we went to the nurses station to put it in the chart. Luckily 'I Know It All' could do his own charting. I sat down and started talking to the nurses, they are always good for hospital gossip! McKenna stood back watching as the nurses introduced themselves.

One nurse sat down next to me offering her hand.

"Dr. Curry, I'm Angel. We met at Dr. Giovenetti's party the other night, I'm sure you don't remember me."

I had no clue because I only had my eyes on one goal!

"Of course I remember you. Did you enjoy the party?"

"I did, how about you?"

I saw McKenna look away as she blushed.

"Yes. The best time I've had at a party in a long time."

"Did you go anywhere after the party?"

"No, I was an old man. I went straight home and straight to bed."

"Gosh, you should have gone out with us! We went bar hopping! We had a great time."

"Call me the next time you go bar hopping if I'm available I'll hop on the train."

"I will, but we don't have to wait to go bar hopping with them we can go without them."

"Great, if you're sure you want to go bar hopping with an old man!"

Angel couldn't have been more than 22 or 23 years old! Fresh out of school.

She leaned over and put her arm on my forearm, as she started to whisper to me.

"Not old just experienced," her tone very salacious.

McKenna got up and walked toward the elevators.

God, that should have made my dick get hard but I could only think of McKenna watching what was going down. Just like she said it did!

"I have to get back to the ER. See y' all later."

I jumped up and ran toward the elevator,

"Dr. Tipton, hold the doors for me!"

I caught sight of her, leaning against the back of the lift looking like she wanted to commit murder and she didn't care who knew it. When I got back to the ER she had her book again.

"Hey super job Dr. Tipton. I'd call that a win win!"

She didn't even look up from her book.

"Yeah, a win win for everyone," she said dryly.

"Funny." I said as I walked away.

The next two nights went by smoothly. We were amicable. Thursday night came and we had a long week end coming and I had nothing lined up. I was feeling a little lonely since Viv was taking Emma to Biltmore House in North Carolina, even though I was off I wasn't invited. I heard from the grapevine (Helen) that Viv had a companion, and it wasn't female. So obviously Vivian thought it might be a bit awkward to have her ex-husband sleeping in one bed and her in the next room with her boyfriend. God, she was such a hypocrite, she would probably try to have my parental rights revoked if I had my girlfriend sleeping with me in the same house as Emma! I was going to confront her about that when she got back.

"Dr. Curry you have a phone call from ICU," came over the intercom.

"I'll get it out there."

As I answered the line I figured I'd have to pick up McKenna again and go help with some procedure there.

"Curry here."

"Dr. Curry this is Angel. I wondered if you're not busy to-morrow night if you'd be interested in doing some bar hopping, or if you'd rather do something else we could do that instead."

"Let me think about it and get back with you."

"Okay! Sounds good. Hope to see you soon Dr. Curry."

"Yeah and Angel it's Rod."

When I hung up the phone I realized I had committed a faux pas! I'm was positive there was only one Angel working in ICU! Jeff Nicely another doc made a clicking sound with his tongue and added, "Nice work Curry."

Nan looked up at me with daggers. "I think I need some coffee."

McKenna dropped her book and walked after her. God only knows what they would be discussing!

I thought about Angel's offer the rest of the night so 07:00 found me at the nurse's time clock! Angel had changed out of her scrubs and looked dynamite in tight jeans and a shirt with a bare mid-riff.

"Hey."

"Hey, how are you," I asked?

"Happy to see you."

"Yeah?"

"Yes very happy," she said as she took my arm leaning in to me.

"Good. I thought maybe we could start early. Want some breakfast?"

"Yes, I'm starved."

"What happens after breakfast," I asked?

"Well I think I might be ready for a nap after that."

"Sounds like a plan," I said as we rounded a corner and ran right into McKenna!

"Oh sorry," she said not even looking at us but somehow I knew she knew who she had bumped into!

Angel was fun. We laughed thru breakfast and when we got to her apartment she practically jumped me! I hadn't had sex in a week so I was ready. We spent the next three days together. I went home Monday morning and got what for from Helen!

"Where have you been! You left that dog alone for three days!"

"That's not true! I came home for clothes and to feed him."

"What about his walk? What about his bathroom break?"

"Jesus!" What was I thinking! "You didn't try to walk him

did you? Why didn't you call me? Who took him out?"

"One question at a time Einstein. No I didn't walk him. You want me to have a broken hip? Don't answer that. I tried to call you but your phone went straight to voice mail. So I called Miss Million Dollar shoes and she took him out two times a day."

I lost it!

"You did what? Why in the hell did you call her?"

She crossed her arms over her chest while tapping her foot, chewing the inside of her mouth! Definitely not a good sign.

"Who did you want me to call? Miss Vivian?"

Well that put things in perspective for me!

"Sorry Helen. I'm sorry. You did the best you could. Did Dr. Tipton ask you where I was?"

"Didn't have to. I think she knew but didn't say a word to me. She is good with that dog. He was a perfect *gentleman*."

I knew the word "gentleman" was a veiled reference as to what his owner wasn't!

"Sorry Helen. It won't happen again."

"What's wrong with you? You've acted weird these last two weeks or so."

I sighed hopelessly!

"I don't know Helen. I've just been off course since the new year."

"Since the new year huh?"

She turned and walked across the hall.

"Oh by the way your package came."

"Okay thanks."

That night at work McKenna didn't mention anything about Posey or her babysitting him. We had six traumas, rare for a Monday night. As a matter of fact the entire week went great. Our next night off was Thursday. Thursday morning I walked thru the ER telling everyone to have a good night off. I had avoided Angel all week because I wanted to keep my mind on my work, being the best mentor I could be. I did want to see Angel later for my overdue dose of hot sex. Who was I kidding, it wasn't hot, just okay. I'd had some worse but a whole lot better and at the top of the list was Dr. Tipton. I had those shoes sitting on my chest of drawers and I decided to go ask Dr. McKenna to meet me for breakfast and I would give her the shoes. She came from the back walking with Nan. I saw her wave at someone behind me. I turned and the resident in radiology stood up returning her wave.

"McKenna are you ready? My brother is meeting us."

"I need to change clothes first, then find a money machine."

"Ken! This is a date, a gentleman always pays!"

I was seething! Who was this asswipe? I could not keep my mouth shut.

"Just like a gentleman always opens the door for a lady."

"Oh good morning sir. Thanks for the reminder. You sound like my dad."

He and McKenna walked off. Nan was busting a gut trying not to laugh!

"What's so damn funny?"

"Nothing SIR!"

I walked off! I was NOT old enough to be his father! I decided to call Angel. She certainly didn't think I was old!

CHAPTER SIX

MCKENNA

After the fiasco in ICU with Dr. Curry and Angel I was done! What I ever saw in him I don't know! He was a dog! No, his dog had better sense that him! I took care of his dog and he didn't even thank me. I wanted to cry all the time, my period was due and I knew I'd feel better once I started and I'd be grouchy until that happened.

One night in the cafeteria Nan and I sat with the crew from Radiology and I met Tony. Right away I knew I would like to go out with him. We talked that night then again at supper the next night and he asked for my number. I had just gotten a new phone so fifteen minutes after I gave him my number he texted me and asked me out. Our first date was to the botanical gardens with his brother and his girlfriend. A sure sign he didn't want me to go to bed with him on the first date.

Tony was from a strong Catholic family, one of seven kids. The youngest so the first time I met his mother I was under the microscope. He called me at midnight so excited- his mother loved me! It was after that we had our discussion about sex. It angered me initially that Mama would have to approve of me before he got into a serious relationship, then I rethought it. We both decided it was a serious step. Playing musical beds was not for either of us. He was trying to protect me. That endeared him more to me.

I was beginning to feel tired very easily, my period was three weeks late. I was thinking of taking a dose pak to start my period. Tony and I had a very heavy make out session and decided we needed to have our first intimate experience. I needed to get on the pill so I had to get an appointment with an OB/GYN. I was able to get in within the week.

Tony and I went out to dinner and dancing. My hormones were hopping! I could hardly wait until we got to my apartment. When we got there he insisted on shaving.

"Ken, I want to have the whole experience with you. I want to eat on you. You don't have to reciprocate but I really want that and I don't want the growth on my beard to chafe you. Okay?"

I started to cry, he was so sweet and tender! I got undressed and got under the covers. The next thing I remember is rolling over to Tony's phone alarm. I jumped up, naked as the day I was born! Tony came from the bathroom stopping dead when he saw me.

"Ken! Jesus I slept outside the covers all night and look what I missed! God if I touch you now I won't leave. I *have* to make this appointment at the bank, it's for a house loan."

I pulled the sheet up over me and walked to him and kissed him.

"Tony, we can meet later this afternoon after my doctor's appointment. We don't have to be at work until 7:00 PM. We can go to work together from here. Okay?"

He grabbed me and kissed me, pulling my pelvis into him. He wanted me! He wanted me!

"I have to go Dr. Tipton. See you later."

"Can't wait Dr. Sansone."

I waved shyly as he left. I went back to bed and dreamed of the hot man I was going to have in my bed later today. Before I laid down I checked the drawer in the bedside table for condoms. I knew it would be a month before the pill would be effective. I didn't want anything to interfere with our plans this afternoon. My hormones were on the warpath and weren't going to be calmed until I had that man in my bed!

I sat on the exam table swinging my legs back and forth waiting on the nurse to come in and put me up in stirrups. They had already taken my blood plus my urine specimen. A pelvic exam was the only thing separating me from my birth control pill prescription.

Dr. Burroughs came in with the nurse, while she got me ready for the exam he gave me the results of my blood work. I was anemic, well that explained my tiredness all the time.

"Now let's see what going on in your abdomen."

He sat down getting ready for the exam. He was gentle, even though he knew I am a doc he told me everything he was going to do before he did it.

"Dr. Tipton I'm going to do a pap smear and take some samples for sexually transmitted infections."

"Okay." I knew I didn't have anything and it was standard procedure now days.

It was over pretty quick. He took off his gloves and sat down to talk with me.

"Okay first things first Dr. Tipton. You are not a candidate for the pill."

I couldn't believe he said that!

"But I don't have any risk factors. I don't smoke, no family history of DVTs....."

"McKenna," he stopped me with the use of my given name.

"I'm sure this is going to be a surprise to you but you don't need birth control of any type. You're about six weeks pregnant."

"Wha.... I... I mean how can that happen?" I shook my head in disbelief. "I mean I know how it happens but I've only had sexual intercourse once in five years and that was New Year's eve."

"Well that makes you closer to eight weeks pregnant,"

"Are you sure? Was that a urine pregnancy test? Do it again, check my blood!"

"We will send your blood to the lab. We'll get the results tomorrow, but you already have some changes to your cervix. Chadwicks. I'll have my nurse call you as soon as we know."

I got home some how, all I could think about was I was pregnant by a philandering jerk!

Suddenly I thought of Tony! I had to call him and stop him from coming over here.

Luckily he picked up right away.

"Hey beautiful girl, I got my loan."

"You did. That's great. Did you look at any houses yet?"

"No I haven't. I'd like you to go with me when I do. We can talk about this later at your place."

"Tony you, you can't come over tonight. I think I'm getting a bug or something. I'm going to call in sick to work."

"Let me come over and take care of you."

"No my sister will be here, she'll help me if I need it."

"Ken I'd really like to see you tonight. We don't have to do anything, I know you're sick. I just want to spend time with you."

"No please don't. I'll call you in the morning if I'm better and you can come over then."

"Sounds good. I've been thinking of you all day and please don't think it's just about the sex because it's not. You are just so special to me."

I started to cry.

"Don't be sweet to me now Tony you're just making me cry and feel worse."

"I'm sorry. If I hear from you I'll come by your place in the morning. Okay?"

"Bye Tony."

"Good bye my beautiful girl."

I called into work while I could still hold it together. I told them I had been to the doctor.

"Oh you don't need a doctor's excuse Dr. Tipton. Take an extra day if you need it. As busy as it is here if you don't take care of yourself you can't do your job. I'll put you down for two days and if you're much better you can call and let me know. It won't hurt Dr. Curry to work by himself a night or two."

"Okay thank you."

That was Vivian's secretary, at least she was understanding.

I went to bed and cried until I couldn't cry anymore. My sister didn't come home which was not a surprise. She spent a lot of nights with Simon. I was exhausted, maybe if I got the iron and prenatal vitamins filled and started taking them I wouldn't be so tired.

I woke up tired after sleeping ten hours. I wasn't going to work that day, even though I didn't have to call in I did. I was off the next two nights after tonight so maybe I'd have it together when it was time to return to work.

I had to end it with Tony. I didn't answer his phone calls for the next two days. I text him the third day and told him I needed to back off from our relationship because it was just going too fast for me. He texted begging to come over but I told him not to call me I'd call him when I had things figured out which- would be never!

I couldn't stop crying no matter what I did the tears still came. The doctor's office called telling me what I already knew- the blood work confirmed my pregnancy. After giving me that good news she informed me if I planned on terminating my pregnancy it would have be done before twelve weeks. I was not happy about being pregnant and it was a mistake but no way would I kill this baby. I said as much to the nurse who called, it was at that point she apologized for being insensitive.

The third day I was off I had a visitor, Dr. Curry. I couldn't not answer my door if I was home sick. If I didn't go to the door they might think I wasn't really sick I just had better things to do. I was a wreck but I didn't care if he saw me like this, it was after all his fault! I was so nervous about finally having sex I didn't realize he hadn't used a condom until he ejaculated inside me. I wasn't worried because I had just finished my period slightly less than a week before. I was more worried about catching a disease. Boy was I mistaken!

I opened the door and realized it must be worse than I thought by the look on his face.

"Good God McKenna you look like **death** warmed over! When was the last time you ate?"

I hadn't eaten in over two days but I couldn't do that now. I had to feed and hydrate myself for the baby.

"I don't know, a couple of days ago."

"You need to lay down. Let me run to that Chinese place down the street and get you some egg drop soup. Your stomach should be able to handle that. It's full of protein."

Before I could say anything he was gone and back. He popped a soup cup from the cabinet and poured it full of soup. He also brought back some bottles of Gatorade and ginger ale.

After he got me settled he told me the reason he was here.

"McKenna I know we've been off each other for a couple of months and I hate it. You are the best resident I've ever had and I've hated working without you the last two nights. Please can we call a truce? I know I've been rude and obnoxious at times, well maybe a lot of the time but please forgive me. Come back and work with me. I promise to be the kind of mentor I'm called to be. If you have a problem I want you to share it with me. God I feel so bad, I come over here, you haven't worked in two days and I find you crying your eyes out. Please forgive me if I'm the cause of your tears because you're frustrated with the way I'm treating you."

"No it's not you personally, it's something else bothering me. I have to work it out."

"It's not that asswipe Sansone is it?"

I snickered, I couldn't help it.

"No it's not Tony. Actually if things were different I'd be with Tony right now. He's a great guy, just the kind of guy I want."

"Then why aren't you with him? I know it's not for a lack of interest on his part?"

"It's just.. complicated."

"McKenna as much as it pains me to say this if you want Tony go get him."

"No, I can't."

"Are you sure?"

"Yes I'm sure."

"Listen I did come to talk about work but I've also been putting off getting these shoes to you. I've had them for months. Each time I thought I'd give them to you something came up so here they are."

He hands me a box from the Jimmy Choo Warehouse. These shoes are brand new!

"Please you have to take these back, I can't accept them."

"Why not? You know I told you there was to be no argument about this. So now we're even."

I started to cry, I couldn't stop.

"No no I can't. Really I can't.'

He sat down on the sofa beside me taking me in his arms.

"Sh, sh, don't cry McKenna. Tell me what to do to make things right."

"It's toooo la la late," I couldn't control my sobbing.

The next thing I knew he picked me up and put me in his lap, trying to shush me.

He kissed my temple, rubbing my shoulders until I guess I went to sleep. I woke up, it was noon and he had fallen asleep too. I started to get up, he pulled me back against him.

"Now are we settled for work?"

"Yes."

"You're coming back?"

"Yes."

"Now tell me why you can't take these damn shoes! They're almost collectibles according to the sales clerk! The damn things are double their original price. So you have to take them."

"I can't take those expensive shoes because I bought mine at a resale shop. I only paid a hundred dollars for them."

He sat bolt upright! He startled me!

"You seriously didn't think I could spend that kind of money on a pair of shoes!"

He started laughing when I said I'd only paid a hundred for them, now he was howling!

"No wonder you didn't get more upset! Seriously you have to take them. Consider it pay for babysitting my dog."

This is the first time he had ever mentioned me taking care of his dog. Now I know he's not an ungrateful newt! He swept it under the rug because I knew he neglected taking care of Posey for a week end of sex with Angel! Humph, maybe her name wasn't even Angel she just acquired it because time spent in her bed was out of this world! Who knew about men and their pussy preference! The one thing I was sure of was that mine wasn't that memorable to him, he could hardly wait to get me out of his apartment!

"That's outrageous! And I didn't do it for you I did it for Poseidon!"

"Well then it is outrageous if you did it for him because he much rather have a pair of your panties to slobber over! Can't say I blame him for that!"

He winked at me and sniffed the air!

I know I turned shrimp red again!

It was good he came. I felt better when he left. Things would be better for us at work for a while. I just didn't know how long I could hide that I was pregnant.

Also there was the problem of Tony.

CHAPTER SEVEN

ROD

I walked away feeling good about my encounter with McKenna. 'Ken' Sansone called her. It must have gotten pretty serious, familiarity does lead to 'pet' names. God if he fucked her! Why wouldn't he? She's beautiful, smart, funny, and would make a great mother! Look how Emmy has taken to her. I just have to face it. I still have that itch for her but that ship had sailed and before it sailed I wrecked it on the rocks! It felt good to hold her. She did relax in my arms, so much so she went to sleep. The darnedest thing was when I went to sleep with her in my arms I had a very erotic dream about her. I woke up with a hard on. I was afraid she felt it and that's why she got up from my lap but she didn't or she wouldn't have stayed when I pulled her back to me. Jesus wait until I tell Helen about the shoes! I'd really like to tell Vivian just to piss her off but then she would know McKenna, 'Ken' slept with me. This is our secret. No one will ever know. I wonder if she told Nan? Nah. Nan would have had my ass on a skewer for that trick. She's really protective of McKenna, I saw that after the party when she wanted to keep her overnight. Yeah, it is still **our** secret.

I'm off tonight. Angel text me at work this morning to go to her place after my shift was over. I told her I had errands to run. We've been on again off again over the last two months. I really don't have an appetite for her anymore. Off hand I can't think of any woman I want in my bed right now, except of course 'Ken', which is out of the question. 'Ken'. I wonder what she'd say if I called her that?

I need to go home and catch some Z's after I tell Helen the shoe story. I'm going to place a little bet with her that she won't tell Viv. That gets her every time! Helen refuses to lose a bet. Nah. It would spill our secret. It wasn't a secret with Helen she already knew.

My two days off were spent with my parents and Emma. It was the week end so we could spend the night at their house. Emma loved it. She wasn't the only grandchild but she was the youngest. My sister and brother both had kids but they were in high school.

My mom had us all close, 10 months between my sister who is the oldest and my brother. Mom waited a while before getting pregnant with me. My brother was 13 months old when I came along! My grandmother was fit to be tied over my mother having three kids in three years! Actually Gran thought it was low class to have more than one child. If she could have caught my dad off guard I think she probably would have cut off his dick! My parents met in their first year of medical school, it was love at first sight for them so when my mother wanted to get married in her second year of med school Gran 'forbid' her to do so! Gran should have known better than that because she and Mom are just alike. If you throw down the gauntlet you better be ready for battle! Not only was marriage forbidden before my mother graduated med school but marriage to my dad was forbidden at any time! He came from a lower middle class family so his pedigree wasn't good enough for Gran. When Gran tossed out all her 'no no's' my mom politely told her to stuff it, not like *that* but it meant the same. She told Gran she and Dad would `elope and she just might be pregnant by that time! Gran could not miss having the society wedding of the year so she agreed to my mom's demands. She still only tolerates my dad and whenever her grand kids do something to displease her she blames the low class genes we got from our father! I do love Gran though, she really dotes on Emma. She says Emma is my mom all over again because she has both parents with pedigrees. I guess my sister couldn't be my mom all over again owing to the 'low class' genes she got from Dad!

Helen was out when I got to Viv's apartment. Viv was there. She answered the door, being her usual charming self!

"What's with your hot shot resident that she missed two nights of work?"

"Well good day to you, the magnanimous Dr. Curry."

"You didn't answer the question."

"You didn't greet me."

"Good morning," she snarled.

"I think the doctor actually told her she has a stomach virus and it's very contagious so she shouldn't come to work. She's puking her guts up, I went to check on her, she wouldn't even let me in the door."

I am not a liar but Viv brings out the baser side of my nature!

"I'm certain she wouldn't let you in the door but not because she's contagious! She's not ignorant, she actually has some sense. I'm sure she's on to you and figured she was safer with you on the other side of a locked door."

"Aw-you do flatter me so! If you were aware of what is going on in **your** department you'd know she and Dr. Sansone from Radiology have a hot romance going!"

"Really? Aw yourself! I bet it hurts that she prefers a younger less *used* man than yourself."

"I think the term is 'experienced' not used. "Don't kid yourself Roderick."

"Oh I'm not! If you want the word used to mean previously owned then I am used. As my original owner you should realize that."

"You are inane! I was as much owned by you as you were by me!"

"While that may have appeared so on the surface, deep

down you were only tolerating me! You wanted a child and I met all the criteria!"

"In case you haven't noticed you have a child too!"

Sparring with Viv always sharpened my teeth.

"I do and I wake up everyday grateful for her and that is the only reason I put up with you and your continual interference in my life! Why do you care who or how many women I sleep with? It is none of your God damned business! I know you had some choice words for McKenna when you followed her into that bathroom at Giovenetti's party. McKenna is an adult, she's got a good head on her shoulders and is capable of making her own decisions. Are you so cold and crass that all you see is a beautiful young woman whom you perceive as competition rather than a talented young ER doctor that can be a valuable addition to our staff. Is your view of what is good for this department so biased that you make decisions based on your own vacuous emotions? I don't know what happened to you. One day we had the perfect marriage as well as a beautiful baby, the next you tell me to move out, get an apartment you want a divorce! I never cheated on you, I respected and loved you with a love I never thought possible and what did you do to me? You cut me! You broke my heart and it took me a long time to come to grips with what had happened, but I pieced my heart and my life back together and I went on. You don't have to like or approve of what I do or whom I see. Do not cast aspersions on the choices I make or who I'm with. You will not, I mean WILL NOT make comments to my daughter about the choices I make in women."

She opened her mouth to speak but I was on a roll!

"Do not deny it! She referred to one of my friends as "is this one of the ladies Mommy said I shouldn't ask about?" Are you so pure you have the right to judge others? What about the little stunt you pulled when you took Emmy to Biltmore? You would not tolerate me sleeping with a woman in one room and my daughter sleeping in the other yet that is exactly what you did!

So stay out of my business! We have no relationship except our daughter shares both our DNAs. And furthermore if I advocate that McKenna be offered a position in the ER at University if there is one available I better not hear of you doing or saying anything to discourage it. Or I will go after your job! Do you understand me?"

I don't think she had ever seen me lose my cool like that, I was beyond reason. I was angry, no I was infuriated! The way she spoke to and about McKenna was only part of the reason, the other part was my own anger at myself. I had hurt McKenna by allowing my own egotistical reasoning to think because I wanted something I could simply reach out and take it! I had damaged any chance for a friendship and worse a good working relationship with one of the most capable residents I'd ever known. Shit I was still shaking when I walked in my shower. I turned on the water and got it almost scalding hot before I stepped in. I had been thinking of McKenna. She appeared crushed, really broken! If Tony had not broken up with her what was keeping her from going to him?

I saw him in the cafeteria two consecutive nights, he appeared wrecked also. As I started to wash my body I realized I had a boulder crushing hard on! I thought about everything but McKenna over the next ten to fifteen minutes but it was determined to not leave until I took care of it personally. God I hadn't taken care of myself like that since I was a teenager and had my first piece! I didn't want my mind to go there but since my ever ready appendage refused to listen to reasoning I went full fledged! I thought of that woman's ass and how it looked when I accidentally walked in on her. Round, firm, high, tight. I imagined I had her ass grinding into me begging for my dick! Her slick wet pussy! Wow it clamped around my dick like a starving Venus flytrap does to it's prey! I finally got welcome relief when I came all over myself, a nd relief felt good!

CHAPTER EIGHT

MCKENNA

Monday night came and with it's arrival was trepidation about Tony. I wanted so badly to see him. He was a warm port from a freezing winter storm but I couldn't approach him. I was already treading water.

We didn't usually get pediatric trauma however a four year old rescued from a silo filled with corn arrived in full CPR.

Her lungs were filled with debris, we could not save her! She was blue even though resuscitation was in process. All I could think about was her last few minutes on this earth, how she had struggled to breath. We worked on her for almost 30 minutes but nothing we did changed the outcome. She was gone when they brought her. Her little heart will never beat again, she will never smile again, her parents will never hear her laugh.....! I knew Curry was as affected as I was and I'm sure it was because he had thoughts of his precious Emma. He went and talked with the family, his voice breaking at one point as the mother held onto her husband and screamed as if she was being disemboweled. The reality was far worse than this. Her heart was being torn from her chest and it left a gaping hole. As we left the "family" room Curry gently guided me in front of him. As the tears rolled down my cheeks I headed for a patient bathroom just outside the ER. I locked the door and the silent sobbing started! I was ashamed at my response because I was a stranger, the hurt and devastation I felt belonged to that mother not me, but I couldn't stop myself. I don't know how long I was there but Curry came and almost pounded on the door, I did not let him in. The next was the janitor with the key accompanied by Tony. He held me in his arms and comforted me. He kissed every part of my face but my lips. After a short time in his arms I felt myself finally getting it together enough to return to the ER when Nan showed up with the driver of the hospital transport van.

"McKenna you're going home now. It's Curry's idea. You should never have come back to work you're still recuping from that damn virus! Here I've got your purse. I'm keeping your car keys. I'll have Ralph follow me to your apartment with it tomorrow morning. Go on now."

She practically pushed me into the driver and I didn't resist. I was exhausted! I fell into bed and didn't wake up until I heard my door bell ring about 08:00. I stumbled to the door, still in my scrubs. I opened it sleepily expecting to see Nan and found myself staring into Curry's chest! He didn't even ask he just walked past me into my apartment. He went straight to the sofa, sitting down he patted the cushion beside him. I ignored him sitting in a chair across from him. He leaned over, elbows on his knees staring at the floor. He was silent for several minutes, then he cleared his throat.

"McKenna I've been in ER medicine for over ten years and last night just about broke me. Jesus all I could think about was Viv and me if that were Emma. Was it wrong of me to think like that? No it was not. There was no problem with what I was thinking only the timing was wrong. One of the things they don't teach in books is how to deal with the gravity and absolute sadness of the job we do. I apologize for the position I put you in last night. I thought you could deal with it. Obviously my thinking was incorrect! You should not have been present when I spoke with her parents. You haven't recovered from what ever is going on with you. I've already put in for a transfer to the ICU for you."

I jumped up, fists tightened at my sides!

"No you can't do this!" I was fighting mad! He couldn't shove me under the carpet like that!

"No! I'll leave the hospital before I leave the ER!"

"SIT Down McKenna! You will do as I say! I am your mentor and right now you are physically and mentally not prepared for the ER."

"Oh so now you're calling me crazy!"

I got in his face so fast! I was nose to nose with him! The tears were falling down my cheeks. One minute I was standing in front of him challenging him, the next I was in his lap He cradled me close. His nose was in my neck, his voice was a whisper yet hoarse.

"God baby no! I don't think you are crazy, I think you are magnificent, mysterious, unselfish, brilliant, and so utterly transcendent that I am awed by you. Your beauty is not only on the outside. That inner spirit of beauty and purity you possess is so rare. I want you to stay in the ER but I fear that whatever is going on right now with you is so overwhelming that you will be crushed under it's weight. I am your mentor and I have to protect and preserve this wonderful gift that has been given to me. Please, no I don't think you're crazy."

I was so caught off guard I didn't know what to do! This was not the same man who asked me to call a cab or who told me I was a conquest to him, that I only garnered his attention because I didn't fall into bed with him. He surely didn't expect me to fall for his bag full of crap, did he? And to put everything into perspective I felt his hard on poking me on my hip!

I came up fighting! I slapped him! I elbowed him in the balls! I propelled myself out of his lap so fast I almost landed on my ass on the floor!

"Get out! Get out! You want me out of that ER you will have to have me removed by having my residency privileges revoked! I'm sure "VIV" would count it a privilege to personally show me the door! You two deserve each other! You are both so self serving and egocentric you make Nero look like a kindergartner! If you are finished with me then I'll request another mentor but I will not leave that ER!"

As he raised his head the look that greeted me was filled with shock and sorrow. He slowly got up and walked to the door.

"If you think that's what this is all about then maybe you do need a different mentor. I won't block you but you will go to ICU for a 30 day exchange experience."

"Oh that's ideal! ICU gets a doc and the ER gets a nurse in exchange!"

"What are you talking about?"

"I'm might be naive' but I'm not stupid! Hasn't your little playmate Angel applied for a transfer to the ER? You think I might spoil your fun because I'm shadowing you? Good bye Dr. Curry. You're standing two feet away from the exit now use it!"

"McKenna..."

I was screaming now!

"Don't you McKenna me! I'm Dr. Tipton! Don't ever presume you are familiar enough with me to call me by my first name!"

"As you wish Dr. Tipton. I shall see you in 30 days. I can only hope your little stay in ICU will improve your attitude! Oh wait, it *has* to improve your attitude because it's impossible for it to get any worse."

"Please close the door when you leave Dr. Curry."

I had turned away from him, I couldn't stand to look at him.

He left without another word between us. I collapsed on the couch in grief. I needed him and I had chased him away! I did care about Tony, but I was in love with Dr. Roderick Curry. Despite all it's nuances and difficulties the feeling I had for him could only be love! I knew any attempt at a relationship other than professional was doomed, even a professional one was going to be difficult at best. Unfortunately it was only going to get worse. Nan told me Nurse Angel Pussy had put in for a transfer to the ER. We had an opening for a nurse on our team so it was official she would be there on Monday. I hadn't puked from this pregnancy but I wanted to throw up now, I barely made it to the bathroom.

CHAPTER NINE

ROD

God I was an emotional mess when I left her apartment! Never had the sting of rejection hit me so hard! It was worse than with Vivian because I hadn't precipitated that event by acting stupid. I loved Viv and was a good husband and father so I didn't deserve her rejection. McKenna was a different story. I deserved any and everything she dished out and I had 30 days to come to grips with it, as did she. I don't know what came over me. I saw her hurt and everything was so clear to me! I was concerned about her as her mentor but now I know it will be a long time before I get over that itch because I love this quixotic woman! How and when that happened I didn't know. But what difference did it make? She hated my guts and that was not going to change especially with the little stunt I had just orchestrated. I had to do it, she is so fragile right now. When she gets stronger she will be unstoppable! The last two weeks have been very atypical as far as trauma goes. We do get children in the ER but usually in the fast track area. All trauma goes to Children's because that's what they do best. They are equipped and staffed for it.

The one wonderful thing about kids is they can be at death's door but if you do everything right they recover so much quicker than adults. Getting that four year old was a fluke. Combine that with whatever is taking McKenna down, it was more than she could handle at this time. I wish she would share with me because it's my job as her mentor to help her weather the storms over her two years here, prepare her to be the best damn ER doc she can be.

I invited Nan out to The Waffle House, I was sparing no expense to see what information I could glean from Nan regarding what's going on with McKenna. Nan has been an ER nurse for twenty six years plus and unofficially she was my mentor-no my savior when I came to University. I was so in awe of Viv I couldn't see the forest for the trees. More than once she stood beside me during a trauma and said, "Get your head out of your ass or you're going to lose this one." I valued Nan not only as a vital part of my team but as a friend and confident.

"You want more coffee?"

I waved our waitress over to our table.

"Yeah but I'd like decaf this cup."

"What's the matter, caffeine keeping you awake?"

This in itself was humorous because as long term night shifters we could sleep any time any where!

She raised her brow at me, "No smart ass but it keeps my bladder on high alert! I just get to sleep and I'm up again. I'm up and I've only slept maybe an hour or two."

"Come on, you're an ER nurse you've got a 12 hour bladder!"

"I do when I'm awake but my body forgets that when it's asleep. Enough of that subject, why did you really invite me here?"

"Super nurse Nan. You hurt my feelings always thinking I have ulterior motives!"

"That's only because you do and I know something is going on with McKenna so shoot."

"That's my problem. I don't know what's going with her, but she in deep with something."

"What do you mean?"

"Both times I've been to her apartment she's been a mess. Crying, acting all crazy."

"Why were you at her apartment?'

"I went to check on her when she called in sick and I took her shoes to her!"

Oops! I slipped up! I saw Nan's eyes narrow when I mentioned the shoes.

"Okay. Again, why did you go to her apartment,"

"I told you I went to check on her because she called in sick for two days. Even Vivian was concerned."

"Hah! That's a good one. Vivian is only ever concerned about Vivian."

"True that."

"Okay, how many times do I have to ask you?"

"Until you specifically say the word shoes."

"Okay. Shoes. This is going to be interesting!"

She pushed forward in her seat, crossed her arms over her chest and gave me her most form-able look.

"It's really quite simple. Posey ate her shoes so I had to replace them."

"How in God's name did Posey get Ken's shoes?"

There it was again, "Ken". A name she would never allow me to call her, I'm sure.

"Simple. She left them at my place."

"Oh this is going to be more than interesting! On what occasion did she leave her shoes at your place."

"On December 31st."

"Un-huh. Would that be the same as New Year's Eve?"

I was rolling the paper to my straw over and over, avoiding her glare.

"Yes."

"Out with it Curry we both have to sleep sometime today."

I sighed deeply. There were only a few people in this world whose respect I really treasured and the woman sitting in front of me was one. It didn't make any difference how I said this I came out looking like a predator, even though my feelings had changed. I knew I loved her but I couldn't share that with anyone, not even Nan.

"It's pretty simple, McKenna came back to my apartment with me after Giovenetti's party."

Her voice lowered, even she sounded hurt.

"There's nothing simple about that Rod. She really had a thing for you and she's not the kind of woman who hands that out to just anybody."

"I know I found that out."

"At what point did you get that little piece of information. Speaking of 'piece'- was it before or after you got yours."

I know this sounded cruel especially in light of what she just said, but it was what it was.

"After I asked her if she wanted me to call a cab."

"Any idea what time that would have been?"

"About 4:00 AM."

She shook her head in regret at my actions.

"You mean to tell me you've spent how many nights with that skank from ICU and you kicked Ken out right after you did the deed?"

"You make it sound really bad when you say it like that."

"So saying you asked her if she wanted you to call a ride before the post-coital glow wore off sounds better?"

"Honestly Nan, we were both a little drunk and...."

"You think saying you took advantage of a young woman who is drunk makes it okay?"

"I said we were both a little drunk."

She pressed her lips together, "Nope, not any better. I can bet you've been in that state many times and made that choice the same amount of times but how many times do you think Ken has been in that situation, a little drunk WITH her boss who has treated her like she's the best thing since sliced bread all evening, a MATURE boss I might add and..."

"Enough Nan, enough. I know what I did was very wrong

because I did take advantage of her in more ways than one. I've apologized to her, I've practically gotten down on my knees and begged her forgiveness but she won't budge."

"How did the dog get her shoes."

"You don't really want to know."

"Oh yes I do."

"Well it started in the cab..."

"Where she couldn't escape."

"Do you want to hear this or not?"

She nodded affirmatively, the look of disgust still on her face.

"Anyway it started in the cab and by the time we got to the door of my apartment we were ripping each other's clothes off. So our clothes were in my foyer and great room.

After I ask her about the cab she got angry and upset at the same time. We had words, she cried and I went across the hall to sleep."

"Did Vivian know you had a woman in your apartment?"

"No, she wasn't there but Helen knew. She answered the door. Interrogator Helen wouldn't even let me in until I told her what happened."

"Smart woman."

"So I came back the next morning about 10:00 thinking she'd be gone but she wasn't.

I thought she was gone because her clothes weren't scattered on the floor any more. On my way to the kitchen to make coffee I tripped over Posey laying in the floor chewing on something. When I told him to go to his bed he dropped his 'chew toy'. It was her black strapless bra. I followed him to his bed and I found her dress unscathed except it needed cleaning. Unfortunately the rest of her things didn't fare as well. He shredded her pantyhose, tore her shoes apart and licked her panties threadbare! So at least he and I share one sentiment about her."

"Don't be vulgar!"

"I just mean we both like her scent. Her shoes were Jimmy Choos."

"Good lord! Jimmy Choos! How did she ever afford those?"

"This is where it gets interesting. She left her purse in the cab, it only had her phone which was password protected and some money. She didn't have anything stored in her phone. We argued about me replacing her shoes. She told me absolutely not. That same day Emmy and I went shopping, I replaced her shoes. The damn things are considered collectibles, they had to be ordered from the Jimmy Choo Warehouse. When I took them to her she cried like the dam had burst. She didn't want me to replace them because she got them at a resale shop for a hundred bucks!"

By this time Nan was laughing so hard she started to cough.

"How much did they cost you?"

"Like twenty two hundred."

"Serves you right and you got off cheap. You lost some bucks. She lost her self respect."

"Nan, it's not like that. I'd really like to have a sexual romantic relationship with her but she won't even listen! She thinks I banned her to ICU so I could finagle and get Angel to work with us."

"Angel! Where would she get an idea like that?"

"I was blown away when she said that so I did some investigating. I found out Angel was 'invited' to apply for that open position."

"Invited?"

"Yeah, Viv's secretary told me she placed the call for her."

"What did you ever do to get that woman's loyalty?"

"I simply treat her as a human being, apparently something Viv isn't capable of doing."

"Does Vivian know about this New Years eve business?"

"No- please there only two people besides you and me who know this, that's Helen and McKenna. I'm trusting you to keep this to yourself."

"What if Ken mentions it to me? What should I say?"

"You can play it by ear, you know her better than I do."

Nan snorted, "I think Posey probably knows her better than *both of us!*"

I didn't look forward to going to work anymore. I had to face Angel on Monday. God what a mess! I'm beginning to agree with McKenna I think Viv is jealous or very vindictive.

CHAPTER TEN

MCKENNA

ICU isn't as bad as I thought. There are some definite positives. Angel is gone so I don't have to deal with her. The nurses in ICU are a tight little clique but they let me in the second night I worked there. I like them, they were great at showing me around, introducing me to their protocols and getting me acquainted with where things are kept.

There's one thing we have in common for sure, they don't like Angel and keep saying how much they're glad she's gone. According to them she bored them to death with details regarding the sexual exploits of Dr. Curry. And Curry was right about one thing, the hospitalist in ICU is an asswipe! He sits and does as little as he can. The nurses do most of his work. They complain that they have a hard time getting him to respond in a reasonable time when a patient is in distress. Add to that, his obvious dislike for me after I talked him thru the art line procedure and we have some interesting nights. Most of the nurses are in their thirties and married but it seems they all have a Dr. Curry story from their single days, except Gwen. Gwen doesn't like him, however she does have a healthy respect for his skills and knowledge plus how good he is with the patients.

Another positive of ICU is I never run into Tony. I did hear he has dated one of the rad techs on nights a few times. I'm glad he has moved on.

After tonight I have one night left and it's back to the ER. I had made rounds with one of the nurses and just returned to the nurses' station when my hospital cell phone rang.

"Hey Dr. Tipton can you come to 620? I don't like the looks of Mr. Stanton."

"I'll be right there."

Asswipe looked at me when I got up but never said a word. He kept his seat.

I found Gwen waiting outside Mr. Stanton's door.

"I don't like his color, he's pale and diaphoretic, his pressure is down a little but his heart rate is stable. He's complaining of pain in his epigastric area. I got an EKG but there's no evidence of an MI."

I went in the room to have a look at Gwen's patient.

"Mr. Stanton, I'm Dr. Tipton. Gwen says you are having some discomfort."

"Yeah, and I got this funny taste in my mouth. Tastes metallic. I can breathe but I still feel like I'm smothering cause something is sitting on my stomach."

I examined him and Gwen's assessment was right on the money, she motioned me out of the room.

"Dr. Tipton, I think this guy is going to crash and burn but I can't put my finger on what's wrong."

"What's his admitting diagnosis?"

"He came in thru the ER four days ago in acute alcohol withdrawal. Yesterday was the first day he even knew his wife."

"He could have esophageal varices, maybe one is leaking. Let's get an abdominal film, CBC with diff and CMP. Get some blood ready, we might have to use some uncrossmatched. We need to get the hospitalist in here. I'll talk to him."

I went to Dr. Reed, who was sitting in the doctor's lounge, his feet propped up with his tablet being the center of his attention.

"Hey I'm concerned about this guy in 620. He's sweaty,

pale, got a metallic taste in his mouth and says he feels like he's smothering. His pressure has dropped a little, heart rate is still okay."

I gave him the rest of the low down. He didn't look up from his tablet so I added, "I think he might be a candidate for a Senstaken-Blakemore. Do you want me to set it up for you in case we need it?"

"Why Dr. Superior, don't you know how to do the procedure? I thought you ER docs know how to do everything. Call me if you need me."

I couldn't believe my ears! Turning around I saw Gwen standing behind me, her mouth gaping.

"That son of a bitch!" she said under her breath.

Five minutes later we had the x ray and blood results!

"Dr. Tipton he's got a stomach full of blood, his HGB has dropped two grams. We're going to have to set him up to put the tube in. I'm afraid he's going to bottom out."

"It's going to take all of us to get that in, we need to give him something so he doesn't fight us and cause the tear to enlarge. Get that hospitalist in here now, get OR on stand-by. Susie and whoever else is available can help us. I need lots of ice for the tube. We need protective gowns and splash guard masks. This is going to be messy. I'm going to go talk to the patient now."

I took a deep breathe and walked in the room, taking the patient's hand I started to explain the procedure to him. He insisted on seeing his wife before we sedated him. As I tried to explain the urgency of the situation he only became more excited. I nodded my head to Gwen to push 10 mg. of Versed. I got gowned up, his pressure was dropping and we hadn't even sat him up yet! As he quieted we sat him up slowly and his pressure bottomed out, I started to pushed the iced tube into his left nostril and the blood just poured from his stomach out of his right nostril! I was trying to keep my voice calm but with all the blood I was having difficulty even seeing what I was doing. I yelled for more suction, an increase of fluids along with something IV to bring his pressure up. I told someone to get the blood started as soon as it got here. Three nurses and I were fighting for this man's life and Dr. Asswipe sat reading his tablet. I was just ready to call a code when someone stepped behind me, putting his hands on my very thickened waist line.

"Are you having a party without me Tipton? You're hurting my feelings! Here- put your hand here...."

He guided me thru the rest of the procedure. My hands were shaking from holding Mr. Stanton's head steady and inserting the tube.

"Here Tipton, duck under my arms, I'll hold.."

I bowed slightly to get out from underneath his arms, God even as scary as things were right then when my butt rubbed against his pelvis my panties exploded!

"What the hell's going on? Dr. Tipton why didn't you call me?"

Asswipe was on the scene! Fussing like he was indignant that I didn't call him and let him know what I was doing!

I was angry! How dare he!

"I......"

"I got this Dr. Tipton. Get out of those bloody clothes. Reed, as soon as I'm finished here we need to have a chat. You choose the place."

I went to change scrubs, they had no XXL. I had to put on mediums! God my waist was getting huge! My boobs were huger, if there is such a word. I had my top hiked up tying my scrub pants when Curry walked in! He took one look at my smaller sized scrubs and grinned a silly grin!

"God Tipton, lock the door! Somebody might walk in here that's never seen you in your all together and be shocked. Pleasantly I want to add. Sit down, I want to talk to you."

I did as he asked. My face was still shrimp colored from his 'all together' remark!

"Gwen told me what went on here tonight and I understand your anger. I frankly am outraged. I wasn't trying to take away your right to say something to him but it's my responsibility as your mentor. Do you understand?"

"No."

"What don't you understand?"

"Are you still my mentor in the ER."

"Wild horses couldn't keep me from it..... Unless you don't want me to."

"I thought...well I thought..."

"You thought what?"

"I thought after ICU you didn't want to be my mentor."

He sat on a table, leaning across he touched my knee gently, his eyes searched mine.

"McKenna I meant what I said. I was concerned for your well being. I don't think I have to be concerned about that any longer from the take charge Dr. Tipton I saw tonight. You saved that man's life while lazy asswipe let his personal feelings alter his judgment and professional accountability. We've all done that but if a patient's safety is in jeopardy it has gone too far. You will have your day in court, the hospital board will meet over this.

Don't worry all the nurses will back you. What Gwen says goes a long way, she called me to let me know how Reed was treating you. Don't blame yourself, he doesn't like me for personal reasons."

"What personal reasons?"

He smiled, "Really? You have to ask? ....I dated his wife before they got married."

A giggle escaped before I could prevent it!

"Yeah it's time you get back to the ER Tipton, you look like you've porked up a bit sitting around in the ICU."

I was shocked he said that! Before I thought about it I playfully smacked his shoulder.

"And I have one more comment Dr. Tipton. I would have

arranged to have an esophageal bleed dropped off in the ER six months ago had I realized it would get you out those tents you wear all the time!"

"What so you can make fun of me getting fat?"

"Fat is no where near what I'm thinking right now!"

He left me standing!

CHAPTER ELEVEN

ROD

My first Monday in the ER without McKenna was blessed with Angel. She followed me everywhere. I finally had a tete' a tete' with Nan.

"Look it's not my job to manage the nurses. You're the shift manager. Deal with her!"

"What would you like me to do? This is her first day so it's strictly for her to observe, trying to get the flow of things. If you don't want her observing you with your patients tell her."

"That will go over good!"

"That's the price you pay for allowing what's behind your zipper to be the wallpaper on every female's cell phone!"

"WHAT!"

"Just kidding, don't get your panties in a wad. Wait! That's your line!"

She was messing with me bad! She was pissed at me over the situation with McKenna and I didn't blame her. I was mad as hell at myself too.

"Okay, I'll handle Angel"

I walked off to find Angel. She was going over our protocols.

"Hey Angel, Megan is almost a fixture here. She's been here for fourteen years. She is great at directing a trauma from the minute it hits the door til it leaves here. Stick with her today and you'll get a good view of how we do things."

Megan was a great at "taking a trauma". The nurse that takes the trauma directs everything so the doc can do his job effectively. If he's going to crack a chest it's essential he has everything in place for the best outcome. She gives everybody a job so even though it appears to be to be mass chaos it really is not.

"Great Dr. Curry, thank you for the tip."

She was a bit too perky for me! God she had to stop watching me all the time. Shit I was going to dinner and it wasn't even 22:00!

After that first night with Angel I prayed for traumas. Not that I was wishing accidents or other bad events on people but it sure made the night go by faster. I also liked the mindless inane events that would come to our side if the other side was extremely busy.

Like the guy who wanted to show off for his girlfriend and decided he's try to spin a wheel on his index finger! Bad idea to start with but not taking the tire off before he started was witless. Then there was the couple in a gas station bathroom using a vibrator! All would have gone well had they locked the bathroom door and some one had not barged in on them, causing the door to propel the person holding the vibrator like a rocket into the wife's rectum! Luckily everything came out okay.

As I ate my dinner I read a book on my phone. The second week McKenna was in ICU Tony sat down beside me.

"Hey Dr. Sansone how's it going?"

"Not so well."

I really did not want to get involved in whatever was going on between them. I knew she really cared about him and that was more information than I needed. So I decided my best course was to leave.

"Sorry to hear that, hope things brighten up for you."

I stuck my phone in my pocket, picking up my tray I was heading out.

"Sir do you have just a minute to talk to me?"

I groaned inwardly and sat back down. Why couldn't I make an excuse and just walk away? I knew the answer to that question was one word: McKenna.

"Sure Tony, what can I help you with?"

"I know you worked with Ken (I just wanted to leave when he called her that!) about eight or nine months before she went up to ICU. Did she ever mention anything about her old boyfriends?"

"Gee Tony, we really didn't have that kind of relationship."

"OH I didn't mean to infer anything improper I just know she held you in high esteem so I thought she might have mentioned something."

"What's bothering you Tony?"

"Well Ken and I were getting very close. I know she was the one, the woman I had waited a long time for. Things were going great, we were going to take our relationship to the next level when everything fell apart."

"You were going to get engaged?" Wow! Things were moving a lot faster than I thought!

"Well I hoped to at some point but I mean the physical part of our relationship."

"So you mean you..you never..."

"McKenna's not the sleep around kind of girl. I respect that. Things were great when I left her that morning, she went to the gynecologist. She called me later that day and told me she had a bug and wasn't going to work. I didn't hear from her for three days, I called she didn't answer. Then she texts me things were going too fast and she had to back off. You don't know about any other guy do you?"

"No Tony I don't."

"I care for her but if she's not interested in me I need to move on. What do you think?"

I wanted to jump up and down and do my happy dance! He had not touched her! Maybe there was a chance for me!

God what was wrong with me? He's tortured, she's falling a part and all I can think is he didn't fuck her yet! I am seriously egocentric just like McKenna said.

"Tony maybe you should reach out to her again. It certainly couldn't do any harm. If you text or call she doesn't have to feel pressured to respond and if she's changed her mind or still mulling it over she will know you still are interested."

"Thanks Dr. Curry. That sounds really good. I value your advice because word on the street is you've had a lot of experience with women."

That shit head! I saw him sitting with another girl about a week later. I wanted to wring his neck. God if she saw him it might wreck her! When I got back to the ER I pulled Nan aside.

"Have you been eating dinner with McKenna?"

"Maybe. Why?"

"I just saw that loser Sansone with another girl in the cafeteria, their heads stuck together. God call her and make sure she doesn't go to dinner for at least another half hour."

"I've got left overs from dinner at home last night. I've been meeting her in the ICU nurses' lounge. I'll call her and schedule a time to eat. She doesn't usually go downstairs anyway."

"Why not?"

"She doesn't want to see you."

"Why not?"

"God I'm not going thru this with you Curry. You can't be that dense!"

"Okay, okay. Insensitive of me to ask."

"That's a better response."

About fifteen minutes later she gave me the ok sign. Three more weeks and she'd be back!

CHAPTER TWELVE

MCKENNA

I had my hair in a pony tail, my contacts in, and my XXL scrubs on and I was ready to tackle the world! The world inside the ER that is! Our shift started at 20:00, I was there at 19:30! I got hugs from all the nurses but one, I was not surprised by that. I didn't care what she did with Rod Curry. I was back home, I wanted to cry, actually Nan and I did cry when we hugged in the middle of the nurses' station.

"Okay, if you're handing out hugs Tipton you might as well include me. I'm as happy as everyone else to have you back. Paul was missing having his shoulders rubbed at precisely 08:00. Nan's missed having someone to order out with her and I miss not having you tagging along telling me what to do. By the way, that Sengstaken-Blakemore tube was a great diagnosis! That patient was lucky to have you working there that night or he might only be someone's memory now."

Before Curry could say anything else the tone went off notifying us of triple car pile up near a bridge with possible submerged victims. Nine victims in all, the tenth was still missing!

Dr. Curry and I worked together as if there had not been that month of separation. I didn't see Angel during any of the actual care but when Nan and I went to supper we followed Angel and Curry down the hall. I wasn't privy to what they were discussing but it must have been humorous to them both. They sat at a table together. Nan and I went to another table by ourselves. That lasted about two seconds. Why Curry moved his tray to our table is beyond me because all we did was listen to Angel talk about her skiing trip over the week end.

We had about five minutes left before we had to head back when Curry scooted over closer to me.

"I'm taking Emma to my parents cabin in Tennessee. I usually take Posey but my Gran will be there this week-end. She positively abhors my dog...."

"Oh Rod I didn't know you had a dog! What kind is it? I love dogs I'd love to see it sometime."

Well guess who loves dogs? Shocker isn't it!

I started to get up and leave but he stopped me.

"Can we talk about this later?"

"Yeah, sure."

Nan and I took the long way back to the ER, Curry was already in Trauma Room 1 with a ninety year old woman who got pushed from a second story balcony by her drug crazed grandson. I went in immediately and started to work. We kept busy the rest of the night with minor stuff. Actually the last half hour of the shift was downtown. I was ready to leave exactly at 08:00. Nan and I walked out together.

"Hey let's celebrate! Let me take you to Waffle House for breakfast."

"You sure?"

"Of course I'm sure. I'll meet you there."

Thirty minutes later I plopped down across from her.

"Tired?"

"Yeah, kinda. There's a lot more walking and sprinting in the ER. I think..."

I heard a distinctive laugh! It was Angel, she was about four booths over. I heard her but couldn't see her so I couldn't see who she was with. I looked at Nan.

"Don't ask, you don't want to know." she sighed deeply.

"I don't care Nan. He's my mentor, that's all."

"Are you sure?"

"I have to be sure. I'm smart enough to know if I let him he'd be in my bed tonight but I'm also smart enough not to do it. He's a player, he's a conscienceless prick and he will go to bed with anything. I'm only an interest to him because I resist him, the minute I show an interest he's on to the next woman."

"I know he feels differently about you then anyone else I've seen him with since Vivian."

"Please Nan I made the mistake of having a huge *crush* on him, but I'm over it. Case closed. Do not mention him or this again."

I wanted to bury my head and cry for a week but I couldn't I had to sit thru torture every night watching Angel fawn all over him and he gloried in it like a pig in slop and that was a very fair comparison.

"Do you want to leave?"

"No the last time I checked this was public property, I haven't seen any 'no trespassing' signs with my name on them . Let's order."

I was on my second glass of tomato juice when Angel walked past. I put my head down expecting Curry to walk past any minute instead he came over and sat beside me using his hip to push me further into the booth.

"Jesus Tipton, scoot it over. You act like you don't want me sitting here."

I looked him dead in his eyes daring him to say something else.

"Okay you don't want me sitting here. I'll move."

He sat down next to Nan.

I continued staring into my phone, Nan didn't say a word. Silence reigned for several minutes.

"Have I done something to offend one of you wonderful ladies?"

"Nope," Nan said looking up at him.

I said nothing.

"Why are you looking at me like I'm sleeping with the enemy," he laughed.

"That's because you are," Nan was practically gritting her teeth.

"Whoa, whoa! You certainly don't think I asked her to come here, do you?"

"Why else would she be here," asked Nan?

I was going fast, I couldn't hold it together much longer.

"Excuse me," I got up quickly and ran to the bathroom. I just made it before the tears came. I can't do this, Curry was right I am too fragile still. I need to go back to ICU where it's nice and safe. I don't know how long I was in there when Nan text me she was going home. I finally got myself together. I didn't have my backpack- maybe she left it with the cashier. I walked out of the bathroom and ran right into Curry. He was waiting by the door. God I needed to get away from him! Please just leave me alone.

He took one look at me and hugged me close, he released me looking down at me. I couldn't look at him, I was swallowing tears, the lump in my throat felt like a baseball.

His fingertips touched my chin.

"Look at me Dr. Tipton."

I looked at him thru tears, I couldn't stop them.

"I'm taking you home, then you're going to talk to me McKenna."

The ride home was silent. He put me to bed with my scrubs on because I wouldn't, couldn't let him see me! He'd know right away. I wasn't ready, I couldn't deal with what he'd say or do when he found out. He sat on the edge of the bed, I laid on my side, my back turned to him. I couldn't stop crying. I don't know what came over me.

"McKenna please talk to me. I can't help you if I don't know what's wrong."

"Go away, just go away. You can't help me. It's something I have to deal with on my own."

"Am I doing something to offend you or hurt your feelings at work or in our personal relationship?"

"Our work relationship is fine, we don't have a personal relationship."

"Only because you don't want a personal relationship with me."

"I'm not another Angel or Heather or any of the other women you fucked so leave me alone."

"I don't know what Heather has been saying but we haven't been together for months, as for Angel that's been a while too."

"I don't care about Angel or Heather, it's none of my business what you do with them."

"I'm not the one who brought up their names. You did."

"I only said their names because we can't have a relationship like you have with them."

"Believe me I don't want a relationship like that with you."

"You fooled me once. I will never trust you again. I even told you how long it had been, you had to have known I didn't want that kind of sex with you."

"I'm sorry McKenna, I can't go back and change what happened, the main reason is I don't want to change it. It was very special to me, you did give me a gift. There is no denying it was very hot but there was a sweetness to it I've never felt before."

"You lie! You only say that because you're in my bedroom now and you think I might be stupid enough to let you in my bed."

"No Dr. Tipton you're very wrong. Even though I might want to go to bed with you again that will never happen because I hurt you in a way I never intended to. You are way too good for me. I'm a rake with very little conscience and I like to take my pleasure where I find it. You and I both know that. Now are you going to share with me what is so devastating to you?"

"No."

"Then my work here is done. Get some rest, it will be Saturday night. You know what that is going to be, we might as well post a welcome sign to The Knife and Gun Club! Go to sleep kiddo!"

He smacked my ass as he went out the door.

"That's a little retribution for being a pain in my ass!"

He got to the bedroom door and turned, "Sure you don't want to talk?"

"No."

"Well you're consistent if nothing else! I'll lock the door on my way out. Your car will be here when you get ready to go to work."

With that he was gone and I started crying again.

Life started again and my secret remained hidden. Dr. Burroughs was super with me. Sometimes my sister went with me, mostly it was just me. Any ultrasound I had the tech always ran extra pics 'for Daddy". I had gained twelve pounds and I was four months, my breast were so sensitive, I was hormone central! I know it's wrong but I so need to get laid! Dr. Burroughs keeps encouraging me to 'keep active', then he laughs because he knows I'm an ER doc.

"Have you felt your baby move McKenna?"

"No. I hope I know what it is when it happens."

"Right after you have sex lay quietly because many times your baby enjoys that little ride and starts to kick. Try it. You might be surprised how easy it will be to recognize that feeling. We can discuss it the next time you come."

"You might pick another topic of conversation for the next time because I'm not sexually active."

"Don't you want to have sex? Surely you don't think it will harm your baby."

He seemed very concerned about my dilemma.

"Oh I want to have sex I just don't have a partner."

"The dad doesn't want to be a part of this? He doesn't want a child?"

"Dr. Burroughs this is almost embarrassing to say but this pregnancy is a fluke. I hadn't had sex for five years, then I basically had a one night stand and got pregnant. He doesn't know about this, he doesn't have a clue."

"When are you going to tell him? Or are you?"

"I don't think he needs to know. It would be a burden on him. That's certainly not something he expected to happen out of that one night."

"Well if neither of you used some form of birth control it's certainly an expected outcome. I mean the man is of normal intelligence isn't he?"

"I hope so, he's also a doc."

He scratched his neck, "Well we certainly hope so. He obviously wasn't thinking straight that night!"

"I feel okay about this Jeff. He has a good family health history and that would be the only thing of concern to me.."

The look he gave me seemed rather doubtful. He changed the subject quickly.

"See you next month. Call me if you have any problems."

I went home, my usual exhaustion chasing me everywhere. Even though I didn't have to work that night I took a nap. While I slept I had a very sexually explicit dream. The main character was none other than Dr. Curry. His touch felt so real. I remembered what his naked body felt like, how it felt to kiss the velvety soft tip of his hard penis. I woke with a start, it was like he had penetrated me with a powerful thrust! My panties were filled with a thick white discharge! My heart was beating wildly, I was breathing rapidly. The feeling that permeated me was so welcoming and warm. I bask in it. I rubbed my belly gently thinking of this little creature that had invaded my body and the man who put it there. I was making light circular movements on my belly, suddenly it was there! A gentle flutter! I felt it, I finally felt it move! A sudden sadness overcame me! The tears started again! It was bad some days, I couldn't turn it off. Fortunately I had been able to hold them back at work.

Curry was cordial to me just like he was to everyone even though there was a distance reserved only for me. The closest he had gotten to me lately happened during a struggle with a guy on MDMA. One minute I'm examining him, speaking with him casually the next I'm laying on the floor! Before throwing me to the floor he grabbed me, shaking me until my teeth rattled! I yelled for security to chase him as I lay flat on the floor. I looked up to see Curry eyeing me strangely. It seemed to me my belly was pretty obvious, when he realized that he was staring at me so acutely he went to his knees.

"Jesus Tipton are you all right?"

I tried to get up.

"Hang tight Tipton, I need to make sure you're not hurt before you try to get up. Is your neck okay? God he shook you like you you weighed two pounds. How about your head, did you hit your head?"

He started feeling around on my body, lifting my arms, looking me over.

"I'm fine. I'm sure I'll feel like a Mack truck ran over me in the morning but I'm okay."

Nan had arrived and put her hand out to help me up when he reached down and picked me up.

"Open a trauma bay," he growled to Nan.

"Get a gown on so I can examine you. You might need an x ray of your C spine!"

He set me down shakily on a gurney.

"No!"

"What do you mean no?"

"Not happening. I'm not putting a gown on and you're not examining me."

He waved me off.

"I don't have to do the exam. Sands can do it."

"I don't even need Sands to do it! I'm fine. I'm a doctor I think I can figure out if there's something wrong with me."

"I know you feel okay but you didn't see it from our side. Jesus he shook you hard."

Nan nodded in agreement.

"It did look pretty bad Ken."

"Not just bad, God damn violent!"

He just kept staring at me.

I jumped down from the gurney.

"I'm fine but I'm going to take five."

"Take all the time you need. Nan can bring you some ibuprofen."

"No, no ibuprofen, only acetaminophen."

They both looked at me strangely, I realized I did say that a little too quick!

"Ibuprofen does a number on my stomach! I almost had a GI bleed from it. I'm fine! You two get back to business. Quit using me as an excuse to get out of work. I need to change my scrubs. He was like spitting on me."

I headed for the doctor's lounge with my cell phone. I changed my scrubs. I dialed Jeff's after hours number.

"Dr. Burroughs."

"Hey this is McKenna. I'm sorry to bother you but I had something unusual happen this evening."

"Don't tell me you had that sex we talked about!"

I laid down on the bed and rolled!

"No! But sex would have been preferable to what did happen."

"Out with it!"

"I got shook by a crazy patient, then he threw me to the floor."

"How do you feel?"

"I feel fine, just sore."

"Ok. I think you're smart enough to figure out if you're injured."

"What about..."

"Stop by my office in the morning. What time is good for you?"

"I get off here at 08:00."

"Just come by when you get off. You don't need an appointment, it will be a quickie."

I felt my face get red! Sometimes my mouth needs a filter. What came out next did not sound right!

"I don't do quickies."

He chuckled, "Neither do .! See you in the morning."

Wow! My face felt like it was on fire! I started to get up, two Tylenol and a glass of water was thrust in my face.

"Here! Hope you feel better. These will hold you over 'til you get off. I mean until your shift is over."

God how long had Curry been standing there! He slams the door as he leaves! How can he do that? It has a thingamajig to keep from doing that!

I was the only patient in Burrough's office, as a matter of fact it was just him and me.

"Come on in, my nurse isn't here yet so we can chat. Tell me exactly what happened."

I replayed the incident for him.

"You didn't receive any blows to your abdomen, did you?"

"No actually, I don't remember having pain as a reaction to anything he did. My neck and shoulders are stiff with some myalgia this morning."

"You've been active all night, get ready for some major aching after you rest today."

"I know, I'll take Tylenol and use warm showers to ease the discomfort. It's like the base of my neck and in between my shoulder blades."

"Here sit down, let me work some of that out."

His hands felt like magic but the magic didn't last long. His nurse Peggy came in the door as the phone rang.

"Dr. Burroughs office.....Yes Dr. Slater, he's right here."
She pushed the hold button.

"Peggy please get Dr. Tipton gowned up, she got tossed around like a rag doll in the ED last night. I just need to do a quick check, no pelvic. Schedule an appointment with the massage therapist downstairs. Get three massages, special attention to bilateral shoulders and C spine. Put it through on her insurance. I'll be in as soon as I take this call."

I followed Peggy back to the exam room. I started to take off my scrub top and winced.

"Here Dr. Tipton, let me help you. You can keep your bra on."

"Do you need a specimen, I have to go to the bathroom."

"Put one in the cup, I don't think we'll need it but just in case."

I was going to the bathroom about every two hours. I left the specimen and came out.

I got on the table to wait.

"Are you and your husband friends of Dr. Burroughs?"

"No. I don't have a husband. Why do you ask?'

"He usually doesn't see people without an appointment unless it's at the hospital."

"I didn't know him at all before I made my initial appointment. Actually I got his name from the registry. He was closest to the hospital where I work."

"Humm......"

Jeff came in before she could say anything else.

"Okay, let's get a quick listen with the doppler."

He heard the heart beat right away. I suddenly was overcome with tears,"

Peggy took my hand, "Are you okay Dr. Tipton."

"Yeees, I'm, I'm fi, fine." I said thru tears.

"Yes Mc Kenna you're going to be just fine," he said gently, "Get dressed and we'll talk about the tears."

I did as he asked.

He returned to the room, standing directly across from me.

"Okay McKeena are you having some difficulty dealing with this pregnancy?"

"No, well....." I sniffled.

"Is the fact the father isn't taking an active role in this pregnancy the problem?"

"No, it's sad but it's my choice. I don't know why the tears are always almost right on the surface."

"I know you work a lot, are you getting out at all?"

"I know that's probably what I need, but I'm just so tired all the time."

"I'm going to give you an assignment. The days you don't work make yourself get out and if you don't do anything but walk it will help, it will release endorphins. Your next appointment is in 10 days and we'll determine the sex of you baby."

He sat down and took my hand.

"McKenna, you are a very brave woman to go thru this by yourself. This baby is a gift, I know down deep you really think it is or you would have made a different decision about this pregnancy. You have two choices, you can cry and mope around and in four months deliver a beautiful healthy baby that you are going to love far more than you ever thought it was possible to love someone, or you can get the best out of everyday there is to experience and in four months deliver a beautiful healthy baby that you will love far more than you ever imagined. So which will it be ER doctor extraordinaire? See you in ten days."

He chucked me on the chin and left.

I still tired easily, I ate everything that did not eat me first! I was beginning to enjoy my pregnancy very privately. Only my sister, her boyfriend Simon and Nan knew. After the shaking incident Nan came to me with some very information seeking questions, so I had to tell her. We went to Tim Horton's for breakfast, neither of us wanted to chance running into Curry and his sidekick Angel.

"McKenna I'm very concerned about you. You look like you are on the point of exhaustion continually, you isolate yourself from any alone activity with Rod. He is obviously interested in you but you push him away. What's going on?"

"Nothing. Absolutely nothing is going on. Curry has no real interest in me, as soon as his conquest is over, he's done with a woman. OTD! My life is complicated enough without letting Curry drive me crazy."

"Crazy how? Crazy mad or CRAZY mad?"

"I'm not sure how you differentiate between crazy and crazy."

She looked at me for a long time, it was sort of like two dogs staring each other down to decide who is dominant! I lost. I looked away because the tears were there again!

"Listen Ken I know about New Year's eve. Curry told me."

The tears overwhelmed me, I kept catching my breath, gasping because I was both angry and sad.

What! He told her! Who else did he brag to! I was going to be found guilty of murdering a certain doctor and then dismembering him! There would be no mistake about the motive because a certain part of his anatomy would be cut into so many tiny pieces it could not even be identified let alone pieced back together! I was getting up right then and taking care of the matter but Nan stopped me! She grabbed my arm!

"Where are you going?"

The tears overwhelmed me, I kept catching my breath, gasping because I was both angry and sad. No not sad, broken hearted. I didn't know how much more I could take! Not only had Curry disrespected me now he had betrayed me! No one was to know that!

"Settle down Ken, it wasn't like that. He's worried about you, he's afraid what happened between you two is eating at you and destroying what little bit of a relationship you have.

He cares about you. I believe he cares more than he wants you or anyone else to know. That stuff with Vivian nearly wrecked him."

"Well now he's wrecked me so I hope he's happy!"

"McKenna you are stronger than this, stronger than one wrong decision, stronger than a one night stand. You have to get over it. So you made a bad decision and went to bed with the wrong man get over it! Move on with your life."

We were sitting in a corner booth which was a good thing because I couldn't control myself! I was like a kid who had a temper tantrum and cried so much it was like I was heaving when I tried to talk.

"I I ca ca can't get o over it! I'm pr pr pr pregnant! I can can't get over it or him."

If I thought Nan was going to be shocked was I in for a surprise!

"I suspected that. Honey I'm sorry but I'm not, if you know what I mean. Tell him. It will force him to face up to how he's really feels about you."

"No! No!"

I grabbed her hands across the table and held onto them!

"Nan please, please you have to promise me you won't tell him. You can't I'm not ready to deal with his reaction."

"Honey I'm not going to tell anyone, not even Ralph. Sometimes I think Rod must be blind. The night you got shook your stomach was pretty obvious laying flat on the floor then your reaction to not taking Motrin and no x rays."

"I couldn't let him examine me, he'd know right away."

"McKenna are you going to keep this baby?"

"Of course what else would I do? I certainly wouldn't give up a child just to make my life less complicated!"

"Babies are wonderful creatures. I think carrying a child, having it form inside your body, feel the life inside you is a life changing event in more ways than one. Be happy about this time. You don't have to let anyone know, let them guess!

Establish a relationship with this baby before it's even born. Talk to it, sing to it, some mothers even read stories to their unborn babies. This is your special time, you will never get this time back again. And Ken I think you'd be surprised at Rod's reaction. He is a good good man, he loves that daughter of his like there is no tomorrow. You don't have to be married for him to go thru this with you. I know when Vivian was pregnant he was on top of the world, he was so proud to let everyone know he was responsible for that belly she sported."

"But he loved her, he was married to her."

"It won't make any difference to him. How far are you?"

"Five months and two days. I find out the baby's gender this Friday at my five month check up."

"Is the baby active?"

"Now that I recognize what the movement feels like, yes it is! On my days off when I try to sleep nights it wants to play!"

"Oh McKenna! You are going to love this baby so much and you are going to love being a mommy."

"I was so upset in the beginning about being pregnant, now I'm just sad I can't tell him.

Sad Nan, just really sad."

"You can tell him McKenna."

I felt better after letting Nan know. My sister practically lives with Simon now. Actually she's decided to move in with him. She's going to help me paint and decorate her old bedroom once I find out the baby's gender. She's excited to be an 'auntie', super excited since the baby started to move. She teases me about my prego belly! When I'm not in scrubs I wear loose tops with leggings. When I go out it's very obvious I am pregnant. I don't try to hide it. I don't socialize with the people from work with the exception of Nan and the odds of seeing someone I work with are pretty slim in a city the size of Birmingham. We don't hang in the same circles.

I took Jeff's challenge about getting out every day I was off.

I did some shopping for the basics. I was anxious to purchase a crib, changing table, and chiffarobe however that was another thing that needed to be gender specific. Two very interesting turn of events happened during my daytime ventures.

I met my sister for lunch at a restaurant in a mall close to her work. She and Simon were gung ho on buying a car seat for the baby so before eating we took care of purchasing that, she arranged to have it sent to the apartment. I felt especially good that day, Paige even mentioned I was getting a pregnancy glow, later when I mentioned it to Nan she agreed! We chose a Greek restaurant for lunch, it was late so there was no lunch crowd. It was the day of my 27th birthday so we were also celebrating that, I even ordered a glass of Moscato to go with my huge Greek salad! I was craving salty foods so I had an entire serving of Kalamata olives on the side. Greek food was very familiar to both of us since the summer right before our senior year of undergrad we saved our pennies and took a backpacking trip to Greece. We were deep in conversation when my sister stopped mid-sentence staring over my shoulder.

"Don't get up because there is a certain co-worker coming with a very beautiful woman at his side."

I purposefully turned in the booth toward the wall keeping my head down as if searching for something in my purse. I couldn't deal with seeing him with Angel it would ruin an otherwise perfect day. I hoped he would pass us by since I was sure he would not recognize my sister after seeing her briefly on the evening after our "dirty deed".

"Dr. Tipton good to see you! It's a bit of a surprise to see you here!"

I looked up to see a gorgeous woman standing at his side. He stopped at our table! How kind of him to rub my nose in his liaisons outside of work as if at work wasn't sufficient to make me feel used! Used and discarded like an old, old, old! Well like an old....... something! I couldn't think clearly with him standing so close, his hand gently gripping my shoulder!

I nodded my head slightly, "Dr. Curry."

The woman was older but beautiful, so obviously out of my class! I didn't want to stare and I didn't want to make the comment that came out of my mouth, but I did!

"Even though it might surprise you residents have brains, brains need nutrition so therefore we eat!"

God that came out snarky! He laughed before turning to his 'date'!

"It's been so good to see you. Give me a call when you and Sam want to put me to shame on the golf course. I'm always up for a public scourging!"

He kissed her on both cheeks.

"I'll tell Viv you said hi."

"Don't you dare! She still needs to apologize to me! Her behavior was so uncalled for. See you!"

She walked off, perfect posture, hips swaying. He hadn't bothered to introduce us.

The next thing I knew he was butt barging my side of the booth! I had to slide over and let him sit down. He put his arm over the back of the booth then leaned forward and offered his hand to Paige.

"Hi. I'm Rod Curry. I work with McKenna."

"Hi, I'm Paige, Ken's sister."

"Aw, thus the resemblance. I think we met before on New Year's day at the Chinese place. Not that McKenna introduced us! Are you ashamed of me Dr. Tipton?"

He asked looking down at me, then letting his hand rest lightly on my shoulder. For a moment there was something in his eyes! It was there then it was gone! Next he did the un-pardonable thing- HE LOOKED DOWN THE TOP OF MY SHIRT! He was blatant about it. Three things happened at the same moment! My face got beet red, my panties got wet and my little invader decided to kick, kick, kick!

"We're celebrating Ken's birthday."

"Well I'm glad I got invited to the party!" (kick, kick)

"This is not a party!"

I wanted to add, even if it is YOU are not invited!

"Obviously not with two people, but three's a party! Right Paige?" (kick, kick, double kick)

"It is in my book."

"McKenna tells me you're in investment banking. How is the investment world faring these days?" (kick, kick)

They started speaking in terms I'd never heard of, so I tuned out, but my little invader continued to kick almost every time Curry talked! Maybe this is a sign I should tell him. I was so turned on, his hip was against mine and it was warm......! I was jarred to consciousness again when he put his hand on my leg! Oh God! Oh God! Oh God! I was so horny I wanted to jump his bones right there!

"Happy Birthday Tipton! I better go before you accuse me of spoiling your birthday."

He reached over to kiss me on the cheek with a near miss of my lips! He needed to go, right now! He was in danger!

He got up and left, I never even said good bye, I just lusted after him! My panties were a serious wreck!

"WoW! He is seriously hot! Sizzling hot and I think he likes you!"

"Yeah, you know what he likes about me. He's already made use of it, I'm just another one on his previous pussy patrol list."

"I don't know, there's something there Ken. I think you should tell him."

"Well I think I'm sure I shouldn't. Subject over!"

"I've gotta get back to work. Hope your birthday lunch wasn't too boring for you."

"It was great. Like old times just the two of us."

"Correction, two and a half of us! I love you Ken and I know you will be such a great mom! Simon and I have already been talking about helping you out by babysitting. Since you started to show Simon has been back on his marriage kick. I do love him and if it's right it will be right in a year or two! Who knows maybe by the time we get married you will have found someone you can't live without and we can have a double wedding!"

"Earth to Paige! When you have a baby you don't have a big shindig you tie the knot quietly then go somewhere and fuck each other to death for two weeks!"

"McKenna Rose Tipton! This baby has to be a boy, you are getting so vulgar! I love it!"

"I love you too. I'm going home and go to bed. I'm exhausted."

I usually took the steps to my apartment, it's an older building with multiple charming features one being a fenced in court yard. I love the ambiance of the building but I hate the creepy elevator! My living room overlooks a park across the street, it has huge windows that let in a lot of natural light giving my whole apartment a cheerful atmosphere. Today I took the elevator because I was sweaty from the long walk home. So many thoughts of Rod Curry crowded out my normal reasonable comfortable tenets. By the time I got to the door of my apartment I was wet and wild! I wanted to call him, tell him everything then spend the afternoon in bed going at it like rabbits! Instead I decided to take a soak in the tub. I laid back to relax. My little invader began to kick, it felt like it was doing somersaults!

"Oh baby today is a special day, you got to hear your daddy talk, I think you liked that!

I liked that! He makes me a total wreck just being near him. In three days I find out if you are going to be a big strong willed boy like your daddy or a sweet little girl like your crazy mommy. I hope someday I can tell you how you got here, how very very much I loved you before you were even born. I hope someday he will hold you in his arms and love you like he loves your sister Emma! Oh if Emma even knew she was going to have a new sister or brother she would be over the moon! I love you little invader. It will be hard but we'll be happy, just the two of us."

The tears were coming like a torrential storm! I couldn't stop them because the sad truth is I am in this by myself. For all my happiness there is also a hopelessness I can't change. After my soak I lay and look at my belly knowing I can't go thru the whole nine months keeping it hidden. I have a real concern about his reaction if he ever realizes this is his baby. He will probably be so angry that I didn't abort it but I couldn't do it! I know all the things a young well educated woman, hell a doctor, should know but I couldn't throw a part of myself away, nor a part of him even if he didn't intend to give it to me.

I began to doze off when my door buzzer sounded. I was sure it was the delivery of the car seat! I hurriedly put on my old fuzzy robe, buttoned it not bothering to tie the sash. Before I could get to the door there was an impatient knock! God can't this guy wait two minutes? I took the chain off the door opening it widely and there stood Rod Curry!

His eyes gave me the once over, settling on the two un-fastened buttons on the top of my robe, showing an indecent amount of exposed breast! He smiled widely and took a step toward me leaning in I was steeling myself for his kiss but instead he smelled my hair!

"Um, you smell good Tipton! Did I interrupt your bath?"

I quickly pulled the top of my robe together. I felt my face getting red!

"Too late Tipton I've already seen the goods, and for the second time I might add."

He laughed cheekily adding, "The first time I had a much better view!"

My temper flared! How could he drive me insanely angry in so short a time?

"I might mention the fact that you enjoyed *"the goods"* so much you couldn't wait to kick me out! Did your pleasure of "*my goods*" enthrall you so little you would have had the cab there to take me home while YOUR junk was still running down my leg! Get out Curry! Don't ever and I mean ever mention my very regrettable indiscretion again or I will go to Vivian and tell her you coerced me into having sex with you!"

If I thought this would make him angry and he would leave I was for sure mistaken!

He howled with laughter!

"Come on Tipton I could be accused of a lot of things but rape is not one of them!"

"I didn't say rape!"

"Well coercion is the same as rape because that means you didn't really give your permission! You wanted it as bad as I did Tipton! I mean I wasn't quite as desperate as you since it hadn't been five years for me!"

I rushed toward him! I wanted to slap him so hard! How dare he bring up something I told him in a very intimate moment to ridicule me! He grabbed my raised arm and pulled me to him, we were both breathing so hard! In a nanosecond he had me in his arms kissing me so passionately! I wanted to give in, crush my body against his but then he would know! I couldn't, somehow I couldn't let him find out this way! In my mind I could see him pushing me away like a scorned woman! So I pushed him away! I could push him back, but I could not push back the tears!

"Get out of here Curry! I'm not one of those women!"

"What women Tipton?"

"Your 'pussy patrol'! That's what women!"

"McKenna," he said softly, "I haven't been with a woman like that in almost three months!"

"Don't lie! I've seen you with Angel!"

"That's just it. Seen me with Angel. I haven't touched her, at least not like that."

"What's the matter Curry? Losing your touch?"

"I am losing my touch Tipton! I'm losing my touch for

anyone but you."

"You only want me because I don't fall down on my knees and worship you. Admit it!"

"Well I do have to admit if you fell down on your knees in front of me I'd like you to do something to me, but it's not worship me."

That made me cry harder because I certainly had fantasized me doing that to him!

"Get out! I told you to get out!"

He reached out to touch me but I stepped back!

"McKenna please, give me a chance," he pleaded almost in a whisper.

"I gave you a chance and you could hardly wait to get rid of me. I felt something for you Curry or I would never have gone to bed with you but that meant nothing to you. It was all a game, a big joke to you. So leave please leave."

I collapsed in a ball on the floor sobbing too weak to stand. He knelt beside me. He gently stroked my shoulders.

"Don't cry Tipton. I'm sorry I'll leave you alone. I've hurt you far more than I realized.

I'm going to put you to bed. Please forgive me. I didn't mean to upset you like this, I only came to give you a card and wish you happy birthday."

He picked me up and carried me like I weighed nothing! He laid me on my bed and sat beside me, I immediately turned away from him. I couldn't stop sobbing.

"Do you want to take your robe off?"

I could only shake my head I couldn't talk.

He pulled the covers over me then laid down beside me on the outside of the covers.

"I'll leave when you stop crying. I'm sorry, I'm so sorry I hurt you."

He laid behind me and spooned my body, he carefully placed his arm over my hip and left it there.

I don't know when I stopped crying nor when I went to

sleep. I don't remember him leaving but when I woke up he was gone and it was dark outside. I got up, ate a PB&J for dinner along with chips and milk heading straight back to bed.

The next two nights at work were super busy with barely enough time for supper let alone small talk. He was polite but distant and that's the way I wanted it, needed it so I could cope with this pregnancy and my feelings for him.

On Friday morning I was excited to leave work! I had my gender reveal ultrasound. Driving there I realized I hadn't invited my sister but I wished I had because I really wanted someone there to share the news.

I knew I was in for a surprise either way but I had my suspicions it was a little girl. I don't know, somehow I just imagined myself with a little girl who looked just like Curry. I had my ultrasound, I was having a boy, a little boy. I held my tears in check. I was excited to discuss it with Jeff and tell him how much better I felt after taking his advice, even though I still tired very easily. I got on the table and exchanged small talk with Peggy while she got my urine, my weight and my vitals. She didn't mention any change in my visit so I was totally surprised when Dr. Slater walked in the room.

"Good morning Dr. Tipton how are you feeling after your very informative ultrasound?"

"I'm excited! I hope being a single mom I'm up for a rambunctious little boy!"

He chuckled, "I'm sure if you are stubborn enough to get thru medical school you'll do just fine with this little guy."

He asked me some other questions, commented on my good blood pressure then bid me good day reminding me to schedule my next appointment.

Peggy was extra smiley with me today!

"Dr. Burroughs wanted me to make sure you are the first patient on your appointment days, so how does 8:30 sound to you?"

"I can come in the afternoon Peggy, I don't always have to

have the first appointment."

She laughed.

"You do if Dr. Burroughs says you do."

She gave me my card with the date and time written on it. I got ready to go out the door. "In case you asked Dr. Burroughs wanted me to let you know he's having coffee at Panera across the street."

"Oh. Oh! Well thank you Peggy. See you in four weeks."

In the elevator I tried to figure out if that was a cryptic invitation to coffee. I decided it was or Peggy would not have said he wanted me to know his whereabouts. So I headed across the street. He was watching for me and stood when I entered. I went to his table. I didn't see any coffee!

"Hey how are you? How does it feel to be having a son?"

Golly! News travels fast!

"Somewhat daunting!"

"You're up for it McKenna. How about some breakfast?"

"Sure that sounds great! I always sleep better on a full stomach."

"Sit. What would you like I'll get it."

I'm thinking gosh what a congenial OB, I'm going to have to recommend him at work.

"I'd like a cinnamon bagel with cream cheese and a small hazelnut with cream only."

"Got it."

I was so excited but I really wished I could go home. I was tired, truly looking forward to having a very erotic dream about Curry. It was hard sometimes to not think very sexually explicit things about him when we were working shoulder to shoulder. God his butt in those scrubs was screaming for me to walk up behind him and feel him up! He always tucked his scrub shirt inside his scrub bottoms, cinched at his hips they fell just right!

"Here you are."

Jeff set my food down. I started to get my wallet out to

repay him. He laid his hand on mine.

"No way. This is not professional, it's personal."

"Thank you,"

I was nervous! What did he mean?"

We drank our coffee in silence.

"McKenna I'm going to have to discharge you to Dr. Slater's care."

"What? Why?"

"You thought your one night stand was embarrassing to talk about. What I have to say now is just as embarrassing to say to you."

"I'm listening."

"I have to discharge you to Slater be cause I've developed very unprofessional feelings toward you. I was attracted to you the first time I met you, I held back because I didn't want to interfere if you had feelings toward this guy. I still don't want to complicate things if there is a possibility now....I know it sounds crazy but I'm very concerned about you and this baby-how you're going to be affected by him and how your career... well your attitude toward your career will change once you have this baby. I know you've told me you want nothing to do with the biological father but does that mean you don't want any involvement with any man?"

I really hadn't said I didn't want anything to do with Curry I just said I didn't want him to know about this baby, however that was a moot point at this time.

"Are you asking me if I'm a lesbian or do you mean am I anti-man at this time?"

"Anti-man?"

Jeff was a hunk! He worked out, had a heck of a bod! Something in his smile and his manner made him very approachable. Yes, maybe I could have a relationship with him, after all he knew what he was getting into.

"Not even really anti-man. My focus is on getting thru this pregnancy with a healthy baby, coping with being the only person solely responsible for him. It's a tall order."

"I know it is McKenna. I can't help you with that right now because ethically I've been in a position to have you be very vulnerable to me. Since I've discharged your care to someone else after your baby is born and your six week check is good I feel it's appropriate to pursue you. God that sounds like we're from the dark ages!"

We laughed together! It felt good.

"I'd like that Jeff but you know every woman falls in love with her OB so you might be taking a big chance turning me over to Dr. Slater!"

"Might be! Nah, Slater's got a hot wife who has already given him six kids! All girls and he's not stopping until he gets that boy! He's tried every trick in the book and she still is popping out girls!"

It was funny!

"I know a lot about you but I want to know you better so do you object to meeting for coffee, only coffee? Just to talk?"

"I'd like that! So we're having coffee, tell me about Jeff Burroughs."

"I'm a tennis player! I love to play tennis! I've tried racket ball and other crap but tennis is still my favorite to play and watch."

"You'll have to teach me sometime."

"I'd love nothing better. I'm a California transplant. I love Birmingham. I came here to medical school and have never looked back. My mom got pregnant with me when she was a sophomore in high school. She and my dad got married, they are still married and seem devoted to each other. After they had me they finished high school, went to college and had careers before they had other kids. So I'm 36 years old with two brothers, 16 and 14 years old!"

"That's terrific! I only have one sister and you met her. Our parents are gone so we're very close. Are you close with your brothers?"

"It seems crazy but we are. My parents are amazing! God when I think of my mom having a baby at 16 I'm amazed I don't have something majorly wrong with me. I mean she had to be so brave! At sixteen she wasn't fully developed, well neither was my dad but somehow they had their heads screwed on right. They struggled but they made it thru. This is a personal question but have you been married before? It wouldn't make any difference."

"No. Have you?"

"Yeah, for three weeks!"

This guy was funny! I hadn't laughed this much since... well for a long time!

"Well I hope our relationship lasts longer than that!"

"I can assure you it will."

"Really? How so?"

"Because I'm not in Las Vegas and drunk out of my gourd! And I didn't meet you in a strip club!"

This not a date was turning out to be fun!

"What did your parents say?"

"What could they say? I was twenty-five and responsible for myself. Not to say they weren't angry at me. My dad said it wouldn't seem as stupid if I was eighteen and just had my first piece of ass but "no you have to make a fool of yourself in the middle of med school." My mom told him not to be so vulgar! I'm sure when I wasn't around they had a good laugh. For several years after that if I got upset about anything my brothers would always ask me if I planned on going to Las Vegas again! The inference to my stupidity was there of course."

We ended up talking for two hours! It was just what I needed to get my mind off of Curry. Jeff and I were meeting weekly for coffee, talking, laughing getting to know each other better. Nothing sexual at all, at least not overtly so. Right before my six month check up I asked him if it would be unethical for him to be with me when I delivered.

He took my hand and kissed it, shaking his head yes.

"As much as I hate to say this, I can't. I count it as a privilege that you would even ask me. While all the nurses and doctors we know would overlook it the hospital board would not."

He still held my hand, "Gosh Ken, I've never felt so honored in my entire life and I mean it."

I choked back the tears. Normally I didn't need a man's reassurance but with this birth experience coming up I did. I was trying to push down this uneasy feeling I had but I couldn't.

The fourth of July week was our rotation for three days off. My sister and Simon went to Miami, really trying to convince me to go with them but I couldn't, it was just too much since I still tired easily. I was spending the time really alone because Jeff was flying to California for time with his family. He hinted at my going since no one there knew of our previous doctor patient relationship, and I really was becoming fond of him. I couldn't decide if it was a romantic thing or I just had horny hormones from being pregnant. What if we got there, got involved in a physical relationship. Would I, could I have sex with him! You bet I could! If I did, that would really muddy the water especially after the baby was born if I didn't feel that way any more. He was a great guy and I didn't want him to be hurt and feel like I did, just screw him because he was convenient like Curry did to me. Thus the decision I would spend the week-end by myself except on the fourth. I was going to Nan's for a cook out with her family. They were great people and I was looking forward to it.

I really was doing okay now. I had regular conversations with Jeff and with my little man. I will have to admit that Jeff is a bit more responsive than he is, however I have to be careful of the things I say to Jeff, little man not so! Nan has heard me talk to him and has warned me not to be surprised if his first words are screw and horny! She is my confidante, she knows how I really feel about Curry although I've never came right out and admitted my deep deep feelings for him. I love this baby, he is already a part of my life. I talk to him as if I was holding him in my arms. He is my everything. I wonder sometimes if it is because I am so in love with his daddy. Would I feel this way if I had not had such strong feelings for Curry the night we made love? She also knows about my hopeless horny hormone appetite! I can say anything in her presence and it doesn't faze her. She's told me several times she always knew when she was pregnant with her sons because she practically stalked Ralph she was so horny for him!

My last day at work was hectic, couldn't prop my feet up, barely got dinner and I had a backache that wouldn't be responsive to the Tylenol I took. The morning of our shifts off I was slowed down from getting out right as my shift ended because I was really uncomfortable. I stood in the doc's lounge absentmindedly rubbing my lower back when suddenly larger hands took over the job.

"It was a rough two nights Tipton. Go home and sleep. Get rested up for your big holiday week-end."

I snickered!

"My big week-end plans consist of propping my feet up, eating all I can eat and then sleeping about twenty-four hours straight."

"Sounds like the perfect week-end except you're missing the two most important ingredients."

"Really? What's that?"

"Alcohol and someone to spend it with, but not necessarily in that order!"

"Dream on Curry, I don't need either of those things to have a great week-end. I happen to like my own company!"

"I like your company too Tipton but you don't like mine. I'm pretty sure by now you hate my guts and I don't blame you."

He chucked my chin and walked off.

Well thank you Dr. Curry! You sure know how to cheer up a gal! I hated him right then, but I wanted him, really wanted him. I wondered how his love life was going. I didn't see him text anyone or talk on his cell phone a lot like he'd done in the past, although I did see Angel corner him from time to time. I saw them walk out together several times. What happened after that I didn't know. I couldn't think about that now, I just had to get home and lay down hoping to get some relief from my back pain.

I stopped for some Chinese food on the way home, I was so tired I didn't even eat it when I got there. I took a shower, got out my heating pad and got in bed. I could eat later. I fell asleep not waking up until the next morning, my bladder must have had a guilty conscience and backed off my every two hour sprint to the bathroom. My backache was still there and a tad more uncomfortable. I got up and did some stretches which seemed to relieve the pain if only for a short time.

I was looking forward to seeing Ralph and Nan's kids again. She had two little granddaughters, Odessa and Oaklyn, who were adorable! Both talkers! If you want to know anything about Nana Nan or Poppy Ralph just ask them! They could tell you interesting things like how many cigarettes Poppy smoked this morning or how many times Nana went to the bathroom or called Poppy 'dumb head'! I personally think they have a future with the CIA! Other than my back I felt very good. I had some energy so I cleaned my apartment from top to bottom. Paige's old room was mid-transformation to a nursery. It was painted a soft blue with white woodwork. The crib and matching chest and chiffarobe was a dove gray. I liked it. It was coming together better than I thought possible. Paige was very artistic, she loved painting. On the short wall she already painted a mural of a big old oak tree with a little rope swing, near it was a tricycle. She painted other items laying on the ground, a bat with a tiny glove next to it, a toy airplane! This baby may not have a daddy but he was going to have plenty of attention from his mommy and Auntie Paige. Paige also did calligraphy. She offered to paint a sign with his name on it for his bedroom. It would have been finished already but the hold up was me! I'm trying to make a definite decision on either McKinley Abraham or Berkeley Abraham. Both first names were my grandmothers maiden names.

Uncle Abe may have been a drunk but he never mistreated us, he protected us, we always had food on the table and a place to live. Every day before school his last words to us as we went out the door were, "Go to school to learn girls, smart girls can do anything they want to do, be doctors, teachers, hell they can go to the moon in a spaceship!" Although life was rough we had the basics and it could have been a lot worse if Paige and I were separated by the foster care system, so I needed to honor him somehow. I was leaning toward McKinley Abraham and calling my little man 'Mac'.

I wanted Nan to take my picture today to put in the book with his ultrasound pictures.

She took a quick one at work in my scrubs! Side view so my belly would show. Today I'm going to put on one of the cute, but short maternity dresses Paige bought for me. It's a soft chambray with red trim, and I decided to wear some red wedge heeled sandals. My hair was down, it seems to have grown tons since I've been pregnant. I also took some shorts and a tank top so I could go in their pool. I made a fruit bowl and some baked beans. Everyone loves my beans and they're vegetarian! Of course I don't tell them that. Who in Alabama with it's strong ethnic cooking influence would admit there was no meat in the baked beans! I was like Jeff, this town was growing on me. Most importantly I'd be having a little 'Bamer'!

My 'Bamer' was particularly quiet today. I knew Tylenol was safe in pregnancy but maybe I'd lay off it for the rest of the day. The party was going strong when I got there. Ralph met me at the car carrying Odessa who reached out immediately for me.

"Nope baby girl, Poppy Ralph is doin' the carryin' today.

Miss Kenna's already got a baby to carry."

"You do!" Her eyes wide with wonderment!

"Yes I do, right in my belly! Feel."

I touched my stomach as she bent over to feel my belly.

"Oh you didn't eat your baby did you?"

She was very concerned!

"No baby, the baby's daddy planted that youngin' there." Wise words from Poppy Ralph! For some reason that satisfied her for the moment but I could sure see the wheels turning on that one. I knew before the day was over someone was going to have to come up with an explanation for that too!

Ralph kissed my cheek.

"Kenny you are lookin' good! Very pregnant but good. Come on we're going to eat soon."

We walked on to meet the others.

"Kenna! You look just beautiful! I've got to get a picture!"

Nan got her phone and took several pictures.

"I'll send them to you."

"Please do, I want them for his baby book."

Nan's kids treated me like a sibling.

Lauren her oldest commented, "Mama always did love you best! All because none of us was smart enough to be an ER doc! She loves you girl! Always bragging on something you did or said."

Karman her youngest daughter followed that with, "Yeah, if one of us got knocked up before we got married Mama would have killed us!"

I heard Nan gasp! Karman put her hand over her mouth!

"Kenna I didn't mean for that to sound like it did, I'm so sorry!"

I couldn't help it, I started laughing!

"Well let that be a lesson to you! See the things you can get away with when you go four more years to school and come out owing half a mil! Gosh, I bet I could get arrested and she'd bail me out!"

By this time everyone was laughing!

"You're probably right about that 'cause Mama always told us if we got ourselves in the slammer we'd have to get ourselves out!"

I was enjoying myself immensely, laughing until I thought I'd pee my pants! We cleaned up after our meal, the kids were going in the pool but I was feeling a lot of pressure in my vaginal area. It gradually increased until I felt like I started having period cramps. I got up from the lounge chair to go to the bathroom and I heard Nan gasp!

"Oh my God Kenna please sit down!"

"Nan I have to go to the bathroom."

"You can't do that, you are soaked with blood in the back! Sit down. I need to get you to the hospital."

"Mama do you want me to call 911?"

"No they wouldn't even be here for 20-30 minutes, I can get her there in 25 minutes! Get some blankets we can wrap her in."

I heard her talking, suddenly it seemed I was an outsider looking in! Instantly a pain gripped me, starting in my back going around to my abdomen.

"Nan, I think I just had a labor pain."

"Hang in there Kenna, Ralph's going for the car. Katie's got blankets to wrap around you, can you make it to the car, it's not even ten steps away?"

"I'll carry her Mama," Paul picked me up and practically ran with me to the car! They laid me in the back seat and Nan got in by my feet.

"Nan stay with your family! It's a holiday. Please."

"Listen to me I'm the one with the most experience here! I think you have placenta abruptio. We need to get the bleeding stopped. Lay flat, don't move!"

After that I laid there quiet, time passing me by, I prayed my little man wouldn't be born today, I prayed Nan was wrong in her assessment of what was happening to me. I tried not to but I started to cry, "Nan little man has been so quiet today. I've had a backache since yesterday I didn't know it could be that, I should have gone then they would have known. Oh" I started panting, "I'm having another contraction."

"Kenna I have to look. I'm going to pull your underwear off, okay?"

"Yes, yes. Nan I feel like I have to bear down! I can't stop it!"

"Yes you can, pant like hell Kenna! We're two minutes out, we've got to be at the hospital before he's born."

Nan was calm, "Just continue to pant honey, don't even think about pushing! No pushing I forbid it!"

I knew she was trying to lighten the moment, I loved her for it!

"I'll be good, I promise. I won't do anything I'm not supposed to."

"Too bad you didn't say that to Rod on New Year's eve. We're here!"

Lauren had called ahead at her mother's instruction.

I remember being lifted, people talking loudly, someone said, "God she's delivering that baby right now!"

I knew all the words they said, I recognized that tone. I'd said those same words when we were trying to save someone. Suddenly I realized I didn't hear a baby cry. I knew, I just knew my little man was gone! I wanted to go with him! He needed me, he was weak and born early, he needed his mommy! I didn't know where I was but Dr. Slater was there, he took my hand.

"McKenna your baby was born too early, he didn't make it. I'm sorry. We couldn't get him to breath or get his heart started. We did everything we could. I'm very sorry. Do you want to see him."

I had to see him! He never took his first breathe! All the things medical science could do but they couldn't save my baby!

I wanted to yell and to scream, "What the hell is wrong with you people! You're doctors, work on him, don't stop. don't stop please don't stop he's all I've got!" The only thing that truly has ever belonged to me and I lost him."

Nan came and stood beside the bed, I had never seen Nan cry in all the horrible things

we'd seen but she cried for me. She held my hand while they laid him beside me. I picked him up, I held him to my chest. If only I could give my heartbeat to him. He was so still yet I had felt him move inside my body. Slowly I unwrapped him and looked at him, he was perfect, ten tiny, tiny little fingers and toes, a dark patch of hair on the top of his head, some over his uniquely formed little ears. He looked so peaceful, his eyes were closed, I noticed little dark fringes where his eyelashes were. He was perfect, so perfect but he never took a breath. I cried and held him until finally they took him from me. Nan stayed with me. I finally slept.

When I woke up Nan was sleeping beside me in the chair, I put my light on and the nurse came to answer it.

"Do you feel rested Ms. Tipton?"

"I'm okay. I need to go to the bathroom and this stupid IV is going to get tangled."

This woke Nan up.

"'Here Ken, let me help you. Do you want to take a shower while you're up?"

"Yes, I guess I'm pretty messy."

When I got in the shower I started to cry, I couldn't stop! I had to leave that hospital without my little man. Nan did her best to comfort me. When my shower was over Dr. Slater came, sat in the chair by my bed and really talked with me.

"McKenna I wish I could change what has happened but I can't. Two things occur when a woman loses a child. The first is blame, she wants to blame herself, her body for not doing it's job, her doctor for not doing his or her job but the truth of the matter is sometimes there is no sign of something going wrong until it happens. I've gone over your ultrasounds and there was no sign your placenta was breaking away, not until it happened. So don't blame yourself or anyone else, blame only slows the grieving process. The second thing that happens is a profound sense of loss. I can't tell you how to get over it or how to deal with it I can only tell you it's going to be there, and is probably there right now. I can give you the names of some support groups, I suggest you hook up with one as soon as possible. I am profoundly sorry. I now need to ask you some practical questions. The first is his birth certificate. Do you want your name as his surname or are you going to provide another name.

"No, his name will be McKinley Abraham Tipton."

"Physically you're doing well, fortunately we did not have to do a section. He was born naturally. Your son was two pounds two ounces and fifteen inches long. We packed your uterus to control the bleeding, the packing is out now. The placenta was intact. You should have very little bleeding because we cleaned it then packed it. You need to come back right away if you experience any heavy bleeding or cramping. I'd like to see you at my office in two weeks."

Nan was there thinking for me, thank goodness.

"Dr. Slater, McKenna is an ER doc. What are her work limitations, when can she go back to work? What about when she goes home?"

"This is treated just like a full term delivery. She can go back to work in six weeks, we'll talk about limitations at that time. For now I don't want her doing much of anything. No vigorous cleaning, no lifting greater than five pounds that's equivalent to a gallon of milk. Get plenty of rest. Do you think you'll need something for sleep?"

"No."

"Continue your prenatal vitamin for at least three months. Call me if you need anything McKenna, and I mean anything. I've been in contact with Jeff, he's pretty upset over this. He planned on coming back on Tuesday afternoon. He really is concerned McKenna, he thinks he missed something with you but he didn't. He'd like you to call him whenever you feel up to talking. He'd like to call you but he doesn't want you to feel pressured into talking to him."

"I'll call him. Right now I don't want to talk to anyone. I just want to be left alone."

"I can understand that, I just don't know if it's the best thing."

"Dr. Slater can you leave a work release for the six weeks, we'd rather you not be too detailed, I'm sure you understand."

"Tell me who and the fax number. I'll fax it from here today before I leave."

"Dr. Vivian Curry, 205-391-5656." Nan wrote that down on a slip of paper as she said it.

"Thanks, I'll take care of this right now."

He walked out leaving us alone.

"Nan go on home. I'm tired I need to sleep. Take care of your family."

"You are my family, you heard my kids. Apparently you're the favorite!"

"How can I ever thank you for what you've done."

"You don't have to thank me. When I come again would you like me to bring you clothes to wear home?"

"That would be super."

"Call me when you're ready to go home."

"Don't worry about it, I can Uber."

"McKenna Rose! If you weren't sick I'd kick your ass!"

"Let me get thru my grief before you start kicking my ass again! If you don't your kids might get their hopes up thinking I'm not the favorite anymore!"

We laughed together! We're ER people, we have to laugh because that's how we protect ourselves. I needed to laugh to protect myself or else I'd remember I'm dying inside.

I'm home now, no more little man. No more kicking me, no more conversations about his daddy and how much I loved them both. I miss him already! No more little man, no more big man! I roamed around my apartment gathering things to put away in my storage space. My doorbell rang. I wasn't ready for company. I was pretty sure it was Nan checking on me before she went home to sleep. I opened the door and Curry stood there. Did he know?

"Hey, how are you?"

He didn't know!

"Can I come in?'

I let him in but I wanted him to leave. This was private grief, he didn't even know little man existed.

"Have you eaten? I'll fix you something to eat. You won't have the strength to get better if you don't leave."

I just wanted him to go, before I told him. I wanted him to hurt as much as I did, but he wouldn't care. He didn't want to leave me with a part of himself, he just wanted to fuck me then make me leave. I did what he asked and he finally left, left me alone without my little man. I wanted to sleep for about a month maybe when I woke up it wouldn't hurt so badly. I stayed in bed. I didn't get up except to go to the bathroom. I slept. I didn't know what time it was, what day it was but whoever was at my door wouldn't go away.

I dragged myself out of bed and staggered to the door. God it was Curry again! I wanted to scream go away but he said he wouldn't leave until I answered my door. I opened the door totally unprepared for what happened!

"He was mine, wasn't he! Oh baby baby why didn't you tell me. I am so sorry."

He pulled me to him and I just collapsed against him, I felt as if Atlas took the world from my shoulders, I didn't have to hid anymore. He started asking me questions. I couldn't stand up. I just couldn't talk to him, I couldn't comprehend what he was saying. He put me in bed but this time he laid beside me.

I was so weak I thought I was dead, but NOT that dead! I felt his erection! God what is wrong with men! Then he cried with me, he did care. Oh Curry things could have been so different! I went to sleep and don't remember what happened after that.

CHAPTER THIRTEEN

ROD

The fourth of July week-end was uneventful for me. Emma and I spent the fourth and the day after with my parents in Tennessee. I was able to take Posey since my Gran stayed in Richmond. I was teaching Emma how to water ski against my father's good advise. As an ENT he thought any skiing at age seven was a gold mine for ENTs and plastics guys. My mother who was much more adventuresome thought it was great. Turned out to be a good time. The only problem we had was keeping Posey in the boat. When ever Emma and I were in the lake he wanted to be there too! After our second day on the water we decided to go into town for dinner. Pizza to be more specific. There was a great Italian place, pricey and on the more formal side but Emma's manners were on par for this type of environment, however Posey's are not, so unfortunately we had to leave him at home. In a strange environment he gets separation anxiety so all four of us felt guilty about leaving him which was the topic of conversation at dinner.

"Daddy if Miss McKenna was here we could leave Posey with her and he wouldn't be sad."

"Who's McKenna," my mother raised her brow as if to say, "Do you have something to tell me?"

"Well she's.."

"She's Daddy's friend but not one of those ladies. Posey

likes her so much he ate all of her clothes.."

"She's a...."

"Even her underwear!"

At this point my Dad excused himself and went to the bar, trying his darnest not to laugh out loud.

"That's pretty funny isn't it Nana?"

"Well it might seem funny to us but I'm sure your daddy's *friend* wasn't happy about it."

"I don't think she minded it, she wore Daddy's T shirt and sweat pants home."

I tried not to make eye contact with my mother. My mother is a mature woman and knows I am a man, a sexual being I might add, so therefore she knows I have an active sex life. She just didn't particularly want to hear about it from my seven year old daughter.

"That's enough discussion about Daddy, how about Emma? I do have to tell you I love your polka dot sneakers?"

"Daddy got them for me."

"Did he let you pick them out?"

"Yes and he got me a backpack and some other clothes just the color of the polka dots in my sneakers."

Thank goodness my mother got her off the subject of my dog's chew toys.

"I love that color Emmy, it's beautiful and bright just like you!"

"Thank you Nana. Mommy hates these clothes!"

My mother gave me a sadistic grin, "Really? I'm shocked that she doesn't like the clothes your daddy bought for you."

"Yeah I know but she'd really be mad if she knew Daddy paid two thousand and two hundred dollars for Jimmy Choos for Miss McKenna!"

There it was! Out in the open! I had no secrets once Emma knew about them. My dad choked on his drink with that little piece of information! I almost had to reach over and close my mother's mouth. My father responded after clearing his throat.

"Emmy what's Helen doing this holiday?"

My daughter who looked so innocent sitting on an adult chair swinging her legs back and forth had spilled the beans! Things could only go down hill from here!

I was glad to be off the fourth, it was the busiest holiday for ERs but I was glad to get back to work. McKenna and I had a good day the last we worked. She is a heck of a doc for being so young. She's a little emotional, has been for last five months or so but God she is beautiful! She has a beautiful spirit, not a mean bone in her body. She's been distant. I know she has a boyfriend. I can't get any information out of Nan, she doesn't seem to know anything. Son of a bitch bastard better treat her right! She's got this glow! I've known about him since the shaking incident. He was the first person she called. The conversation wasn't even about her being shook. It was pillow talk! Talking about quickies! God I wanted to reach thru the phone and choke the asswipe out. I'd tried to take care of her but she wouldn't even let me touch her. Jesus does she ever hate me. I know what I did but I don't know what I did. Sounds complicated and it is. I just wish she could, or would forgive me.

I dropped my backpack off in the doctor's lounge. The schedule for next month was hanging there next to July's schedule. There was a line thru McKenna's name for the rest of July and half of August! What the hell! I practically ran to the nurse's station, Kelly the unit clerk stopped me.

"Dr. Curry, the other Dr. Curry wants you to call her in the morning about the schedule."

"She'll hear from me when I feel like calling her!"

I was angry, frightened, and disappointed because my first thought was McKenna just quit! Why would she quit before talking to me. Anything out of this ER was shaky but we had a solid working relationship. At least that's what I thought. I had to track down Nan.

She was getting report from a day shift nurse. When she saw me she looked away, I had to find out what happened!

"Nan I need to see you immediately? Are you finished with report?"

The day nurse smiled brightly.

"We sure are Dr. Curry, you've got her undivided attention!"

I took Nan's hand starting to lead her down the hall. I saw tears. I put my arm around her shoulder and took her to the doctor's lounge. As soon as I shut the door she turned away.

"Please don't ask me anything."

"God Nan what's happened to McKenna?"

"Please it's just too sad to even talk about!"

She put her hands over her face and wept!

"Nan you have to tell me! You don't know how I feel about her. Talk, please I'm breaking up inside."

"Her, her baby di, di didn't make it!" She could barely speak thru her tears

"What are you talking about? What baby? Where? When?"

Nan looked at me like I had two heads!

"You really didn't know she was pregnant?"

"Pregnant! Hell no! Pregnant?"

I started to pace. I couldn't believe what Nan just told me could be true!

"When did you find out?"

"Only about a month ago. She told me after she got shook."

That's why she called that asswipe so quick! She wouldn't let me examine her because I would know she was pregnant by some asshat who probably has no idea what a wonderful woman she is.

"Did the shaking? Surely the shaking didn't cause any problems with the baby?"

"No. No it didn't. I've got to go, I can't talk about this with you anymore."

"Is she at home?"

"Yes, but leave her alone. She's hurting bad enough."

"You think I'm going over there and intentionally upset her?"

"She's too fragile right now to talk to you or anybody."

"The father?"

Nan shook her head and more tears started to roll!

God damn it to hell! Son of a bitch bastard got her pregnant and skipped out on her! You better bet I was going to see her and I was going as soon as my shift was over!

She answered the door and she had on her ratty PJs!

"Hey. How are you doing?"

She looked pale, she had been crying. Her hair was hanging down on her shoulders. She was so beautiful! I wanted to tell her but I couldn't make a comment like that at a time like this.

"Can I come in?"

She shook her head and stepped away from the door. She went to sit on the sofa. It was covered with a plethora of baby clothes, mostly blue with some green and yellow interspersed.

I got down on my knees in front of her. I took her hands, she refused to look at me.

"McKenna can I do anything?"

"No."

"When did you get home?"

"Nan brought me home today."

"Have you eaten?"

"No. I'm not hungry."

"You need to eat."

"I can't."

"I know you don't feel like it, but you need to."

She shook her head no. Her eyes were so vacant looking, I wanted to hold her and comfort her. I wondered why asswipe wasn't here taking care of her! God I was a low life but even that is beneath me.

"I'm going to get you some soup

"I won't eat it."

"Yes you will because if you ever want to get rid of me you'll eat because I won't leave until you eat and take some fluids."

That was enough incentive! I left two hours later, she was back in bed sleeping after eating some chicken noodle soup and drinking some fluids.

I went home and tried to sleep. I just couldn't piece things together. Who was the elusive asshole? I needed to talk to Nan. I'd catch her at work tonight.

I called Viv when I got up, after my shower and some coffee.

"I asked you to call me this morning?"

"I know what you asked. I had a headache and I couldn't risk it getting worse and having to call in. What's up?"

"What do you want to do about your resident?"

"I'm not sure of what you are speaking."

I was being an ass to her but right now I didn't care. Surely she knew what happened to McKenna and made no comments to allude to the fact that she might have some human emotions! Right to, "What do you want to do about your resident!"

"Well she 's going to be off for more than a month. Do you want to terminate her and take on another resident?"

"What is wrong with you? The woman has suffered a loss! No I don't want to take on another resident! This conversation is over!"

God how unfeeling can she be!

We were about four hours into the shift and it slowed down enough for me to go to dinner. I tried to get Nan to go. She wouldn't so I took her into the nurses' lounge.

"Did you see McKenna today?"

"I stopped before coming in. She said you'd been there but.."

"But what?"

"Curry how dense are you?"

"You know I'm pretty stupid sometimes so give me a clue as to what you're referring to."

"She was six months, almost seven Curry so this wasn't a miscarriage. That was a formed baby."

"I know my anatomy and physiology so you don't need to go into detail."

She gave me a disgusted look and started to walk away.

"You are hopeless."

I held her arm.

"Six months? That can't be!"

"Well it was and it was a boy- a baby boy Curry."

I had to sit down! I felt like I had been hit in the chest! I couldn't breathe! My heart pounded! How could this be true?"

"Now you're getting the picture."

"I I I didn't know. Why didn't she tell me?"

"There you are turning stupid again! Maybe she couldn't get Angel to shut up long enough to tell you!"

"Come on Nan, that's been over a long time."

"You listen to me and you listen to me good Curry. You stood right out there in that nurses' station and made a date with that skank not even a week after you had her in your bed! You are a useless prick sometimes! Do me a favor, forget about her! You broke her heart and she never recovered from it. You went from one woman to another and almost rubbed her face in it, so how do you think she felt. Stay away from her or you will have to deal with me!"

I spent the longest night of my life in the ER. I left as soon as I could.

I knocked on her door four times and she didn't answer. I'm sure Nan had informed her I was on my way."

"McKenna, I'm not going away. I'll sleep out here today if I have to. Let me in."

When she opened the door she looked so pale. She had been crying. I didn't even ask her if I could come in I stepped in and pulled her to me.

"He was mine wasn't he?"

She relaxed in my arms, sobbing as if a great weight had been lifted off of her!

"Oh baby, baby why didn't you tell me? Why?"

I had held it together as long as I could! The tears fell silently down my cheeks.

"Why McKenna? Do you hate me so much you would rob me of a son? Rob Emma of a baby brother? Why?"

"I don't feel good, I can't talk about this now. I have to lay down. Just go and leave me alone. I don't have a baby any more there's no reason for you to stay."

"I'm not leaving. I wanted to stay many times before and I didn't even know about the baby. I'm going to put you to bed."

Picking her up I started down the hall to her bedroom. I passed a bedroom newly painted blue. I knew I needed to close that door later. I laid her down covering her up, she started to shiver so I took off my scrubs crawled in behind her spooning her body. God it felt good to be laying close to her body. My body responded, I couldn't control what was happening to me. I hoped McKenna didn't notice!

"If you try anything Curry I will cut that thing off when I feel better!"

I laughed but I knew she was dead serious!

"He has a head but no conscience, please forgive him. My intentions are purely honorable. Now rest. Are you getting warmer?"

"I don't think so I'm just so cold."

I got closer to her, putting my nose on the back of neck I inhaled deeply! I craved her scent, and I wanted that baby even though knowing about him was new to me.

"He kicked me a lot." She whispered into her pillow.

"He liked to torment his mommy, probably more like his daddy than you wanted him to be," I couldn't help but chuckle. "How much did he weight?"

"T, two pounds two ounces. He was fifteen inches long

Curry. Only two pounds and he never took a breath. Jeff said he was going to be big when I had my last appointment."

She began to cry again, I held her tight.

"Do you have pictures?"

"Yes."

"When you're feeling up to it later I'd like to see them."

"In the last level 2 he was sucking his thumb."

I really had to laugh this time!

"Must be a daddy gene because Emma sucked her thumb too. I'd like to see a picture of you with your pregnant belly, God I know you were just beautiful."

She made a small noise, I wasn't sure how to interpret it. I put my arm over her, gently rubbing her stomach. She started crying again, putting her hand over mine she grasped it tightly.

"Sh, sh baby. I know there's nothing I can say or do to make losing him hurt any less.

McKenna you have to let me share this loss with you. Please don't shut me out. I know now why you cried, but I can't figure out why you didn't tell me. What kind of a man do you think I am?"

"Please, I'm so tired I can't talk about this now."

"I did give part of myself to you that night McKenna. I gave part of myself to you and it became a living child, a part of you and a part of me. So don't shut me out."

Her only response was her tears. I kissed her neck and her shoulder, pulling her hips back to meet my pelvis made me wish I could end every day like this. Eventually her crying subsided, her breathing became even and I knew she was asleep. I thought about the night my son was conceived. She was so responsive, when I caressed her breast, just rolling her nipples between my thumb and index finger made her gyrate her hips. It had been so long for her and God she was so ripe! The first time I didn't wear a condom and I nailed her! I thought about her ass and her tits, I started to get hard again. I knew now it didn't matter how many times I scratched that itch I'd still want to scratch it everyday for the rest of my life. I only had to convince her of that. I drifted off to sleep thinking of Emma's reaction to a baby brother.

I was awakened by McKenna getting out of bed and staggering to the bathroom like she was drunk. She was covered in bright red blood from her hips to the back of her knees! The bed was soaked and where I laid against her was saturated as well. This was too much blood!

I found her leaning against the wall sitting on the toilet.

"Curry I'm so cold and I'm so weak, I don't think I can get back to bed."

She started shivering, her teeth were chattering! I had to do something about this bleeding! I was sure she had retained placenta.

"I have to get you some clean everything McKenna. Where are your pads?"

"Don't Curry, don't be nice to me now because I'll cry and I don't have the strength to do that."

"Listen to me baby. I have to take you to the hospital and I have to call your OB, who is he, or she?"

"Jeff Burroughs but Dr. Slater delivered me because Jeff is out of town, call the after hours number. I just need to go to sleep. Please let me sleep."

I found the number and left a message with McKenna's cell number. I had to clean the blood from me then get on my scrubs so I took her phone into the bathroom with me.

As soon as it rang, I picked it up.

"McKenna are you okay? Ken I've been so worried about you even though I discharged you to Dr. Slater."

"This isn't McKenna. This is Rod Curry."

"Are you...What's going on with McKenna."

"I'm sure she's got retained placenta, her bed was soaked in blood and so was she. I'm bringing her in immediately."

"I'll have Dr. Slater meet you in the ER. Are you an ER

doc?"

"Yes."

"An honest answer. How is she?'

"I can't waste time talking."

I hung up and carried McKenna to the car. I was scared. She was barely arousable.

"McKenna I need to call your sister."

"She's"....She drifted off again!

"Mckenna, talk to me!"

"Florida......Simon."

Shit! She needed family! I needed family!

I ran every light and broke every speed limit there was in the city of Birmingham. Where was a cop to do a police escort when you needed one! I couldn't wait the twenty to twenty-five minutes for a life squad. I called her name several times and gently shook her to get her to respond on the way there. Thank God Slater was there with blood waiting when I got there. She soaked thru the blanket that I had wrapped around her.

Blood had even pooled in the bucket seat of my car! God how much blood had she lost? It was my fault, if I had been watching over her instead of being so interested in sleeping with her I would have noticed the excessive bleeding. I was told someone would come get me as soon as possible. They *assumed* I was her significant other but didn't ask me for any information since she was discharged less than 48 hours ago.

I had her phone which was not password protected so I looked up her sister's number.

"McKenna! What's going on! It's hotter than hell here in Miami you should have come! The beaches are great! Oh wait, you've got a pregnant belly you're not very proud of! When are you going to let the douche in on your little secret."

She said all this before I could even say hello!

"This is the douche Paige."

If I expected her to say something I was sorely disappointed, she didn't. When I found myself actually having to say what was going on I floundered! I foundered because my child, a son did not survive a premature birth and the woman I loved was bleeding out because of my stupidity!

"I'm with McKenna at the hospital..."

"Oh my God it's too early! Can they stop the labor?"

My voice broke as I spoke again.

"It's too late. He was born about thirty-six hours ago and didn't make it."

"Oh no, how is Ken?"

There it was again! The person who should be closer to her than anyone else on this earth and I still couldn't call her that!

"She's a wreck emotionally but she's retained some of the placenta as a result she's having some pretty serious bleeding."

"I'll get the next flight out!"

"Paige I don't know how much longer you were supposed to be gone but she's not really up for company!"

"I'm not company!"

"I'm sorry. I know that. I just meant I'm going to be here, where I should be taking care of her."

I couldn't last much longer, I had to get off this phone.

"I'll keep you posted. I'm sure she'll be here for a day or two depending on how low her hemoglobin is."

"Okay."

"Good bye Paige."

"Bye. Rod?"

"Yeah?"

"How are you? I mean, this was your child."

"Thanks for asking Paige but you should really just be kicking my ass instead of being concerned about me."

"I know what happened. She can't be budged once she makes her mind up about something and she was determined not to let you know."

"Sadly she had her reasons and they were correct. If I had been half as observant about things I would have known what was happening to her. I gotta go."

I hung up. I had another call to make, I needed my mother.

"Mom I need you and Dad to come to Birmingham right away. Do you think you can do that?"

"Rod is everything okay with Emma?" Her voice sounded full of panic!

"Everything is fine with Emma, I just need you right now."

"Okay, we'll use your dad's friend Charlie's copter if we can."

"That's great. Can you come to Princeton OB?"

"Rod!"

"Mom just meet me in the ER waiting room."

One hour later my mom sat down beside me and took my hand, kissing it and pressing it to her heart.

"What's wrong baby boy? I'm here."

It was almost like the day I found Harry our dog laying on the side of the street after some son of a bitch bastard hit him with his car and left him to die-I was twelve years old. Too old to cry out loud, too young to absorb the hurt like a man!

"God Mom she might die!"

"Who Rod?"

"Mom you know I'm a player and for that I'm a rotten son of a bitch bastard. I was with a woman for one time. One time Mom and she wasn't that kind of girl. She didn't sleep around, she had feelings for me and I tossed her aside! I haven't not used a condom since Viv and I separated but I didn't that night and she got pregnant."

"That surprises you?"

"Yeah, well I guess I didn't think my sperm were that potent. She didn't seem worried and she's a doc."

"Maybe she intended for it too happen."

"God no Mom! Jesus she is not devious like that. I didn't even know she was pregnant until the day before yesterday. She didn't tell anybody except one friend at work and that was only after some drug crazed nut case shook her and threw her on the floor. She wouldn't even let me examine her, get x rays or anything."

"Dr. Curry, Dr. Slater."

He stood above us with the news I so desperately needed to know. He extended his hand in politeness. I stood up taking his hand quickly! I needed to know what was happening!

"It was a little hectic for introductions before. You were right, she had a uterus full of blood plus what she had lost, that was about three units. She's had two units and I've ordered packed cells. She's still pretty groggy but you can see her if you want."

"Thank you. Dr. Slater this is my mother Dr. Emma Curry I'd like to take her with me."

"Sure. Sure. I know there's nothing legal so I don't know how long it will be before you get kicked out. I know you're the sperm donor...."

"Now wait a God damned minute! I ....."

I was already on edge! He had no right to make a statement like that!

My mother took my arm, "Rod that can be discussed another time. We're here for a different reason."

"I apologize Dr. Slater. Thank you for what you've done."

My mother was right but fuck him I was more than a sperm donor! I love that woman. Even though it was lust on both our parts when I got her pregnant that did not take away the fact that I love her and want to be a part of this. I love that baby even though he was gone and the thought of her having to go thru labor then losing him cut my heart out. We would have been a family, this is what I want. I know McKenna lost her parents early and grew up in a dysfunctional home but as she said she came out okay. I know deep down she wanted me to love and cherish this baby and I would have. If she thinks for one minute this would be an embarrassment to me. Wow is she ever mistaken! I would have let everyone know that belly she was wearing was my creation.....I had to stop thinking about this, actions speak louder than words and now was the time to act.

He nodded his head, turned and walked away to join another man who strangely enough seemed very interested in what was going down between the two of us.

"McKenna, how do you feel?"

I bent over and kissed her forehead as I took her hand, kissing it also.

"I feel tired very tired and empty especially empty."

She turned her head away from me, the sobbing started again.

"I know baby and I'm sorry, I'm very very sorry."

She cried some more. I was at a loss for what to do so I stood there and held her hand. She turned back to me.

"You don't have to stay. There's no baby, there's nothing, so go. Go away and leave me alone."

"McKenna.."

"No Curry, leave. You were never a part of this anyway."

"McKenna I'm Emma, Rod's mother and you can tell me to butt out but I think he needs to stay. You need to hang on to one another to grieve your loss together. He didn't know McKenna or he would have been there. I know my son and he would have been there for you."

"I told you to go away Curry! Go find Angel, I'm sure she's waiting outside the door for you."

She was still experiencing some latent effects of the anesthesia, not really grasping what was being said to her.

"Listen to me Dr. Tipton, you'll not tell me how to feel or what to do! I'm not leaving so get used to it."

"McKenna it was nice to finally meet you, I hear my grand dog is in love with you."

She reached over and kissed Ken's cheek then she kissed my cheek, whispering in my ear, "Don't leave, no matter how hard it gets, don't leave."

My mom was a hard taskmaster but she loved me and knew me better than anyone, including the woman with whom I shared my soul and my bed for over two years. I would heed her advice because I know it was not only given from love but from experience, I was sure of that.

I stepped outside after McKenna went to sleep, she was still recovering from the anesthesia and might not even remember any of this in the morning. I got my cell phone out, I had to make three calls. The first to Paige, it went to voice mail.

"Paige I know you don't recognize this number. It's Rod Curry please give me a call back. Thanks. Just so you don't worry McKenna is doing well physically. She did lose a lot of blood but it's being replaced. Talk to you."

My next call was to Nan.

"Nan."

"Curry what's going on? I just got back from Ken's place and her car is there. She didn't answer the door. The neighbor told me she saw you carry her out."

"She had retained placenta and lost over three units of blood. They did a D&C, she's getting blood now."

"That's a lot of blood! How is she doing otherwise?"

"I don't know. Why didn't she tell me? Why didn't you tell me? Do I seem that shallow that I would be responsible for getting a woman pregnant and then walk away from her?

Regardless of how it happened it was my sperm and we were doing what humans do when they procreate! God she has gone thru so much by herself and it didn't have to be this way."

"Come on Rod we've already gone thru this! Should I ask Angel how many times you screwed her? And God knows how many other women!"

"Nan, I love her."

"God Curry are you out of your freakin' mind? She's done

every guy on the night shift at University!"

"No I mean I love McKenna."

"Now you've just decided that? Why? Do you feel guilty? Do you think you owe her something now! God you infuriate me!"

"Listen Nan I know this is a piss poor excuse for the way I acted and McKenna is partially right in that her appeal to me was she didn't throw herself at me, she was unattainable. That was true in the beginning but the longer I was around her the more I realized I'd made a huge mistake in the way I treated her. She's right I did wait until a woman made the first move so I didn't have to feel responsible for how the relationship panned out. If I didn't want to call them again I didn't have to feel obligated because I didn't make the first move!"

"You expect me to believe that bull shit!"

"You can believe what you want, I never saw it that way either until McKenna pointed it out to me. The second part to that is the last woman I had pursued burned me! I didn't think I'd ever recover from that but I did. I determined I'd never be the pursuer again because I never wanted to be vulnerable to that kind of hurt. Like I said this is a piss poor excuse but I was reeling from McKenna's rejection and I had to prove I was still capable of attracting a woman strongly enough for her to make the first move."

"I don't know why she still loves you because I personally think you are a shit case!"

"Why Super Nurse Nan you do flatter me! I'm being very serious because if it was humanly possible I'd kick my own ass."

She laughed, "Curry I don't know if I should kick you in the nads or kiss you! If you want that woman go get her."

"I am! I'm calling in for the next two nights. I'm staying here even if she tells me to leave. If she has me put out of her room I'll wait in the hallway. After those two nights , we have a four day stretch off, we'll take each day as it comes."

"I'm proud of you Curry. I think I might finally see a man shedding his protective adolescent shell!"

"Don't say anything at work until I have a chance to discuss this with McKenna and see how she wants to go about this."

"I won't. Curry I love that girl like a daughter, don't hurt her again."

"You have my word."

"Vivian this is Rod."

"I know who it is."

"I won't be at work my next two scheduled shifts I have a family emergency."

"You better come up with a better excuse than that, we're already down a resident."

"That resident doesn't count in the staffing pattern until her second year."

"Well I think if you check her contract you'll see her second year started July 1st."

"I'm not coming in! If you want to terminate my contract over this than feel free to do so. If you want to check my reason for not coming you may call my mother. You know she wouldn't lie for anyone. She will tell you it is a family emergency."

"I was a part of that family and if someone is in crisis I think I should be told."

"Shit load of bunk! That's what that is! You didn't care for my family, hell you didn't even love me and I was your husband!"

"Roderick when are you going to stop bringing every conversation between us back to that unfortunate divorce?"

"When you quit using that connection between us to run my life. I've told you I'm going to need the next two shifts off."

"But I have no one to cover you!"

"I've worked my ass off in that ER for ten years! We always cover when people need to be off. But then you are not a team player so you wouldn't understand that principle. If you tell me I can't have this time off then I'm terminating my contract immediately without notice."

"But Roddy, I have no one to cover for you."

"Cut the Roddy crap, I've been impervious to that name for a long time! Here's a novel idea for you- work it yourself! I'll fax my termination letter before the end of the work day."

I cut the call! God how she could get under my skin after all this time is beyond me! My phone vibrated, I had a text message.

"You are covered. Do I need to prepare Emma for something?"

"No."

I walked back to the room and her bed was empty. I saw the bathroom call light blinking.

"McKenna, do you need help?" I stood outside the door.

"Yes please, I'm still so weak."

I walked in and found her sitting on the toilet, leaning against the wall, soaked with sweat and ghostly pale!

"God baby, what do I need to do to help you?"

"I need a pad from that package over there."

She indicated where the package was, I got the pad for her..

"Now what do I need to do with it?"

She started crying!

"Curry I don't want you doing this for me it's not like that with us."

"Mc Kenna, I'm a doctor this stuff is not new. Please baby, let me help you."

"Unwrap that pad and press it in the double lining part of my underwear."

"How does it stay in place?"

"It's got sticky on it once you remove that backing."

"Okay. Not what?"

"Hold on to me when I stand up so I can pull my under-wear up."

"I got a better idea, you hold on to me and *I'll pull your underwear up! I'm the underwear specialist in this bathroom.*"

She stood up, wobbling and she held on to me as I pulled her panties into place. I gave her a hug and a quick kiss on her forehead. She didn't pull away.

"Curry you are ate up! Just help me back to bed, I'm still so weak today."

I did her one better, I picked her up and carried her to the bed and set her down. She got under the blankets, sighing as she closed her eyes. I know she probably didn't want to talk but I had to know, I had to ask.

"Didn't you ever want to tell me when I made comments about you porking up?"

"I guess I thought you'd put two and two together and figure it out."

"God I was clueless! In retrospect it all makes sense but I never thought I'd nail you in just one shot."

"Stop! Please don't make it vulgar, something beautiful came out of that."

"My intent is not to make it vulgar, I'm just kinda proud of myself doing it in one go round."

"I said stop."

She started crying again.

"McKenna turn around and look at me, please. If you don't feel like turning over I'll go to the other side of the bed. I need to talk to you and I want to look into your eyes as we speak to each other."

She didn't move from her fetal position so I went to the other side. I sat the chair by the bed, sitting down I laid my hand on her cheek.

"Eyes please."

She opened her eyes, the tears teeming down her cheeks.

"Baby listen to me. I'm sorry I hurt you, I'm asking for your forgiveness. I'm sorry we lost our son, I know the loss is much more acute to you then it is for me. I think we both know the reasons for that. I still don't understand why you didn't tell me, I would have been very proud, I could have gone to your doctor's appointments. I ...."

"That why I didn't tell you, that's a fake relationship. You'd be forced into having a relationship with me."

"You know that's not true! How many times did I beg you to at least give me a chance!"

"That was a chance to get in my pants not at a relationship."

"Well I see you've added another skill to your repertoire besides ER medicine."

"What's that?"

"Mind reading! That is not what I wanted and it's not what I want now. McKenna I love you! I want to marry you and give you babies, I want to leave a part of myself with you every time we make love."

"Go away Curry, I don't want to be your flavor of the month! Go to Angel or whoever is your current fuck buddy! I'm not like that."

Good! She was getting back to her usual snarky self when it came to conversations with me!

"McKenna I haven't been with a woman in over four months."

"Why not? Losing your touch?"

"I haven't been with another woman since I realized you are the only woman I want in my bed."

She laughed at me!

"Yeah like you're going without sex for four months! What do you do?"

"You don't want to know."

"Yes I do. I don't believe you!"

"Well I still have two hands and a very vivid memory of what you looked like when I walked in my bedroom as you were coming out of the bathroom. Baby, your ass and tits could start a war!"

She asked. I told her. Now she was acting all offended by

what I did!

"You are disgusting!"

"Come on McKenna, don't you think of how hot it was between us! I can truthfully tell you I've never had a woman rip my shirt off because she was so hot for me before that night. And on the same note I've never left another woman's clothes laying in my foyer! I've always undressed them in my bedroom or their bedroom."

"What do you want from me Curry?"

"I want your heart first, then I want your body and in that order only."

"How do you propose to do that?"

"I want to take care of you, I want us to be together as often as we can. If you will consent I'd like you to move to my apartment."

"No."

"Why not?"

"Flaunt that in Vivian's face, no way! She already hates me!"

"Okay, let me move some things to your apartment."

"What about Posey?"

"My parents will keep him for that six or so weeks."

"What about Emma?"

"What about her? She's crazy about you. I'm not hiding this McKeena, I don't care who knows. I've given this a lot of thought and I really want this to work out. What do you say? I know we've got some hard days ahead, I want to be there for you and with you."

"I can't."

"Why?"

I was not prepared for what she said next!

"Because I'm already in a relationship with someone else."

"Who the hell are you seeing?"

"See, there you go acting like a hot headed teenager. You have no hold on me!"

"I'm not acting like a hot headed teenager! Well yes I guess I am. I can't deny being jealous, because I am. May I ask who he is? I'm assuming it is a 'he'."

"It certainly is, and he's a doctor. I'm not going to tell you at this point. What are you thinking right now, why are you looking at me like that?"

"I'd like to kiss those beautiful lips. I missed you like hell! We are so good together."

I reached over, cupping her chin in my hand I raised her face to mine! Before I realized it I had her against me! She only let that kiss last a few seconds! Jesus it was intense! She pushed me away. I ran my nose down her neck, inhaling her scent. We both were breathing heavy!

"You remember the day of my birthday and you sat beside me?"

"Umm."

"My little man did the strangest thing. Every time you talked he kicked me!"

I was both surprised and delighted! Surprised because she shared it with me, delighted because I am the man who put him there.

"Get outta here! He did? He really did?"

"Yes."

She started crying again. I had tough questions for her, I might as well get thru it.

"McKenna is he buried somewhere?"

"Yes."

"I need to see where. Did you give him a name?"

"Of course! McKinley Abraham Tipton."

"Can I add my name, to the end of your name, McKinley Abraham Tipton Curry."

"That's such a big name for a little guy so I was going to call him Mac."

"I like it. Mac Curry." I choked to get it out.

I picked her up from the bed, I sat down in the chair with

her in my lap. We both slept until they brought her dinner.

While she ate her dinner I stepped out to call my mother, when I returned a guy was sitting on her bed, holding her hand, he looked familiar but I couldn't place him. When I saw him I turned starting to go out again.

"Hey Curry, you don't have to leave."

"I've got calls to make I just wondered if you wanted something from the gift shop."

"I'm good. This is my very special friend Jeff Burroughs. Jeff this is Curry."

So I'm not good enough to have a first name. Fuck that! I extended my hand.

"I guess she doesn't remember my first name, seems we've never been on a first name basis have we Dr. Tipton? My name is Rod and it's nice to meet you, Dr. Burroughs. I think we spoke on the phone last night. If you'll excuse me I'll get my calls completed."

I was seething! What an asswipe! Just what did 'very special friend' mean! What special privileges came with that title!

I went to the cafeteria to get a cup of coffee. God I was weary. I couldn't imagine how McKenna felt. McKenna, a beautiful name for an even more beautiful woman, but she was only McKenna to ME! Everyone else called her Ken or Kenna! Even that asswipe Tony whom she was with for about two minutes! Then it hit me! She ended that relationship because of the baby. She hasn't let another man touch that part of her since we made love! I wondered if "very special friend" had crossed that ring she had drawn around herself. Maybe she wants me to know he has so that's why she introduced him that way! OR she was rubbing my face in 'it'. Treating me the way I treated her as Nan said. I thought back over the last six months and the probably six or so women with whom I'd gotten under the covers! The more I thought about it the less I liked myself.

What had I become was a womanizing prick! I treated

women as entertainment getting my pleasure when and where I wanted it. I didn't know why the mere sight of me didn't make her physically sick. Fuck! It disgusted the hell out of me. Why had I let myself become this way? I was taught to respect women! My mother wouldn't even let my dad smack her on the ass in front of us kids because she thought it disrespected women, patting their backside like you did a cow or a horse to get them to respond to you. I was despicable! I could use the break-up of my relationship with Viv all I wanted but the ugly truth was there. I was responsible for my own behavior. I, Roderick Crawford Curry am an ugly disgusting roach! I had busted my ass to become a top ER guy. I was invited to speak at conferences and symposiums all over the country. Professionally I was a shining star, personally I was a fallen star! Enough introspection! I'd start right now to reshape my personal relationships. I wanted to start now with my mother. I called her, it went to voice mail.

"Mama this is your favorite baby boy, I'm still at the hospital with McKenna....."

"Rod, we're out to dinner with Helen and Emma.," she interrupted my message.

"That's great. Was Emmy surprised to see you again so soon?"

"She was. It's a bit sticky trying to explain why we're here. I just told her a friend of yours became suddenly very ill and you were at the hospital. I'm not sure how to handle this."

"That explanation will suffice for now. I'll be in and out of my place for the next week at least. I asked McKenna to come home with me but she refused. She used Viv as an excuse but that's only part of it I'm sure. I'll be at her place until she kicks me out. Thanks for what you said to her."

"Sweet boy from the time you were a baby you have always required more physical attention than your sister and brother. But you give as much as you take and I know you would have supported McKenna thru this regardless of the relationship had you known."

I appreciated my mother recognizing there might be at least some amount of altruism in me and my reasons for doing things.

"We.....well we talked about him. She named him McKinley Abraham Tipton Curry."

"Oh, so she is going to allow you in."

"So far. She shared something with me that she didn't have to about him."

"Can I ask what?"

"She and her sister were having lunch on her birthday, I met them only by accident, I stopped to talk with them. I sat in the booth by her.....she said every time I spoke he kicked her."

"That is a precious memory for you."

"She will let me see the ultrasounds and other pictures she took when she can deal with it. He weighted two two and was fifteen inches long. If I remember my facts on fetal development he was a little larger than normal. She didn't look pregnant, at least not in the baggy scrubs I always saw her wear. How did I miss this? Everything at work, for the most part went well. She just seemed to cry all the time when we were alone. I begged her to talk to me and tell me what was wrong and she just kept saying it was something she had to work out on her own. One time, one 'mistake in her judgment' as she calls it and we create a child! A son. She said that was such a big name for such a little man, she called him her little man so she was going to call him Mac. Mac Curry."

I was blubbering like an idiot in the corner of a hospital cafeteria and I did not care. This had to be killing her. I had to get back to her!

"I gotta go Mom. Thank you."

I didn't give her time for a response I headed back upstairs. This time I did get stopped and questioned as to my relationship with the patient.

"I'm her significant other."

I saw that ward clerk's eyebrows raise as she rolled her eyes but she let me through. McKenna was staring into space when I entered her room. She had packed cells running. I walked to her, wanting to kiss her lips but I settled for her forehead.

"Is this it for the blood?"

"Dr. Slater was here, as soon as it is in I can go home."

"They're not going to check your hemoglobin and crit again?"

"It's 8 and 24."

"That' a little low."

"This is not the ER and you're not in charge here so if they're happy with it I'm happy with it. I know Jeff wouldn't let me be discharged if it wasn't safe."

It shot out of my mouth before I even thought about it!

"I wouldn't be so sure, they sent you home with retained placenta."

"What's the matter? You don't want me going home this soon because you feel obligated to 'take care' of me?"

I had spoke in error and I knew it, there was nothing to do but apologize.

"I'm sorry. That was both unprofessional and unkind, I should not have said it."

It was strangely quiet here in this room. The ER is always hustle and bustle so quietness in a hospital seems odd. There was one more touchy subject I had to bring up. Doing it here it would probably be less confrontational, at least I hoped so.

"McKenna, even though you, Nan and I are the only ones who know about this now that's not going to be the case for very long. So how do you want to approach the work situation?"

Before she had a chance to respond a nurse came in the room to check her packed cells infusion. I stepped back so as not to be in her way.

"You've got about half an hour before this is finished. Are you doing okay? Do you need anything Dr. Tipton?"

"I'm fine thank you."

She turned to leave then stopped abruptly!

"Rod Curry! How are you! What are you doing here?"

Kitty Cameron, about five years ago. Moonlighted in the ER at University. The ER was not the only thing she moonlighted!

"Kitty how are you?"

"I'm fantastic! Is this your wife? Don't tell me you finally got married!"

"This is not my wife yet but I'm working to amend that situation."

McKenna sat with her mouth posed in a position that could catch flies!

"How is everything at University? That was the greatest bunch of people I've ever worked with, especially the doctors. Are you still nights?"

"Yep, still nights. Things are going well. Nan's still night charge, the docs are all the same, except for residents there is not much changed. Still crazy busy most nights. What are you doing in OB?"

"To work the ER as long as you and Nan have, well it takes a special person to deal with other people's devastation day after day. I had to get out after three years, I was having nightmares about some of the stuff there."

"I'm not sure about how special we are but we sure have a warped sense of humor."

"I'd agree with that. It was so great seeing you."

She leaned toward me and kissed me quickly on the cheek! She had a few words of advice for McKenna as she left the room.

"Hang on honey, you've roped a wild one!"

I chuckled as she left.

"I'm supposed to think that's funny? It only goes to show what a horse's butt you've been for a long time! Have you slept with every woman who's worked in that ER?"

She was piqued! I really should be trying to soothe her rather than rile her up. I didn't.

"Not all of them. Not Nan or Dotty."

"That's because Nan is married and Dotty's probably older than your mother!"

I loved that snarky side of her!

"Come on, surely you've heard of December to May relationships!"

"You're disgusting Curry! Get out of my face!"

"Come on baby, some people would say I'm too old for you but I'd love you to the moon and back."

I saw the tears come to the surface again before she turned away from me.

"Don't just don't."

I closed the gap between us by sitting on the bed and bringing her into my arms.

"Just don't what?" I asked as I whispered in her ear. "I will love you to the moon and back, I promise. Give me a chance."

"I told you I'm already in a relationship with Jeff."

I wasn't moving I continued my hold on her.

"McKenna what can he do for you that I can't? Why him and not me?"

"Because I don't want a relationship with you Curry. You made love to me and you threw me out! I worked side by side with you for six months, even if what we did was nothing to you, just fucking and nothing else did you have so little regard for me as a friend, as a human being that you'd just throw me out! Even stray cats are allowed to hang around longer than that after they've been given a saucer of milk! You hurt me."

She turned away and wouldn't let me touch her and if that wasn't enough there was a delivery of flowers from the relationship guy! You talk about fucking things up! I'd done that since the beginning of my relationship with her. I was an ass, a roach, a prick or anything else you wanted to call me but I wasn't going to leave and I wasn't going to force myself on her.

CHAPTER FOURTEEN

MCKENNA

I felt someone shaking my shoulder and calling my name, I opened my eyes to see Dr. Slater looking down at me.

"What....where am I. Where's Curry?

"It's Sam Slater."

"I know. Why are you here?"

"You're in recovery McKenna. There was a small piece of placenta left and you almost bleed out. It's a good thing that guy was there with you or you wouldn't have made it. You lost almost three units of blood."

I should have been grateful to Curry but I wasn't. I didn't want to take my own life I just didn't prefer life over death right now.

"Thank you."

I know my tone was flat. I didn't care if he knew I was at the bottom of the greatest depths I'd ever experienced.

"So I guess Curry dropped me off and left."

That sounded like a question, it was not. It was a statement. A statement of the fact that this wasn't the first time Curry had left me stranded after.. after....after he put little man inside me. Curry was up and gone but little man was supposed to be mine for the rest of my life.

"No he's in the waiting room. There is someone with him. I know he was just the 'sperm donor' so to speak but he was very concerned."

I had to ask the next question! If he had Angel out in that waiting room so help me God I was getting out of bed, going out there and finishing him off with whatever I could get my hands on!

"Who's with him?"

"I'm assuming it's his mother."

His mother! Why would he bring her into something like this. I didn't want to see her. How was he going to introduce me? So Mother here is McKenna, she couldn't hold onto your grandson long enough to give him life."

"Do you want me to have him sent away?"

As much as I hated Curry right now I did love him and I did need him. I needed his physical presence right now. I felt so empty and cold. And I was tired, so very tired and sleepy.....

"McKenna, baby how are you?"

I opened my eyes to his voice. He reached down and kissed my forehead and held my hand.

"I feel tired, really tired and empty especially empty."

"I know baby, I'm so, so sorry."

I couldn't stop the tears. I couldn't look at him. I not only had failed my little man I had failed my big man too. I could see the hurt in his eyes.

"You don't have to stay Curry. There's no baby now, there's nothing."

"I'm not leaving."

"I said go! There's no baby, there's nothing. You were never a part of this anyway."

"Dr. Tipton I already told you I'm not leaving."

"McKenna I'm Emma, Rod's mother and you can tell me to butt out if you want to, but I know my son and he would have been there had he known."

"Go, leave me alone."

"No baby, I'm not leaving."

"McKenna it was nice to finally meet you, I hear my grand dog is in love with you,"

Then she kissed me! Why would she kiss me? She probably thinks I'm a slut and I just did this to trap her son, like she said, he'd be there if he knew. It was so much to take in, I was just too tired to think about this any longer. I wanted to sleep. I needed to sleep.

I woke up with a full bladder. I couldn't wait so I got myself and my IV and somehow made it to the bathroom. I managed to empty my bladder but I was too weak to stand up.

I tried but I felt like I was going to black out. I put my bathroom light on and waited. I was beginning to fade fast. I didn't want to fall and hit my head on top of everything else that was happening to me.

"McKenna, do you need some help."

God it was Curry, I did need help but not from him! I didn't want him to see me like this, but he was there right beside me.

"What do you need me to do?'

I started crying.

"Curry I don't want you to see me like this, don't help me."

"I'm a doctor, I know about this just tell me what to do."

"Can you get a pad out of that package. Unwrap it."

"What do I do with it now?"

"Stick it to my underwear."

"How does it stay there?'

"It's got sticky on it."

It suddenly dawned on me, for him it was like he did this for me all the time. He wasn't uncomfortable at all!

"What now?"

"Can you hold me up so I can pull my underwear up?"

"I've got a better idea. Why don't you hold onto me and *I'll* pull your underwear up.

I'm the underwear specialist in this bathroom."

Did he say that? Am I imagining that? How could he act

like everything was okay between us! He picked me up, carried me back to my room and we settled in the chair. My head was on his shoulder. This is all I wanted on New Year's eve, just to lay against him and feel secure and I did until he started with the cab thing.

I was exhausted from just going to the bathroom. I just was too spent to do anything but lay there. He cuddled me! I was so tired......

I think he must have slept too. My dinner came, he helped me with it before leaving the room.

I wasn't hungry but I was weak so I ate. When he returned he was like chatty Cathy!

He wants me to move in with him! He said he wanted my heart and my body and in that order. If I'm in close proximity to him like that as horny as I've been he'll definitely have my body way before he gets me to admit he has my heart! And he wants a relationship! Too late, too too late!

"I can't be in a relationship with you because I'm already in a relationship with someone else."

"Who is he?" He barked! Well that went over well!

"I assume it is a he."

Smart ass! He knows I'm straight as an arrow, straight as the one he ran thru my heart!

"His name is Jeff Burroughs. He's a doctor too."

Then he really put on the pressure. He kissed me! A hot hot kiss! Maybe it wasn't little man who made me horny! I wanted to jump his bones so badly I had to pull away. This was the most alive I'd felt in a long time! Then he asked me a question that broke my heart again.

"What can he give you that I can't give you?"

I loved him but I didn't know if I could get over the hurt. First his rejection of me, then the precious life that had developed inside my body, having to keep it a secret because he obviously had lost interest in me. The proof of that was the parade of women he strung in front of me. It cut me and the only comfort I had was the life I carried inside my body, now that was gone too! I didn't want to go on, I learned to live without him, now I had to learn to live without my little man. With the promise of his life gone, now all my dreams were gone. It was too much. I had to sleep again.

"Ken, hey sleepyhead. Wake up!"

I opened my eyes to a little piece of comfort! Jeff was here. I sat up quickly which only resulted in my getting so dizzy I had to lay down again.

"Easy there McKenna! Lay down, I'll sit right by you on your bed."

He leaned over giving me a rather sexy smile then kissed me full on the lips. He lingered for a moment inserting a little taste of his tongue! God if that was someone else's tongue I'd want it all over me!

"I didn't think you could do that here!" I whispered loudly.

"I didn't either but the sight of you filled me with such hunger for you. Damn the hospital board! I've missed you so much." He whispered in return, his voice more controlled

"I didn't think you'd be back until Monday or Tuesday."

"I was extremely unpleasant company for my parents. My father finally told me to get my ass on a plane and get back to you."

"You told your parents about us?"

"Yes and they want to meet you the next time they come to Birmingham."

He took my hand and held it to his lips.

"Enough of that. How are you doing with this?"

"I guess I got thru the very worst I could imagine and that was going home without him.

Now I have to go home without him again."

"I can come stay with you or you could come to my place."

"As strange as it seems Curry is going to stay a couple of days with me. According to Sam I would be dead if I was there by myself. I just remember going to sleep because I was so tired and weak, the next thing I knew I woke up here again."

I saw Curry walk in the door then turn abruptly to leave again.

"You don't have to leave Curry."

"I'll come back later. Just checking to see if you wanted anything from the gift shop."

"I'm good but come in and meet my very special friend Jeff Burroughs. Jeff this is Curry."

I could tell by the look on his face he wasn't happy with Jeff being here.

"I do have a first name, it's Rod. I guess she never felt we were close enough to be on a first name basis."

Wow! That was almost saying it was like a drive-by fucking session! We didn't even know each other! That jackass!

"Nice to meet you Dr. Burroughs. I've got calls to make."

He left. He deserved what he got! How many women did he rub in my face? I'm sure he's wondering what is going on between me and Jeff sexually. He can wonder all he wants about me. I <u>know</u> what he did with those women.

Jeff left shortly after that. It was like Curry planned it, he came in the door almost immediately after Jeff's departure/

I think Curry was upset about Jeff.

"Come on McKenna. I can give you everything he can."

"Curry you've slept with every nurse in that ER. A good example is Nurse Kitty."

"That was a long time ago, and I haven't slept with every nurse in that ER."

"Name them!" This was show down time!

"I haven't slept with Nan, or Dotty. Also Sally, I've never slept with her."

"That's because Nan is married and Dotty is old enough to be your mother and I'm almost positive Sally is lesbian."

"Come on McKenna I haven't been with anyone since I figured out you were the only one I wanted in my bed, that's like four months!"

"I don't believe you, tell me how!"

"Well I still have two hands and a vivid imagination as to how you looked when you came out of my bathroom that morning. Your tits and ass could start a war!"

Ugh! Gross! Why would he think I wanted to hear that! I meant how he *talked* himself out of having sex.

"Curry you are disgusting! Get out of my face!"

"Baby you know I can love you to the moon and back."

I felt like my heart had been pierced when he said that. I know he could but only until he got tired of me. I had to tell him why I couldn't be in a relationship with him.

"Don't just don't even say that."

"Why not?"

So I told him all the ways I hurt, how he hurt me and the very worst was my little man was gone from me forever. I'd never hold him in my arms, I'd never hear him cry, I'd never feel life in his little body and that in itself left me almost without a heart it was now so broken. And last, he'd move in, he'd take my heart, when the chase was over, when I loved him, adored him and would have given myself completely he'd come home one day and tell me to call a cab. I would not, could not live thru that rejection again! And when I finished he looked at me in a way I'd never seen before then he walked out.

CHAPTER FIFTEEN

ROD

How could I even look at her? How could she bear to even look at me? I had devastated her and the only thing good to come out of it was our 'little man'. Now he was gone. I should walk away and never see her again, release her from her contract with the hospital, but I can't. I need to make this right. I need her, we need each other to get thru this. I know her hurt is much deeper than mine, and I can hardly bear it. We each have lost a part of ourselves. I needed to talk to my mom and Nan.

"Nan do you have a minute to talk to me?"

"What's going on? Is Ken doing okay?"

"She's heartbroken but she's dealing. She's going to be discharged later today. Before I take her home do you think I should go to her apartment and put all the baby's things away. Like maybe put them in the room that was to be the nursery?"

"Yes make them accessible to her. It might help her to be able to touch them or just know they're close. How did today go?"

"She talked to me, she told me about an incident when he responded to my voice. She said he kicked every time I spoke. He was sucking his thumb in one of the ultrasounds, Emma was a thumb sucker! God that bothered Vivian, you would have thought the world was coming to an end! My mom told her that it was very important for a baby to be able to comfort itself. I wanted to add that's why little boys fondle themselves but I knew either my mom or Helen would have killed me!"

"No wonder she kicked you to the curb! I've never figured out what your appeal is to women. You're not that great other than your smile, and your body, your brain, that hair that looks like you always just got out of bed!"

Nan could make me laugh anytime, I was down really down for what I'd done to McKenna.

"Did you mention how good I am with my hands?"

Now she laughed, "Oh sorry I also forgot to mention how unassuming you are too!"

Suddenly I felt like a knife went thru my chest, I didn't care what any woman thought of me I just wanted McKenna and she hated my guts. Maybe if little man was still inside her body she would have gradually accepted me. She worked in that ER everyday, giving 110% and I never even noticed! If I was being truthful with myself I'd have to say every time I looked at her I saw her nude body, it didn't really give me time to study her. The only time was when that idiot shook her, I did notice her rounded belly but I was so worried about her being injured that I didn't think it thru. Then I went to give her some Tylenol and she was talking to someone about quickies!

"Nan do you have any pictures when she was pregnant and not in those awful scrubs."

"I have one taken on the day she lost him. She was absolutely glowing! I'll send it to you."

"Thanks. I'm going home to get clothes so I can be at her place for a few days and put the baby clothes away then I'm going back. Can you call her and keep her company by phone?"

"I'm on it! Curry?"

"Yes?"

"I'm on your side, you know that don't you. But I'm only on your side because I really do think you love her. When you were a husband and a father you were the best man I've ever known outside of my husband."

"She thinks I'll walk out on her again. Ask her to "call a cab" as she puts it. I'm not.

I was still very much in love with Viv when she told me to move out. She had cooled a little to me but I thought that was due to her mom's illness. She still was my world and it became that much better when we had Emma."

"Lose the past Rod. Be the man you were before you decided to chase every skirt at University Hospital."

"I'm looking for him."

"Get off this phone and go find him."

Two minutes after we talked she text me a picture of McKenna, standing profile, showing that round compact belly and the most beautiful smile I ever see her wear!

I wanted to give her that smile again and I didn't care if it was the next 'first time' we made love! When I got to McKenna's I remembered the messy bed and towels, even the bathroom floor was spattered with her blood. I took the sheets off the bed, put them to soak in the washer with bleach I could wash them later tonight after she went to sleep. I couldn't find another mattress cover so I called my mom.

"Rod I thought you might call earlier with some news about McKenna."

"Sorry Mom. She's doing well. They're going to release her tonight. I'm at her apartment now cleaning the mess. The blood saturated all the bed linens clear to the mattress. I can't do anything about that right now but can you run to Macy's or some place and get a good mattress pad? I have an account there just put it on that."

"Blankets? Anything else?"

"Just get whatever I'll need to dress her bed. It's queen sized."

"What color is her bedroom?"

"Some shade of a true gray, medium."

"Give me her address, I'll bring the new sheets home and

launder them before I put them on the bed."

"I'm coming over there to get some clothes for a few days, I'll give you the key then."

Emmy was waiting for me when I opened my apartment door.

"Daddy!" She flew at me.

I picked her up, she was light as a feather, long skinny legs!

"Hey Petals, how's my favorite girl?"

"I'm good Daddy! Poppy has been teaching me how to play dominoes. He says I'm pretty good for a beginner."

"Well I'm sure you are 'cause Poppy doesn't hand out compliments easily."

About that time Posey rounded the corner and dived right in the middle of both of us!

Emmy was squealing, "Get him off Daddy his kisses are wet! Uck!"

I personally thought it great fun but called a halt to Posey's shenanigans. He gave me that Poor Pitiful Pearl look.

"Sorry buddy, I have to talk to Petals about something serious."

Emmy settled on my lap, looking at me with those serious beautiful green eyes.

"What's up Daddy?" She looked seven but sounded like she was seventeen!

"Nana and Poppy are going to be staying here for a few days to keep an eye on Posey and to enjoy being with you. Daddy has a friend who was in the hospital and he's going to taking care of his friend for a few days."

'Is she your second favorite girl Daddy?"

"Is who my second favorite girl."

"McKenna, silly! You said she's your friend. Mommy told Helen she's in some kind of trouble, something about not being able to find her baby 'cause she lost it."

"Emmy you misunderstood Mommy. Miss McKenna is

not in any trouble. She did have a baby in her belly but she had some problems.........he was born too early so his lungs weren't fully formed, he didn't live."

This was killing me! I wanted to tell her that the baby was her little brother but now was not the time.

"That's sad Daddy, so sad."

"Yes it is Petals, very sad. She's very sad so that's why I'm going to stay at her apartment and help her."

"Why doesn't her husband help her?"

"She doesn't have a husband."

"Then how can she have a baby if she doesn't have a husband? Who planted the seed?"

This was getting tricky!

"Emma Elizabeth I think I owe you an ice cream cone for beating me at dominoes! Shall we go get it now?"

My dad reached for her hand.

She jumped up, babies and husbands forgotten! I knew I'd have to answer it the next time we talked.

As I walked out of my apartment door I got a text from McKenna.

"Being discharged. Don't come, will call an Uber."

I wanted to mess with her and ask if she had an objection to cabs but this wasn't the usual snarky ready to bite back McKenna. So I didn't.

"Will be there in 10. Don't call Uber!

It actually took me 15 minutes and I honestly was afraid she'd be gone when I got there.

She was laying in a fetal position tearful again. I went to her, pulling her into my arms.

I kissed the top of her head. Her hair was sticky, she needed a shower. I'd help her at home.

"Thank you for not calling an Uber. I'm glad you waited for me."

"I wasn't waiting for you. I didn't have any clothes. Did you bring some?"

"I brought this big dress like thing with some underwear."

I emphasized underwear and wiggled my brows, she swatted at me then laughed.

"If you got in my underwear drawer you know it's all maternity stuff."

"Not quite! I found some very interesting items on the very bottom!"

"Curry you are a pervert! Going thru a woman's underwear. That's a serious mental health problem."

She blushed a bright red!

"Not just any woman McKenna. I want to know all about you, what you like what you don't like."

"Let's get one thing clear, I *don't like* you going thru my underwear drawer."

"You could go thru my underwear drawer any time. I wouldn't care."

"Therein lies the difference, I do care! Don't do it again."

"Got it mam, shall I assist you in getting dressed?"

"Can you pull that curtain, untie my gown in the back then get out of here. Oh and you have to sign my discharge instructions because I had anesthesia. Your *friend* Kitty is my nurse, I'm sure she'll be delighted to help you with that and anything else you want!"

God she got snarly! Pay back time!

"Are you sure you don't need some help?" was my request as I pulled the curtain back, Jesus she was standing there naked!

"Get out of here or I will call an Uber!"

"Are you sure you want to do that. I just might take all your clothes, that back seat could get pretty sticky with no panties!"

"Please just go away and let me get dressed,"

God I loved this woman more every minute I spent with her! She sounded a little stressed so I decided I'd give her a break for now.

I did go to the desk but Kitty accompanied me back with a wheelchair for McKenna.

"Dr. Tipton I need to go over these instructions with both of you. Ready? You will need to call and make an appointment at Dr. Slater's office in two next weeks. For your activity, no step climbing more than twice daily, no lifting over 5 pounds, no tub baths, no sexual intercourse for six weeks. You may have anything you want to eat but no alcohol for 48 hours after your anesthesia. If you are taking birth control pills you can resume them when you get home, just take them as prescribed. Do you have any questions, Dr. Tipton? Rod?"

"You okay McKenna?"

She nodded her head but I saw tears in the corners of her eyes.

"We're good. I'll get the car. Where shall I meet you?"

"Back by the emergency entrance. Oh here. Take her flowers. I poured the water from them, they will be fine for transport home."

I took them but I wanted to throw them in the nearest rubbish can!

The trip home was quiet.

"Would you like to stop for some take out? I didn't check your cabinets to see what there is to eat."

"I'm not hungry, I won't eat this evening."

"Do I need to stop at the drugstore for anything?"

"No."

I wanted to carry her up the steps to her apartment but she wouldn't have it.

"No way! I'm not an invalid. I just had a baby, it's a normal physiological function of a woman's body."

I tried to talk to her about her lack of energy due to her blood loss but she would not hear any of it.

When we got to her apartment my mom had really worked her magic. Everything was spic n span! She had some atomizer thing going and I'm glad because when I was there earlier

PHYLLIS LYNN

it smelled like blood, something McKenna was very familiar
with.

She looked around.

"Where's little man's things?"

"I just put them in his crib. I can put them back on the sofa
if you want."

"No that's fine. I just can't bear to part with them yet."

"Keep them as long as you need to baby. Can I get you
something?"

She collapsed in a big overstuffed chair.

"I'm sad Curry. I don't know how I can deal with all this.
I'm so tired and exhausted I can barely stand up. My body
smells and I can't take a bath, I don't have a shower chair to
use the shower. I want to go to sleep and never wake up. I'm
not suicidal I'm just too tired and weary to put any effort into
living. Why did this have to happen? I loved him and wanted
him so much, he was the only good thing to come out of that
night."

Her cry was like a keening. I couldn't not touch her.

I picked her up and put her in my lap, she was like a rag
doll. Her head laid against my shoulder.

"Baby listen to me. I know how you feel about that night,
how it has hurt you, but you are so right about giving a part of
yourself to the other person in the physical act of love.

Don't get angry at me but I'm very happy that I gave a part
of myself to you that night. I feel all warm inside when you
talk about him, just because I didn't know about him from
the beginning doesn't take away the hurt. I love you and I
can think of no greater privilege than to implant my seed in
you. I was so caught up in your beauty and spirit that night. I
have never forgotten to use a condom, never. You were, are so
beautiful to me. Do you want to know why I asked you to call
a cab? Not because I wanted to get rid of you, I was a coward
and I knew you'd have a hangover in the morning and I knew
I had taken advantage of you! God when you told me it had

been five years! Five years and you ended it with a prick like me. I'm sorry, please forgive me for hurting you like that."

"Curry what would you have done if I had told you?"

"Before three months ago I would have not been upset, but I wouldn't have been thrilled. I know I would have expected and wanted to be a part of his life. Make no mistake I would have been proud of him. Being a father is wonderful thing. I can't even begin to describe how I feel when I look at Emmy."

"But you loved Vivian and wanted her."

"Tipton I've had feelings for you for a long time, I realized three months ago that I love you. At first it was admiration for you. You are smart as a whip and not only do you have book learning you know instantly what to do about your diagnosis. That night I came to ICU, God that took guts to go against that fucker! But you were right and that man would be dead now if you hadn't acted. I was so elated that I wanted to pick you up and swing you around with joy."

"If you had you would have realized what I was crying about, my waist was thicker and God help me my boobs were bigger!"

"No God help me because I felt the difference when you ducked down to go under my arms. I hate it when I wax poetic like this but I am a tits and ass man."

She giggled!

"Oh that's very poetic, watch out Shakespeare here comes Curry!"

"I'm going to put you in the shower, and I'm getting in with you."

"No, no you can't. I don't want you to look at me. My ass is *big* and I have flab on my belly."

"Okay if you don't want me to look at you put blinders on me and I'll use my hands to make sure you get nice and clean."

"Oh no you don't! I'm not that stupid."

"Seriously though, this shower is therapeutic. I'm keeping my tight y whiteys on."

As I put her down she staggered.

"See that's why you shouldn't shower by yourself tonight."

My phone rang, it was Emma's ringtone. It was my good night call. At home I walked across the hall to tell her good night when it was Viv's week, of course Viv didn't come to my place when it was my week. Her loss my gain!

"Hey Petals! How was the ice cream?"

"I was so good Daddy, Poppy let me get two scoops 'cause I beat him two games."

"Let me guess, chocolate and strawberry!"

"Yes! How did you know? Did Poppy tell you?"

"No darlin' you get the same thing every time."

"Can I say good night to Miss McKenna?"

I had her on speaker phone, McKenna nodded yes.

"How are you Emma?"

"I'm well thank you for asking. How are you?"

"I'm okay, I'm a little tired."

I was not prepared for what Emma said next!

"I'm sorry about the baby, I'd tell your husband sorry too but Daddy said you didn't have a husband. So I'm going to say I'm sorry twice to you. Okay?"

"Okay. Thank you Emma."

She handed the phone to me and almost staggered into the bathroom. I followed her I didn't want her to fall. She dropped down onto the toilet seat. I had to hold her up.

"Emmy, I love you, Sleep tight. Daddy's throwing you a kiss."

"I'm throwing you one too! I love you, night night Daddy."

The look of hurt and betrayal in her eyes pierced me. She spoke so softly I could barely hear her.

"Why Curry? Why did you tell her."

"McKenna I didn't tell her."

"She said you did. Why would she lie?"

"Let me help you get your shower then we'll talk."

She jerked away from me so violently she almost fell to the

floor. I caught her and pulled her against me, she hit me with her fist, she made contact with my nose! It started bleeding. I caught her wrist and she started to bite me.

"Baby don't!"

The deep gut wrenching sobbing started again!

"Leave me alone, leave me alone."

"McKenna you don't have the energy for this. You can be angry at me all you want, you can hit me and call me every name you can think of but not tonight, not tonight, please baby not tonight."

To my surprise she stopped! I turned the shower water on and helped her get undressed.

I smiled as I helped her take her maternity underwear off.

"Laugh all you want! You did that to me! You didn't care about me but you did that to me anyway."

I wasn't about to argue with her.

"Yes baby I did. Here see if the water is too hot for you. If it's not get in. I'll be there as soon as I get undressed."

"You have to keep your underwear on! You promised I don't want to see that thing."

I got in with my briefs on. Sometimes I think I'm just evil, I couldn't seem to stop myself. I pulled her back against me and whispered, "Yes and you kissed it so sweetly."

I don't know what I had expected but certainly not what she did! She turned and pressed her naked body against mine.

"I know I did, I know but that was when I wanted you! I don't want you now."

She started crying again, deep racking sobs, it was killing me. She sobbed and I washed her body. When I finished I dried her off and took her to bed.

"Don't cry McKenna tell me what to do. Tell me what you want me to do, please. Anything, I'll do anything except leave you alone for the next couple of nights. Tell me baby and I'll do it."

"I can't tell you because I don't want you to do it, but I need it so badly Curry I need it."

"I can't have intercourse with you. You know that."

"Put your mouth on me, make me come with your tongue." She whispered as if someone other than me was listening.

"Make me come! Little man made me so horny, I'm sorry I won't ask again, just this once. Please. I'm not nasty, I'm not even bleeding anymore, they cleaned me out so good."

"Don't McKenna, don't beg. It should be me begging you. I want to do this, but don't get angry at me if I have an erection. I can only talk that fella down for so long than he has a mind of his own."

"I won't. You have to take off your underwear."

"Oh Lordy McKenna Tipton! You took A&P, you know what that's going to do to me."

"I know. I want to see your desire for me, if you have any."

"Dr. Tipton, I'm shocked you are not more observant. It's quite the joke in the ER that I don't develop priapism when I'm within ten feet of a certain resident!"

She ignored my comment.

"Now Curry, I want it now."

"I will but I want to kiss you all over, I want to experience your exquisite velvety soft nipples that become like hardened beads when I nibble on them. Alright?"

"Yes, please now." As she looked at me the pupils of her eyes were so big her eyes appeared black.

I took off my briefs and sat on the bed. I pulled her onto my lap, she straddled me. Then it started, God this woman was beyond horny! I kissed her and her tongue invaded my mouth, she literally sucked my tongue, my dick was going crazy. I swear I didn't move an inch and it touched her pussy! I jumped, she jumped, it was hot. I continued down her neck, she ground her breasts in my chest! I laid her back on the bed, I rubbed my cock over her stomach, her breasts set me on fire. I couldn't be gentle! The harder my teeth ground on her nipples the wilder her hips got.

"Now Curry now. I need you. Do you even want me."

"Oh baby! You don't know how long I've dreamed of having your body under mine like this. Lay still. Enjoy what I'm doing to you, let me please you McKenna, that is my greatest desire. God I love you!"

She spread her legs for me, I inhaled her.

"I love your scent Ken, I love you!" I couldn't tell her enough how I felt about her.

I teased her lightly with my tongue, I kissed and sucked her pussy from every angle I could. I felt the need to come mounting in her, finally as I sucked and bite her clit, she went over the edge! Her face was so beautiful when she came. She kept murmuring over and over, "Curry you are so good, so good."

I held her. I spooned her body. My dick rested right in the crack of her ass. She ground her ass into my pelvis, God it was torture but I felt good because I made her come! I kissed down her neck, her shoulder, she raised her shoulder in response. She seemed relaxed, like she was right where she should be.

"McKenna let me explain to you about tonight. I didn't say a word to Petals until she told me Vivian said you were in trouble, that you lost your baby. I told her you weren't in any trouble. She thought the term 'lost' meant you had to find him. Then she asked me why your husband wasn't helping you find him so I told her you didn't have a husband. I want to marry you baby. There's nothing to hide as far as I'm concerned. People will talk, the worst are hospitals. I'm the culprit here if there is one. We had a relationship and you got pregnant, no one needs to know how long it was or when it was. I do want Emma to know about this, about us. She will be over the moon, so will Helen."

"Vivian?"

"What about Vivian? We didn't do anything that Vivian and I didn't do except go public with our relationship. Don't worry, anything said that's negative will be squashed by Nan."

She began to cry, "My arms are empty Curry, after all my excitement and secret dreams, my arms are empty. I want my baby, I want my son."

The afterglow was over, the contentment of the moment over, the beautiful woman laying beside me was feeling devastated again.

"McKenna I know the pregnancy was a shock to you. I know you hadn't planned on your life being altered by another little human being so..."

"What are you trying to say? I should be glad this happened because it was an unwanted pregnancy!"

I could feel her hurt and uncontrolled rage coming to the surface again, emerging from where she hid it from me and everyone else. I need to be gentle with her, get her thru this any way I can.

"No, no. I'm trying to say I'm forty-two years old, I'm ready for another child. I wanted Emma to grow up with a sibling. Have a relationship with a sister or brother that is unlike any other relationship she'll have in her life. I know having another child will not replace what you felt for little man but I want to marry you and give you another child."

"I can't marry you Curry."

"Why not."

"Because I just can't."

"Because of the asswipe sitting on your bed today?"

"Don't be like that?"

"What jealous? I died a thousand deaths when I saw you with Tony that morning in the ER."

"That's why I can't marry you because I can't have that kind of sex with you."

"What kind of sex?"

"The married kind of sex."

I started laughing, she became angry!

"What is married sex?"

"Vaginal intercourse."

"Then how am I supposed to get you pregnant? With a tur-key baster?"

I was getting a little upset now.

She sat up, her sensuous back side barely visible by the light from the street.

"I told you, you hurt me. You paraded all those women in front of me and I knew what you were doing with them, to them. I would feel dirty letting you be inside me again."

"McKenna! What the hell is wrong with you! Millions of people have sex everyday! There is nothing dirty about it. Tell me what is wrong."

She got out of bed, crying.

"What's wrong with me? I'm damaged Curry, I'm damaged goods. You threw me away and I can't get past that."

She grabbed her robe, leaving me sitting! My mouth open in shock!

I couldn't let her cry anymore. I put on PJ bottoms, got nightwear for her then went to find her. She was laying on the sofa crying her heart broken cry! I sat beside her.

"Come here baby, let me get you dressed for bed then let me hold you in my arms. No more talk about anything, I'll just hold you."

She didn't respond verbally but she let me get her dressed. She watched every move I made but was silent. I carried her to bed, laid beside her enfolding her in my arms. I held her close to my body, she didn't push me away, but she was board stiff. When her body relaxed I knew she was sleeping. I knew los-ing her little man was the catalyst for this see-saw behavior. Would she accept me when this was over?

I held onto her during the night marveling at the way her body draped itself over mine!

She backed that great ass up against my hip, I turned to spoon my body around hers, she took the arm I laid over her hip and tucked it close to her breast. I lightly rimmed her nip-ple with my fingertip. I couldn't help myself I got instantly hard. I nudged her with my hard dick, she turned to me and whispered, "Do you want me to make you feel good Curry?"

I did want her to make me feel good! I wanted it in the worst way but the bigger picture was for her to want me to make her feel good with vaginal penetration.

"McKenna I do want you to make me feel good more than I can every express, not tonight. You've had a rough enough day. Tomorrow we'll talk about this. The light of day might make us feel differently about how we want out relationship to be."

"It's now or never Curry! Tonight I'm hurting and I'm seeking comfort from you, tomorrow we have no relationship."

"Then it's never Dr. Tipton. Like you just said, you're hurting tonight and I would be taking advantage of your grief and I won't do that. I've made enough mistakes in our relationship."

"I told you we can't have a relationship..."

"I know. Oh how I know. So go back to sleep, let me cuddle you while I can. May I kiss you good-night?"

"Not tonight Curry. You don't want me to make you feel good and kissing would make you feel good, so no."

I love a challenge, there was 'I dare you' written all over that one little word, "no".

Instantly I had her body laying under mine, I laid between her legs. I pressed my hard dick against her pussy. I covered her face and neck with kisses! Sloppy kisses, hot tongue searching kisses, kisses that made us forget what we were not supposed to do, turning us into pleasure seeking lovers! She pushed my PJ's and briefs down in one motion. I ripped her gown down the front, when I placed my fingertips inside her panties to feel her wetness she urged me to take them off. God! I looked at her beautiful body spread out under me I almost came on her belly!

"Take me, take me now," she begged, "please, I want you inside me. Fuck me like you've never fucked any other woman!"

Hearing her say "fuck me" brought me to my senses! What

was I doing? I was basically about to rape a woman who gave birth to my son a little more than four days ago. I couldn't take advantage of her vulnerability like this. I had to stop. I rolled to my back and pulled her body on top of mine, I buried my face in her hair. I was so turned on emotionally and sexually that I could hardly speak.

"Baby we have to stop, I don't want to hurt you physically. Your vaginal tissue is still so engorged and delicate, I could tear you with my thrusts. I love you so much that I can't do this to you."

She stared at me, almost thru me. I waited for her response.

"Okay," she said flately.

She got up, picked up her torn gown then wrapping it around her she laid down beside me. She turned away from me getting into a fetal position, she didn't move or speak the rest of the night.

I got up before her. After draining the water from the blood soaked sheets I started the washer. I checked her cabinets and made a list of things we needed from the grocery store. I made a cup of coffee with the Keurig, sitting down to drink it I noticed a message from Vivian. 0730 today. Might as well return her call and get it over with, I didn't even read her message. I pushed her number, I had her on speaker since I was moving around the kitchen. She answered immediately. No hello, no thank you for returning my call only outright vehemence!

"Well Dr. Curry you've gotten yourself into quite a pickle."

I wasn't in the mood for her attitude, so typical of inserting herself right in the middle of my affairs.

"I'm not sure to what you are referring Vivian."

"I know what your little family emergency is! Every nasty thing you do comes to light Roderick! You are a predator!"

"Let's see if I've got the situation to which you are referring correct.."

I paused significantly.

"Young inexperienced attractive resident comes to the

ER. That resident attracts the attention of an older emergency medicine mentor. Behind the scenes things get pretty hot, a sexual relationship develops.....Do I need to elaborate anymore?"

"You left out unwanted pregnancy!" She was sarcastic, almost sneering thru the phone.

"Don't you mean marriage?"

I heard her catch her breath!

"You married her?"

"No but I wasn't talking about McKenna and me. I was describing what happened between us! Get off your high horse Vivian! What happened between McKenna and me is no different then what transpired between us. It is a mutual relationship. McKenna and I plan on getting married, the baby was what we both wanted! Losing it to prematurity was traumatic to both of us but Kenna is devastated. I will be back on my next scheduled shift unless of course you think I should take emergency FMLA. She needs this time, her body needs to recuperate. Iit is no different than a full term delivery. Now do you have anything else you want to say?"

Silence. I was about to end the call when she responded.

"No. I am sorry Rod. I had no idea things had advanced to that stage. Tell Dr. Tipton I send my condolences."

She actually sounded sincere!

"Thank you Vivian, did you need anything else?"

"No."

I ended the call. I looked up to see McKenna leaning against the wall for support. She turned around, walking unsteadily to the bedroom. I heard her crying. I decided to not interrupt her grieving. No matter how much you love someone grief is still private. Two people can be grieving, standing right next to one another but eons apart.

CHAPTER SIXTEEN

MCKENNA

After I unloaded everything on Curry he just walked out. His face paled, he blinked back tears then he just walked out! I hurt him, I wanted to hurt him because he hurt me! I hurt because he pushed me away after making sweet love to me. I thought he cared, not love certainly but more feelings than he would have for a hooker! Isn't that what men do after they get what they want from a hooker-they send her away. His semen was running down my leg, but not enough. Not enough to keep little man from growing in my belly. Would he have looked like his daddy? Emma is a little image of Vivian except for her beautiful little lips! Full and sometimes pouty like Curry. I just needed to see him open his eyes, to hold him close to my heart! But I couldn't! He was gone, my little man was gone! I couldn't fight back the tears, so I buried my face in my pillow and cried until I had no more tears.

Where was Curry? Maybe he wasn't coming back! I didn't know how long he had been gone but Nurse Kitty (more like Nurse Titty!) strolled into my room announcing the doctor had discharged me.

"Oh did Rod leave to get a break?"

"I thought I was the one being discharged. What's the deal with *Rod*?"

At least she had the decency to look uncomfortable.

"Oh I didn't mean it like that! If he's taking you home.."

"And he is."

"If he's taking you home I need you both to get instructions since it's not been forty-eight hours since you had anesthesia."

"He's coming."

I had no idea if he would ever come back but I couldn't let her know that because obviously after he had her he didn't send her away! No he didn't send her away because she still had it for him that was pretty obvious the way her face flushed when she kissed him and that smile she gave him. He didn't have to do anything, he just stood there and with the slightest provocation she would have jumped in his arms!

"Can I get your clothes and help you get dressed?"

It hit me! I had no clothes, I had mentioned it to Nan. Maybe I should text Curry to bring clothes.

"I don't have any clothes. I was bleeding heavily, they cut my clothes off. So I have to wait for him to bring me some. Thank you for offering to help."

"No problem. You must be a very special person."

"Why's that."

"Well don't look like you want to kill me again when I say this, okay?"

Wow! I didn't know I was that obvious in the way I felt about him.

"Okay."

"There's not a woman I know who wouldn't give everything to have Rod Curry look at her the way he looks at you. Vivian is a tough act to follow! She's got it all going on!"

"Yes she does, she's got it all except Curry."

She laughed and looked at me, shaking her head like she couldn't believe I had just said that!

"Right on! She's so smug and condescending! Call me when you're dressed and ready to leave."

Kitty might just have it right! At least I'm not the only one that's ever been judged by Viv!

I text Curry I was ready to leave and I'd call an Uber. I don't even know why I even text that, I wasn't going anywhere without clothes,

I laid down to think. So Curry was the catch every woman wanted, why did he want me?

I was nothing but a rookie! He was known in all the ER circles as the guru of emergency medicine. I knew my second year of medical school that I wanted to practice emergency medicine and set my sights on doing a residency with Dr. Roderick Curry. I didn't know how old he was, where he went to medical school not even what he looked like! That didn't stop me from being attracted to him the minute I was introduced to him. He was a great mentor, making me feel comfortable to make decisions right off the bat. I really had no interaction with Vivian until the New Year's eve party.

Curry's arrival interrupted my thoughts.

"Hey thanks for waiting for me!"

"I wasn't waiting on you Curry I was waiting on my clothes." I intended to sound piqued.

"Would you like some help?" he wiggled his eyebrows!

"Untie my gown, pull that curtain and get out of here.... Oh, you need to see your friend Kitty. She wants to give you some discharge papers and I'm sure anything else you want too!"

I was grouchy I knew that. I got out my underwear to put them on, I looked up he was peeping inside the curtain watching me. God he was a pervert!

"Get out of here Curry or I will call an Uber!"

"Keep it up and I'll take your clothing. That back seat in an Uber can get pretty sticky with nothing to cover your ass."

I giggled! How could he make me feel so angry and frustrated one minute, the next he was this delightful funny man I couldn't get enough of? I watched him flirt with other women cutting me to the core! I wanted to hit him and jump his bones almost at the same time. Little man's presence in my life made me so horny <u>for him</u> that had he asked me to go to his apartment after working with him all night I would have gone with him! My feelings for him are so complex maybe, just maybe without little man those feelings will go away. I already feel so empty inside. Without both of them I will be a vacuum, a huge bottomless vacuum!

He returned with Kitty and the wheelchair. He got the instructions, I got in the wheelchair and we left. I dreaded going home. All the little reminders of my little man were gathered there. And to make matters worse he went thru my underwear drawer! I thought I had hidden all my sexy things down pretty deep but he found them, he was the pervert of all perverts! I realize down deep Curry really was trying to be kind to me, he even offered to carry me inside, I told him I wasn't an invalid I had just had a baby. There! I said it and didn't cry! I only could experience two emotions at this time- overwhelming sorrow and lose for my baby, a part of me I no longer had OR intense sexual desire for the man who unintentionally gave me my reason to go on living.

When I walked into my apartment I could see Curry had been working on it. The blinds were drawn only letting in the light from the setting sun, the smell of something fresh hit me. He stood watching me, waiting for my reaction. How could I be upset when he was trying so hard to make this easier for me. My sofa had been covered with baby clothes was now unencumbered except for some throw pillows. I had surrounded my self with all his things when I came home. Going thru each and every piece, fingering it, smelling it for a scent that was not there was my way of saying good-bye, now it was gone.

"Where are my little man's things?"

I was trying to stay calm. He stepped close to me, putting his arm around my waist.

"I just put them in his crib."

I know it is insignificant but Curry saying 'his crib' made me realize he was real to him too. That was a huge comfort to me. Even so I was still feeling lost.

"I'm not sure I'm ready to put them away for good."

"I know baby, you can go and get them any time you want. They're just out of sight for now but not out of reach."

I fell into a chair, I couldn't stand any longer. I guess even though my blood volume had been replaced I still experienced feelings of hypovolemia. Hypovolemia and emptiness!

"Curry I just have no energy. I don't want to hurt myself but I'm not sure I have the energy to go on living. I feel so ucky, I need a long soak in the tub, I can't do that and I'm too weak to stand in the shower. I don't even have a chair to sit on in it."

He picked me up and put me in his lap, his touch was soothing and so comforting. He held me close to his body.

"I'll help you shower. It will be therapeutic only, I'll keep my tighty whities on."

He kissed my hair and despite my pathetic state of hygiene he inhaled my scent!

"Here, I'll start the water."

He stood me up and I staggered, I was fighting, trying to overcome this feeling of profuse fatigue and weakness. He walked me to the bathroom, settling me on the toilet seat. His phone rang.

"I'll be right back, it's Emmy for our good night time."

I was so thirsty, I needed a drink. I started to the kitchen for a glass but only made it to the end of the hall, I had to lean against the wall for support. I could hear Curry talking on speaker phone.

"No darlin, Poppy didn't tell me. You get the same two flavors every time."

"Daddy can I say good night to Miss McKenna."

He looked up and saw me, raising his brow in question, I nodded affirmatively.

"Hello Miss McKenna how are you?'

"I'm fine, just a little tired,"

"I wanted to say I'm sorry for the baby. I would say sorry to your husband too but Daddy said you don't have a husband so I'm saying sorry two times to you."

He told her! He told her our secret! I wanted to scream at him but I couldn't.

"Thank you Emma. Good night."

I just turned back to the bathroom. He betrayed me! That was our secret!

"Good night to you too."

I had to get out of his sight! My heart was beating a mile a minute, I couldn't get my breath!

He came to me right away.

"You told her! You told her about little man."

I was barely hanging on, he put his arm on me to steady me.

I didn't want him touching me! I pulled away from him almost falling. He caught me and pulled me close to him.

"I didn't tell her about the baby McKenna."

"She said you did. Why would she lie?"

I pushed him away, I hit him in the face, he grabbed my wrist.

"Don't McKenna, you can fight me in the morning you don't have the strength tonight, please not tonight, not tonight baby."

There was such sadness in his voice, and he was right I could barely stand after that burst of anger and resentment. I needed him right now, so I stopped resisting.

"I'll start the water, when it's hot you can get in. Let me help you get undressed."

He was being so so sweet and gentle with me. I had to stop this now.

"I don't want you to look at me, my belly is flabby and my ass is huge."

There! That ought to make him want to turn away.

"Well forgive me when I wax poetic like this but I am a tits and ass man all the way!

Your ass and tits could start a war."

Just like that, it was right between us again!

"Yeah, watch out Shakespeare here comes Curry."

I raised my arms and he took my dress off, then my bra. He stooped down to help me with those big maternity panties, he smiled.

"You did this to me Curry, you didn't even care about me and you did it to me."

"Yes baby I did. Now get in the shower. I'll be right there to help you.'

"You have to keep your underwear on, I don't want to see that thing."

I don't know why I said that. I did want to see 'that thing'. The amazing vector that delivered my little man, put him right in my body!

He stepped in behind me, pulling me back against him. He whispered softly, his lips touching my ear, "Yes and you kissed it so sweetly."

"That was when I wanted you. I don't want you now."

That was a lie! I did, and I wanted to do it again. I did want to see him, I wanted to see if he was hard for me, I wanted him so badly but all I could do was cry! He washed and dried my body and took me to bed. I couldn't stop the crying.

"McKenna, please baby tell me what to do. I don't know what to do to help you, just please please tell me. I'll do anything you tell me except leave you alone for these next few nights."

"I can't tell you because I don't want you too but I need it so badly."

Somehow he knew me, he knew what I wanted and needed.

"I can't have intercourse with you."

"I want you to satisfy me with your tongue. Make me come. I'm not nasty, I'm not bleeding anymore." I felt so ashamed to admit my need to him but I couldn't hold back now.

I had wanted and needed him for so long, now he was here and I felt like I would wither away if he didn't make love to me somehow, someway. I was drowning in my desire for him I needed that life raft of touch that only he could give me.

"I want to do that to you but don't get angry at me if I have an erection. I can't stop it but I'll keep my underwear on."

"I want you to take it off. I want to see your desire for me if you have any!"

"Oh baby, I want you so badly you will see my desire."

He sat on the edge of the bed, picking me up sitting me down in his lap. I straddled him. He was already so hard.

"I will make you come but I want to kiss you all over, taste your body before I taste that delicious pussy."

I couldn't hold back, his words released that flame that had been burning inside since we made love that very first time. I wanted my mouth on him! I sucked his tongue so hard there was no mistake what I needed to do to him! I said I didn't want to want him like this, who was I trying to fool?

"Let me do this to you, please you, so you'll never want another man to touch you. Your desire will always be for me, your dreams will always be about me. Our lives will be so intertwined being together will be our greatest satisfaction."

He laid me back, taking his time, looking at me like he was memorizing every inch of my body. Had he looked at me this way the night he put little man inside me? This look made me more desperate for him. I couldn't help it, I raised my hips and spread my legs for him! His full sensuous lips sought out every inch of my body! Kissing, licking and biting me! The way he lay between my legs was perfect positioning for him to thrust inside me! That's what I really needed and wanted but it was too soon. As I felt the weight of his body leaving mine I opened my eyes. He looked at me, licked his bottom lip thoroughly, then lowered his mouth to me. The first touch of the tip of his tongue lightly piercing my opening released something inside me. I moaned, it felt so wonderful but it was almost painful! I felt the need to bear down, just like I did when little man left my body! So I did, the more I would raise my hips and bear down the deeper the painful pleasure that ripped thru me! I didn't want it to end but I couldn't hold back any longer, I was there, he was bringing me there just like the night he gave me little man! I can't even begin to describe the feeling of euphoria I felt!

"Oh Curry you made me feel so good, so so good."

I was weak again but in a very different way for a far different reason. I wanted to be near him, I wanted his body touching mine, this was the way it was to have been that night! He spooned my body, his erection laying against me, he nudged me, I pushed back hard against him! He was in just the right position to enter me and even though he had just made me come I would have welcomed him again, any way he wanted to take me. I relaxed against his body, he kissed my neck, my shoulder with small tender kisses. That gave me the shivers! He made me feel like I really did mean something to him other than being just another participant of his pussy posse!

"McKenna I want to explain to you about Emmy's and my conversation, please listen to me. I didn't tell her anything until she told me Vivian said you are in trouble, that you lost your baby. She had no idea of the meaning of 'lost' only in the sense you couldn't find your baby. I didn't want her to think you had done anything wrong because of Viv's statement. I told her I was staying with you for a few days to help you, she asked why your husband didn't help you. In her seven year old world you have to have a husband to have a baby. She understood you were, are sad so that's why she wanted to tell you she is sorry. Don't be angry. I love you. I want her to know about the baby, I want to marry you. She will be over the moon, so will Helen."

"What about Vivian?"

"What about her? I don't care what she thinks, we've done nothing wrong. I want our relationship public, no one needs to know when it started, they only need to know we love each other and this baby was not an 'oops'!"

"It doesn't matter! I don't have my baby anymore, my little man is gone. All my secret dreams are gone with him. My arms are empty, I'm empty. I want my baby, I want my son."

I was losing control again, my little man was gone and soon my big man would be too! I know he won't stay.

"McKenna listen to me. I know you didn't want this pregnancy. It was as unplanned as a pregnancy could be....."

He was acting like all this wouldn't have happened if I just had done away with my little man! Got rid of him before he became my little man, before I could talk to him and he could hear me, before he could move inside me! I could feel the rage and the desolation building inside me again!

"Are you trying to say because it was an unwanted pregnancy I should be glad it happened?" I gritted my teeth with anger.

"No, that's the last thing I meant! I love you I want to marry you and give you another child. I know that child cannot replace little man, nothing can take his place. I'm 42 years old I'm ready for another child. I want Emma to grow up with siblings. Nothing about this is a mistake!"

"I can't marry you Curry?"

"Why?"

"Because I can't have a relationship with you."

"Because of that asswipe sitting on your bed earlier?"

"No because I can't have a married relationship, I can't have sexual intercourse with you."

"How else am I supposed to get you pregnant? With a turkey baster?"

He was losing his patience with me.

"I can't let you be inside me again, you hurt me Curry. You paraded all those women in front of me, I know what you did with them, to them. I would feel dirty if I let you be inside me again."

"McKenna millions of people have sexual intercourse

everyday! What the hell is the matter with you?"

He didn't need to ask that question! He already knew the answer, but I was going to say it anyway.

"What's wrong with me? I'm damaged goods Curry. You threw me away and I can't ever get past that."

I had to get away from him, I was breaking down again, soon he would know I'm not only damaged goods but I'm also crazy! I put on my robe and left. I went to the living room. Where else could I go? I couldn't bring myself to go to little man's room. It was still too soon, the hurt still too fresh.

I felt like I had cried my life away. Since the first of the year crying was my most expressed emotion. I don't know how long it had been before he came to me since time wasn't important to me anymore. Time, another useless commodity! No matter how much or how little time I had, time would not bring my little man back to me.

"Let me help you get dressed. Sh, sh, no more talk tonight, just let me hold you close, we can draw strength from each other."

His voice was gentle as was his touch.

This was going to be a one way street, I had no strength everything depended on him.

I fell asleep quickly. Our bodies were entwined when I awoke, he was still sleeping.

I slowly turned to my side, backing up against him. He laid his arm over me, I was certain he was asleep until he gently fondled my nipple! Pregnancy hormone attack! I ground my ass into his pelvis, more specifically his erect penis! I could not deny my love for this man, I also could not deny my need for him. He had made me feel so good, he asked for nothing in return but I wanted to reciprocate.

"I want to make you feel good."

"I want you to make me feel good more than anything but this has been a hard day for you. Tomorrow we might feel differently about this relationship."

"I told you we have no relationship. I want you and need you tonight. Tomorrow we have nothing, it's now or never."

He kissed the tip of my nose.

"Then I'm afraid it will be never Dr. Tipton. I'd be taking advantage of you and I'm not going to do that. Now may I kiss you good night?"

"No. That would be making you feel good and you don't want me to make you feel good so the answer is no."

I thought the issue was settled! I blinked and I was under his body! Where his skin touched mine it felt like I was burning for him. He kissed me roughly! I responded in kind! How could I not? There was no stopping now! We were like feral cats clawing and biting at each other! He ripped my gown from me, I was naked underneath. I pushed his boxer's and PJ's down, finally his rigid penis was against me, ready to push inside me, to give me what I needed and we both wanted! I needed it to be different with me, different then any other woman he'd ever been with.

"Take me Curry, take me now! Fuck me different than you have any other woman."

Abruptly he stopped! He rolled us so that I was laying on top of him, his breathing was quick and raspy, he buried his face in my neck and hair, he kissed me with such timidity. His voice shook with desire and restraint.

"I can't do this to you now, I love you and I will hurt you, and not just physically. I want it so bad but I can't."

I heard the finality in his words, there would be no argument from me. If he didn't want me, he didn't want me and I couldn't change that. This was a turning point for Curry and me. It seemed he turned off or covered up any feelings of affection or love he had for me as a woman.

He stayed with me constantly for five days. He only left to go to the grocery or to pick up carry out. He stayed close to me, he was thoughtful of me. He took me to my OB appointment, he didn't ask to go back with me but he did ask if everything was okay.

The sixth night he had to work, his mother came to spend the night. I was angry that he ask her, I didn't need a babysitter. I was old enough to stay by myself. I couldn't say anything to her or in her presence so I text him.

"Don't treat me like a child Curry! I'm not seven, I'm twenty-seven. I can stay by myself!"

An hour went by, he had not answered my text. I was sure he was ignoring me so I text Nan. She didn't answer me either then I knew they were crazy busy.

I was laying in bed, the tears flowing, I couldn't stop them. I was so sad and lonely. I knew I better get used to it. I didn't have my little man and soon my big man would be gone. I heard my message tone, it was from Nan:

"I am working with one sad man tonight! He's very quiet, everyone here knows he is hurting. Everyone but Angel. She tried to talk to him in middle of nursing desk, put her arm on him. He practically dragged her to back! He came back quick, she came later, she had been crying, she deserves it. Miss you, hugs and kisses from everyone. Curry says you're taking it day by day."

A second ding:

"I miss you! It's going to be a long six weeks- in more ways than that.□

Yes, I'm very aware you are 27 not 7 else our relationship would be very inappropriate and I love you far too much for that! I'm concerned because you still wake up at night terrified at something and you pace looking for someone or something. I have an idea what is happening but you are not coherent at the time, I'm sure you don't remember it in the morning. So I haven't said anything about it. We'll talk about it when you're ready.

Oops! Trauma coming.

Will you marry me?"

I couldn't help myself, I giggled. I loved him but he would

send me away. I put my phone with that text over my heart and gently rubbed my hand over my stomach, holding onto something that was not there. I went to sleep like that, I woke up with Curry's mom laying beside me. She was awake, just watching me. God! What's with this woman?

She smiled at me, I couldn't help but return it.

"One doesn't have to look too long or too deep to know why my son is so crazy in love with you."

I shook my head slowly, "No he just feels guilty and obligated to me because my little man is gone."

"I would agree with the guilty part. He does feel guilty because you had to go through having your little man alone. He wants to be with you but not out of obligation McKenna. I don't usually use this language but Rod does not 'bull shit' about anything!"

"Oh I would disagree with you. You've obviously never seen him when he's trying to impress a woman. You'd probably be shocked at your baby boy's behavior."

"Oh I doubt that. Women hear what they want to hear. You've obviously not been pulled in by his line of crap."

"Oh but I have, that's how little man got here."

"Mc Kenna I'm going to be very honest with you. My son felt guilty quite a while before he knew about the baby. You can ask Helen because he admitted he had hurt you. He was sorry by the time he walked across the hall to spend the night. She noticed the difference in my son from that night on and knew before he did that he would want you for his wife. Helen is not easily fooled, she knows Rod probably as well as I do. She was the nanny for my children from the day I brought my daughter home from the hospital. She retired when Rod went to high school. The day he found out Vivian was pregnant with Emmy he called Helen. They've always had a special bond, she does not mince words, she shoots straight from the hip as she says.

Rod is hurting far more than he lets you know because he

feels he has to be the strong one. He's put his life on hold until he finds the right woman. Believe me he is going about it the wrong way I've told him that many times but he is responsible for his own behavior. How he has lived has finally become problematic for him because you only have seen him as a womanizer and refuse to look at him any other way. But he's a big boy now and has to figure out how to solve this dilemma."

"It doesn't make any difference how I feel about Curry, I'm damaged, we're damaged. Little man is the only thing that has ever truly been mine, now he's gone and so is my heart. Sadness is the only emotion I feel, crying is the only emotion I can express so regardless of how Curry feels about me I can't return that feeling. I am broken, I don't even know if I can be fixed. I'm not suicidal, I'm not going to hurt myself in any way but I don't have the will to live right now, I don't have the energy to live and I don't have the energy to care that I don't care to live."

Emma had tears in her eyes, she reached out and touched my cheek with her hand.

"Dear girl, you need to talk to someone. Rod loves you but I'm not sure his love is enough to get you thru this. Come eat some breakfast, and don't say you're not hungry."

I got up and followed her to the kitchen, I ate some toast and drank some coffee. I just had a need to check on little man so I went into his room, I ran my hands over his crib and changing table trying to feel him. I got his clothes out of the crib, folded and refolded them. I don't know why I thought I could feel life from objects that have no life in them, no heart to beat, no tears to cry, no eyes to see his mother, no mouth to put to my breast and suck milk from my body! It was nothing, there was nothing! I picked up a tiny quilt I made for him and held it to me as I rocked back and forth. My body shook with loneliness and tears. I couldn't stop. I don't know how long I was there until Curry came for me.

"Oh baby, come here. Let me hold you, let me try to absorb

some of your sorrow. Sh, sh I'm so sorry if there was any way to bring him back even for one minute for you to hold in your arms I would."

He picked me up and carried me to the bed, he laid me down and spooned my body. I slept. He was still sleeping when I heard soft knocking on my apartment door. I was dressed and very glad I was when I opened the door to Jeff!

"Can I come in?"

I stepped back, nodding my heard. He stepped in and took me in his arms.

"Hey Ken, how are you doing? And don't tell me fine because I know that is not true just by looking at you."

"I'm in a terrible funk and I can't get out of it. I'm not hungry, I apparently have nightmares, and I've no will to live."

He kissed me, it was soft, it was slow and unhurried, it filled my spirit with peace!

"Thank you, I've been looking forward to that since I saw you in the hospital. Are you staying by yourself?"

"No Curry or his mother is here."

"Have you been out of this apartment other than to go to your doctor's appointment?"

"No."

"Put your face on or what ever you do before going out, I'm taking you to Panera for coffee. No argument, go now I'll wait here."

The day was beautiful, he held my hand as we walked the four blocks. We talked for two hours, over nothing! I had my first real laugh since that day at Nan's house. I ate a sandwich with a cup of soup which is more than I'd eaten in almost two weeks. I got a call from Curry! He must be up, it was two o'clock.

"McKenna are you okay? Where are you?"

"I'm with Jeff, having coffee at Panera and lunch."

"Would it have killed you to leave a note?"

I didn't reply to that.

"I see. Have a good lunch with Jeff, maybe you can work on that relationship."

He cut the call.

"What did he say?"

"He just said have a good lunch."

"Really, I would have sworn he'd be pissed you're out with me."

"He's fine."

"Ken, how is it with you two?"

"What do you mean?"

"You can tell me it's none of my business but do you have a sexual thing going with him?"

I don't know why I couldn't be honest with Jeff, I was honest with Curry. I guess I didn't care if I hurt Curry but I did not want to hurt Jeff.

"No, strictly platonic on my part. I can't ever have a relationship with him because he hurt me too badly, I can't heal from that. He knows, I told him."

"He was fierce Ken when you were bleeding out. He did a brave thing putting you in his car and taking you to the hospital himself. If he had waited on a life squad you probably wouldn't have made it."

"He's an ER doc, we're trained to make split second decisions, I'm sure it didn't bother him at all."

"Maybe not as a doctor but I saw him and as a person he was very affected."

"I don't want to talk about this."

"Okay, what topic do you want to talk about."

"I want to talk about a date."

"What date is that?"

"I want you to take me on a date. I want to be wooed and won by a handsome OB doc whose patients all fall in love with him."

"I only care about one previous patient, right?"

I knew 'previous' referred to the ethical question of the

beginning of our relationship.

"Right."

"I'm on call for the next two nights but I'm not on Saturday, do you think you can pencil me in on your schedule for that night?"

"My calendar is pretty full, but I'll save you a spot."

We both laughed at that ridiculous comment! He knew I didn't keep a calendar and if I did it would be wide open.

"Great. I'd like to take you to dinner then to a theater show. Have you ever heard of *Kinky Boots?*

"I saw the movie, I thought it was great."

"I'll get us tickets, we'll have to dine early because the show starts at 8:00 PM."

"Thank you Jeff, you're my hero!"

"I hope heroes get a good night kiss."

"They do."

"Even on a first date?"

"Especially on a first date.

Half way thru that conversation my phone pinged with a message, I was sure it was Curry. I didn't look at it, I didn't need his negativity.

The walk home was nice, it was cooler. Jeff talked some more about his family, they were coming in three weeks and he wanted me to meet them. I agreed. Why? I don't know except this had been such a nice afternoon and I felt indebted to him. He kissed me at the door, it was a toe curler, but not a panty wetter! Only Curry held that distinction!

I let myself in, if I was expecting fireworks I didn't get any because he wasn't even home, however there was a note.

"Hey baby (why did he have to call me that! I'm sure he called every woman he ever dated by that name), hope you and your very special friend had a good day. I missed you when I woke up. I'm indebted to Jeff because you did indeed sound like you were enjoying your afternoon.

It's my evening with Emmy so we're going roller skating,

she was excited she thought you might feel well enough to go with us. I will leave for work from my apartment, tonight you will be going solo, my mom thinks it's best. I have to defer to her because I know I'm not seeing things straight when it comes to you.

Have a good night.

Oh, will you marry me?"□ □ □"

I had to laugh! He has such a magnificent brain filled with all kinds of knowledge and he sends me goofy symbols!

I showered and got dressed for bed. I couldn't sleep so I put in a movie. Why did I ever choose *Fifty Shades of Grey?* I watched the scene where he takes her virginity three times and her initiation into the red room five times! My panties were a wet mess! I wanted Curry inside me so badly I ached! While I was watching one of my 'repeats' I got a text from Curry.

"Are you okay?"

"I'm okay. Watching Fifty Shades."

"Want me to come home?"

"I think it is in your best interest to stay at work."

"No, it is in *your* best interest for me to stay at work."

"LOL"

"Dream of me."

Curry didn't have to tell me to dream of him because I had one of the most "X" rated dreams of my life. Curry was all over me, in every orifice I possessed! Doing things to me you only see in porno flicks!

I thought I was still dreaming when my nipple was being sucked on, a familiar weight pinned me to the bed, while driving his pelvis into mine!

I felt his fingers touch my wet swollen lips, he moaned, he helped me slide my nightgown and panties off. He kissed down my body, leaving my skin wet. He separated my legs, bending my knees to open me up. He licked and kissed the inside of my thighs until I quivered all over.

"I want to taste your delightful pussy. Please say yes

McKenna."

"Yes, yes."

He touched every part of me with his tongue, he grabbed my hips and thrust his tongue inside me, he licked me all over and teased my clit until I raised my hips and put my hands on his head and pulled him to me, he bit and sucked me until I cried out in pleasure, it was like I'd never felt like that before! He sat back on his heels studying me intently right after he made me come, I could see his erection, he put his hand on it and stroked it. I couldn't stand not touching him any longer. I sat up and pushed his hand away.

"No I want to pleasure you."

"McKenna no, I don't want you to do this because you think I expect it because I don't, experiencing your body makes me happier than I've ever been."

I looked up into his eyes, I saw love! I saw adoration! I saw desire! I wanted him to be mine and mine only.

"No, I want to, I've never done this before you might have to guide me."

"Baby, whatever and I mean whatever you do will please me beyond belief!"

"Lay back, I want to feel you over every part of my body."

He laid down and I kissed him, dragging my nipples across his lips I moved quickly, as he tried to put his mouth on me, I moved away.

"Oh have you turned into a tease? Because I'm already about to explode from eating your pussy."

"Sh, let me please you."

He started to speak again, I stopped him by burying my tongue in his mouth, then I sucked his tongue, he reached to stroke himself, I watched! That was one of the most erotic things I'd ever seen. I remembered how he told me he thought of me and stroked himself to satisfaction. I had to touch him with my nipples. I placed my nipple over the tip and stroked him touching me!

"Oh God Kenna, you are driving me crazy!"

I straightened up, still holding him, I shook my head and whispered, "Not yet."

I got between his legs, I flexed one and I nibbled on the inside very close to the hand that was stroking him.

"Kenna please I need to be inside you, please!"

"Not yet, I want to kiss you, I want to taste you."

I positioned my wet pussy against his flexed leg. I kissed the tip, then licked it gently.

He hissed!

"Please let me inside you now."

"Not yet."

I put my mouth over him taking him as deep as I could in my mouth, I stroked him.

"Rub your pussy against my leg baby."

I moved my body up and down on his muscled leg, I took him deep in my throat. I was so caught up in the pleasure I was getting from pleasing him and me at the same time!

"Enough baby, please no more. I'm going to come and while I've dreamed of you doing that to me, not tonight."

I pulled away, my mouth was dripping with saliva, I loved the taste he gave me. He pushed me gently back on the bed, settling between my legs.

"Watch as I push inside you McKenna Tipton, watch as we become one!"

I can't explain how that made me feel as I watched his body disappear inside mine. I was so wet and ready it was almost effortless.

"I love you Dr. Tipton, I never want you to think of or want another man to do what we're doing now. You are mine. Mine McKenna mine! Do you understand?"

"Yes, harder, faster please."

"Oh God I'm going to come, please be ready, I can't wait, I can't! I have to pull out."

He pulled away from me and for the first time I saw what

had given me little man, I saw it gush forward then gush forward again. He moaned and collapsed beside me.

He whispered, "Oh baby that was so beautiful. I've never experienced anything like tonight in my lifetime. Please tell me it was special to you too."

"Yes."

That's all I could say. He kissed my face and neck, he raised up and smiled.

"I better get you cleaned up."

He went to the bathroom returning with a warm washcloth and hand towel, as he cleaned his semen from me a great sadness descended on me. I started crying and I couldn't stop.

"McKenna baby, what's wrong."

I pushed him away! I couldn't stand it! I wanted my baby! I could have all the sex and pleasure there was to experience but it wouldn't bring my baby back to me. I wouldn't let him touch me. I couldn't do this again, He had to leave, he had to leave me alone.

"Get out Curry!"

"What? What's wrong McKenna? Please, please don't push me away."

"No get out! I want you out of my apartment and don't ever come back here again. I don't need you, my little man is gone! Gone! And he's never coming back now you leave."

I fell to the floor sobbing, He tried to touch me but I wouldn't let him. He left, just like I knew he would. I laid for three days, I didn't eat, I didn't drink, I didn't bathe, I didn't answer my door or my phone for those days either. On the fourth day my sister came, letting herself in with her key. If I expected sympathy I didn't get it!

"Get up McKenna, go on get up. Get in the shower, wash your hair and brush your teeth, put on clean clothes. I'm fixing you food and you're going to eat it. There are people who love you and are worried sick about you! You think you're the only one who hurt when you lost little man? No, I care, Simon

was hurt, he wanted to be an uncle, Nan is hurt and hurting be
cause she thinks she let you down, and last is a man you have
shut out because you blame everything on him! He didn't even
know about him McKenna, he's loved you and tried to make
up to you, but you want to wallow in self pity. You go back to
work in two weeks, I've made an appointment for you to see
a psychologist this afternoon so get up and get dressed. After
you eat we're leaving."

So I went to see the psychologist, it only changed how I
looked on the outside, how I reacted to other people, but on
the inside I was just as dead as before. I went back to work, I
kept everybody at a distance. Curry stayed away, I could see
the hurt in his eyes but he continued to be the best mentor a
resident could ever want. He was pleasant, if he was seeing
anyone he kept it a secret. Angel did not give up, I saw her
flirt with him and every other guy in the department. My due
date came, I dreaded going to work but it would be no big
deal no one knew but me. I ate dinner in the doctor's lounge
by myself. Nan asked me almost every night to go to supper
with her, sometimes I went. There was nothing exciting about
the cafeteria. I saw Gwen and the girls from ICU occasionally,
Dr. ICU asswipe was there all the time, I guess the meeting
with the board didn't change him at all, he still did nothing,
the nurses continued to do his work. Tony had a new squeeze.
She was hanging all over him at dinner one night, I found out
later they got engaged and bought a house together that week.
Curry sat by himself almost every time I went to dinner with
Nan. It was strained between Nan and me. I knew she wanted
to say something but was holding back. October 7th I went to
work, the only person I saw and had a half decent relationship with was Jeff. He helped me keep my head above water.
He texted me that night he was on call and there seemed to
be a myriad of women who were able to keep their babies inside their bodies until they were healthy and ready to meet

the world, and now he was helping deliver them. He text me something humorous then he called me. I was talking to him when Curry came in the lounge.

"Sorry Tipton, didn't know you were here, I'll only be one second."

He got something from his locker and was gone again.

I talked to Jeff for a few minutes then realized my break was over. I picked my lab coat up to put it back on when something fell out of the pocket. It was a white card sized envelope. "McKenna Rose Tipton." I recognized the handwriting so I tucked it away in my locker. I didn't intend to read it, I'd trash it after I got off work.

The night stayed busy so when our shift was over I was ready to head for home and bed. We were off that night so I wouldn't sleep too long, besides Jeff was coming over for dinner and I needed to go to the grocery. I hadn't even decided what to make. I opened my locker and stuffed my stethoscope inside, as I locked the door and slammed it shut the envelope fell to the floor. I picked it up, stuffed it in my pocket leaving as quickly as I could.

I laid on my bed and cried, I still hurt badly and I hurt the people around me but I didn't know how to stop the cycle. I picked up the card and opened it. It was a blank note card with the initials rCc on the front.

My Dearest McKenna,

I almost feel like I am intruding on your very private life but I have some things I need to say to you. You may not want to hear them, but I need to say them.

I want to apologize for starting the vicious cycle which has led you to almost a life of solitude. Had I realized my attraction to the itch I couldn't scratch would be so damaging to you I would have cut my own heart out before causing you all this sorrow.

I know today is the day our son was expected to make his

debut into this crazy mixed up world. Today was the day you would have held him, kissed his little cheeks and put him to your breast when he cried. I can barely look at myself in the mirror for what I've done to you. McKenna, I did not throw you away, I never intended for you to feel that way at all. I love you and even though you shun me and shut me out every day I can't get past how I feel about you. I want to lay with you and start another life in your beautiful, mysteriously intoxicating body. I look at you, I long for you, I want you with a passion I have never experienced with any other woman, even Queen Vivian must take a bow to you in that category!

I want you McKenna, there is no other woman for me. I thought my life was wrecked and had ended when Vivian told me she wanted a dissolution but I was sadly mistaken because the day that I laid my heart out to you, the day you surrendered yourself to me was the most wonderful day of my life and it was also the most devastating day of my life. I don't know what I did to make you reject me. I beg you to please tell me so I can make it right because I cannot believe that you would love me so freely and completely and not love me with a love that is for a life time, and a love that could overcome any obstacle placed in it's way.

My heart aches for you, you know what my body does for you. McKenna, McKenna my love, if I could only hold you in my arms tonight and make sweet sweet love to you one more time. Your mind captivates me, your body thrills me beyond any words I could ever say, but your heart is cold to me.

Always yours,
Curry

It was handwritten, I turned to my side, my body shook with torrential sobbing! I clutched his words to my heart, bringing my knees to my chest as I tried to make the physical me as small as I could. So small I would shrink to nothing and the hurt would have nothing to adhere to so it would go away.

The first feeling I experienced when I woke up was a fog accompanied by a headache. It was my worst in over two years. My vision was blurred, any movement of my head was paired with a wave of nausea so strong it didn't take me long to completely empty my stomach! My first thought was Jeff, I couldn't keep my commitment to him for dinner. I barely found his number on my phone I texted him "h/a". He would know what that meant, medical slang for headache. I tried to sleep to be out of awareness of the pain.

My next realization was Jeff washing my face and neck off with cool water. He placed an ice pack against my throat to help with the nausea.

"Ken, I'm going to give you an injection for your headache. I'm placing this under your tongue to dissolve, it's a muscle relaxer, the muscles in your scalp and back of your neck are rock hard, I'm positive this is a tension headache."

"Yes," I could barely whisper without it sounding like a herd of horses thundering thru my head.

"Here let me clean your arm off where I'm going to stick you."

I felt a prick.

"There, you'll sleep most of the day. I'll take a rain check on tonight. I can send Peggy over for the day. Lisa is there doing the books she can answer the phone and get my patients ready to be seen."

"No," I mouthed, "better alone."

He took my hand and put it to his lips.

"Ken it's been three months and it's still as fresh to you emotionally as the day you lost him. I love you, it kills me to see you like this and not be able to do anything. Sweetheart you have to get some help."

I mouthed 'okay'. He settled in the chair setting in my room, it was a left over from my living room during my med school days, it was ratty like my PJs and just as comfortable.

"I'm staying until you go to sleep. I'll call your sister in case she tries to contact you. I have my number up on your phone, just push it if you need me. You don't even need to say anything. Got it."

"Yes," I mouthed.

I woke up at 8:00 PM. I had slept almost nine hours! I was sweaty and thirsty. I turned to my back and felt something crunchy under my shoulder. It was my love letter from Curry, the first I had ever received from any man. I read it again and again. I showered, drank two bottles of water, then ate left over Chinese. I brushed my teeth, put on a pair of shorts and a tank top, put my hair on top of my head and laid down on my bed. I read it again, I had a tingling in my nipples where they rubbed against the ribbing of the tank top, the panties I had just put on were wet with my secretions!

One minute I was laying on my bed, being overrun with need for my big man, the next I stood outside his apartment building in the dark. I opened the door to the hallway and the door man nodded and let me thru, he was the same one I met when I took care of Posey. I got on the elevator to his floor but when I got to his door I stood not knowing what to do. I knew what I wanted right then, but I didn't know what would happen tomorrow. I closed my eyes and knocked softly on the door. I didn't ring the bell. He answered the door in his PJ bottoms, no shirt. I jumped into his arms, he held me close, his hands under my ass supporting me, I wrapped my legs around him. He kissed me sweetly, it was a lingering kiss.

"Oh McKenna I've missed you so." There was such longing in his voice.

My reply was, "Take me to your bed and make me know I am yours."

"Yes baby yes!"

He took my top and shorts off, dropping them on the floor. I raised my hips for him to remove my panties. He crumpled them in his hand, holding them to his nose he took a deep breath. He didn't drop them to the floor, he put them under his pillow. He smiled impishly at me.

"I'm confiscating those for my personal use."

He stood looking at my naked body, he pushed his pajamas down, his erection escaping. He stroked himself, then lowering his body he brushed it against my opening, sliding it up and down. He moaned dropping to his knees he started to consume me, he didn't stop until I screamed out his name.

"This is only the first of tonight. I'm going to fuck you now and I want you to know I don't have a condom."

He stood up and stroked himself again, I sat up, I put my hands on his ass and pulled him to me.

"McKen..."

Before he could say my name my mouth covered him, he gasped as I sucked on him hard, he touched my hair lightly, his legs shook. I pulled my mouth away and looked up at him, there was something wild in his eyes.

"Fuck me now, just like you've dreamed about."

"I can't McKenna, I can't do that to you."

"Yes you can. I'll make you stop if I don't like it."

"I don't know if I can, I really don't think I have that much control."

"You don't, but I do. Fuck my mouth Curry, please."

"Sh, don't even say that."

I put my mouth on him, and pulled him to me, his hands cupped my head, he moved slowly in and out of my mouth, then he seemed to lose himself. I could taste the cum, I wasn't sure I could swallow that so I pulled away, he pushed me back on the bed, kissing me, wet kisses, deep kisses, tongue fucking my mouth kisses. Then he turned me over. He pulled me to the edge of the bed, pulled my hips up.

"Lay your face and shoulders on the bed, if you don't want to come this way, stop me and I'll take you in the missionary position. You understand baby?"

I nodded yes.

He grasp my hips, he ran the tip of his erection up and down my wet anxiously waiting lips. He bent over and bit me gently, he positioned himself and drove his dick in me so hard and so deep I felt almost like I lost my breath with the impact. Then he started to talk to me!

"Oh baby, you don't know how this looks, you're so swollen with want and so very wet, so wet. When I pull all the way back and drive my dick in you I feel like I own you. God what a precious possession you are. I have your body but will you give me your heart?

Will you baby?"

I had never experienced love making like this, I was very inexperienced but I knew even after twenty years of this I would never tire of it.

"I want to fuck you so hard, I want to punish you for shutting me out, for cutting me off because I do love you McKenna and I can't live without you!"

He made me come twice, the second time just as good as the first!

"You are mine McKenna and I'm going to make you come one more time, this time I'm going to come with you."

God I didn't want this to end but I felt the change in him. He was not a quiet lover! I knew when he came and I was right there with him.

"Jesus McKenna, it's a wonder I didn't kill you! That has been building up since the last time we made love."

I was surprised, here was a man who had a very active sex life and he hadn't had sex in over three months!

"You've not been with anyone."

"Nope, just me and my hand when things get really bad. I am in love with you. I don't want any woman but you. I know you don't believe me but I only have eyes for you.

I want you in my bed, I want you to be my wife. Will you marry me?"

I couldn't tell him this was my itch I couldn't scratch, but now it was scratched it was over. I needed him to give me one wild night of sex and it was over with. It had been three months but that is nothing in a relationship and I knew he would leave me. The only reason he hadn't left yet was because the chase was not over! I loved him more than I ever thought possible but he would leave me and I couldn't take take rejection again. It was better to look at him from afar and think about how things could be than to think about how things had been.

We made love twice more, each time it was more satisfying. He was tender with me, he was ferocious in both giving and taking love, he was beautiful, his laugh or his smile caused a light to turn on inside me, his heart was kind, his mind was exceptional, he was... he was...he was every thing that I wanted and needed but I had to go.

It was 05:00, he held me close and whispered in my ear.

"What are we going to do if you got pregnant tonight."

"Nothing because I have Plan B in my purse."

I said this with no feeling as I was being torn apart on the inside.

He sat up, the look in his eyes was almost like I had betrayed him!

"Say something Curry. Out with it."

"McKenna why did you come here tonight? Am I your booty call? Are you giving me a taste of my own medicine, so to speak. Talk to me."

"I came here because I thought today of all days we might be able to comfort one another. You recognized it as a special day in your card to me, and yes I came here for the sex"

"So what happens after this?"

"Nothing happens Curry. We're done for good. Everything I touch I mess up starting with the baby you gave me."

"McKenna that is not true, what happened with little man was not your fault, it was no one's fault, it was an act of nature. I love you, we can work this out. I don't care if it takes five years, ten years, I'm willing to do whatever it takes, however long it takes. We can leave here, if this is too painful for you we can go somewhere else. It doesn't matter where I practice, you are what matters."

"That sounds very altruistic Curry but we wouldn't last a year. Even if we got married the chase would be over, you might not divorce me but you would eventually cheat on me and that would destroy this last little piece of my heart that I'm desperately trying to keep."

I got dressed in my shorts and a tank top, I didn't even ask for my underwear.

"Thank you Curry. I know things would be different if my little man waited until today to be born. Thank you for comforting me. I'm assuming you got as much pleasure out of it as I did."

He followed me to the door, opened it as the consummate gentleman would, stepping back so I could walk thru it unhindered.

"Are you still seeing Jeff Burroughs?"

I couldn't look at him, "Yes."

"Again what can he give you that I can't?"

"Peace," I walked away with the tears streaming. I was dying inside.

For the next two days off I shut myself off from everyone, I was trying to prepare for going back to work. Work resumed as usual, my relationship with Jeff resumed as usual. Thanksgiving was coming up, it had been over a month since my night with Curry. I was hornier than hell. My period for October was late, I took a test and it was negative. I cried as if I'd lost another baby.

The most passionate Jeff and I ever get is kissing and touching. He wants much more, he knows that I'm not capable of giving 'more' at this time. He's willing to wait. I went with Jeff to California for Thanksgiving. It was nice, very nice. The day after Thanksgiving I helped his family trim their Christmas tree. Jeff was very touchy that night and I reciprocated. I was ready to start my period, so I was very horny. Jeff came into my bedroom that night and we made love. It was nice, not hot, not wild, not spicy, but very nice. He was gentle and kind with me. He was elated over the experience. I climaxed but was not satisfied. His parents went Christmas shopping on Saturday afternoon, his brothers were gone somewhere, he was doing some kind of CEUs on line so I went to my room to read. I fell asleep, but was awakened by his kisses.

"Ken come take a shower with me. We don't have to make love but I want to look at and experience washing your body."

This was a different Jeff! He did wash my body then he dropped to his knees and ate me out good and proper! Then he had me steady myself against the shower wall and he took me from behind and that awakened memories! I ended up fucking a memory! He didn't know that and he never would. That night we shared the same room, I was both ashamed and angry at myself, he was a much better man than I deserved. We arrived home late Monday afternoon and I had a note stuck in my door. It was from Curry asking me to dinner on Wednesday evening, he made it obvious to me that it was professional.

We worked Monday and Tuesday night just like we had before little man. I think the difference was me. Being with Jeff and having a sexual relationship seemed to have a calming effect on me. Wednesday was our off night. I was six months away from my two year mark as a resident and was looking forward to at least being offered the option of staying on at University as an ER physician. It would be a big boost in salary and benefits, as a resident I only received a stipend and mediocre medical benefits.

When I left work on Wednesday morning Curry reminded me of our dinner. I thought he would offer to pick me up but he didn't. I was feeling better so I was giving more attention to my personal appearance. I gave myself a facial, actually put some Hollywood curls in my hair and decided to wear a teal and black dress along with my new Jimmy Choos. It was my first time to wear them. I took time with my make-up, I kept telling myself I wanted to look my best if I was going to be offered a job here, but deep down I wanted Curry to want me. Want me just for just a little while like I wanted him every day of my life, to experience both the pain and the pleasure that accompanied those feelings that swept over me and carried me away like the waves carry insignificant grains of sand into the sea.

Curry met me at a busy but exclusive steak house, it had him and Viv's name written all over it class wise.

I was taken aback when he greeted me in the vestibule. He was wearing a black pinstripe three piece suit.. His shirt was a light blue, almost the color of his eyes. His tie was a blue, gray, and black geometric print. He was also wearing that killer smile. It came to mind that this was like a date but with all that Curry and I had experienced we never had been on a date! He took my elbow as we walked to the table and held my chair, it was at that point I realized he probably helped himself to a nice gawk at my boobs,

"You are beautiful as always Dr. Tipton."

We made small talk during dinner, he hadn't mentioned anything about a job. He suggested we to go to the bar for drinks after dinner as it was "a bit more private".

Then it started. He congratulated me on my stellar performance as an ER doc and for my leadership capabilities. Then he went into meeting with a friend who was CEO for a small conglomerate of medical services in Fredericksburg, Va. This CEO was looking for a rising star to head up his free standing ER away from the main complex. I couldn't figure out the connection between why I was here and his friend's business. Finally he got to it.

"Dr. Tipton I've given you a letter of recommendation as

well as a letter from Dr. Curry on what an ideal candidate you are for this job. Tate wants to meet with you, and if you both agree the position is yours. He'd like you to start on January 2nd."

"But my residency contract is not completed until July 1st."

"I am releasing you from the remainder of your contract siting you have far exceeded what is expected from you."

"You want me to leave in a month?"

I could hardly breathe, my heart was jumping out of my chest! He didn't answer me.

"I asked you, do.you.want.me.to.leave.in.a.month?"

"I don't think that is the issue here McKenna. I've taught you everything you need to know and this is a great opportunity that may not be on the table in June or July. So you need to take advantage of it while it's available."

I had tears streaming down my cheeks, I was mad, really, really mad but the hurt went deeper than the anger!

"You still haven't answered me! You do want me to leave don't you! This isn't an opportunity for me it's an opportunity for you! For you to get rid of me! Because I'm a constant reminder that you fucked up!"

His voice seemed very controlled, I'm falling apart and he sits there looking so innocent like the cat who swallowed the canary.

"I don't want you to leave, because whether you are here or not I live with the reality of what I did to you."

"Then change it!"

"I can't."

"Yes you can!"

"I can't, it's already been signed off by Dr. Giovenetti."

"And Vivian! I'm sure she's finally getting what she wants! She's wanted me gone since that little party in the bathroom. You ruined me and now you just want to send me away."

"No baby, I don't want to send you away."

"Don't you 'no baby' me! I have a contract and I haven't

done anything to break that contract."

"McKenna you are self destructing before my very eyes, I can't let that happen to you."

"I'll fight you all the way Curry! You're not getting rid of me that easy! I'm staying!"

"Then I'll send you to ICU for your remaining time."

I couldn't hold it together any longer, I sobbed and sobbed. I know people were looking at us! So what if he is embarrassed, he started it! He moved to my side of the booth, pulling me close to him, he seemed oblivious to what anyone else was saying or doing.

"Come on baby, let me take you home."

I don't remember anything else until I felt his body spooning mine. I cried so many tears. We laid close to each other, both fully clothed except for our shoes.

"McKenna I can barely live with myself knowing what I did to you. If you feel that strongly about finishing up your contract I'll withdraw my letters, but you will go to ICU. You flourished there before and asswipe needs to think he has some competition for his job. You're already far more qualified than he is."

"Curry I can't go now. I have to leave my little man here and I can't do that yet. He still needs a headstone. He deserves that so people who see his grave will know he was loved and he is missed."

"He was mine too baby. Let me do that for you and him. If you will go with me we can at least do that together."

"What will you say if they ask who you are."

I heard him chuckle.

"I want to say, I'm her lover and he was our love child, and we'd like that put on the stone."

I giggled.

"Curry you're ate up!"

"No, you're the one who needs that."

We stopped and stared at one another. Something changed

between us.

"I'm sorry I embarrassed you in that bar."

"McKenna Rose Tipton I don't care where we are or what you are or aren't doing I'm so proud to be with you. I'm never going to be embarrassed!"

Sometimes I say things I shouldn't, they just slip out!

"What if I was humping your leg?" I couldn't hold back the snicker!

"Nope, but you'd probably be very embarrassed at what I'd do in response."

We were silent for a long time, I had to ask. I knew I would be disappointed but I had to ask.

"Curry, do you...well are you?"

"Am I what?"

"Do you have someone else, is that why you want to send me away?"

I had a lump in my throat the size of a golf ball

"No McKenna, there is no one else."

"Then do you not love me any more?"

Before I could blink my eyes he was on top of me. Kissing me, he pushed his erection into me, I was so sensitive, I cried out. His hand fondled my breast.

"Damn it to hell McKenna can't you see I'm being eaten alive everyday, every single day. I can't touch you when I'm with you, I can't even let myself look at you or even smile because I cannot trust myself. You came to me for comfort the day little man was due and I took advantage of you. I pushed you to do things you did not want to do. I'm sorry. I say I'm sorry but I know if given the chance I'd do the same things again. I'm starved for you. I'm so selfish I almost prayed you'd be pregnant after I made love to you the night you came to me. I know a baby is not a band aid for a relationship but your pain is still so acute....."

I didn't want him to feel guilty because I did want him, I wanted him badly but the fear of him getting tired of me and leaving me was crippling me emotionally! Big time.

"I wanted you to do all the things you did to me. You'll leave me and I can't survive that. I can't."

"Do you have someone else McKenna?"

That was not a question I expected from him, I couldn't look at him.

He asked again so softly it was almost a whisper.

"Has someone claimed your body since we were together? Have you laid with another man?"

I looked at him, he knew. He knew what I had done to us. He was not the one to drive a stake between us- I was.

He got up, sitting on the edge of the bed he put his shoes on. He sat with his head down, I didn't hear a sound but the tears fell to the floor beneath him. He cleared his throat as he sat up straight and squared his shoulders.

"There is nothing further for me to say or do. I can't change the past, neither can you.

I will forward your recommendation to Tate Williams. He is a good man, a family man.

If you need help moving I'm sure plenty of the guys in the ER would be very happy to help you."

He stood up, I grabbed for his hand, he pulled it away.

"Curry please listen to me, it's not what you think?"

He didn't even turn to look at me.

"Did you allow another man to put his penis in your vagina."

"It wasn't like that. I......"

"You fucked another man McKenna! You made me feel guilty because I had women before I knew about little man. I haven't touched or fucked or even looked at another woman since then. I don't want another woman even now. We need this separation so I don't have to watch you being happy with someone else although I do want you to be happy. I love you that much and as much as it pains me I want you to have a child by another man if that makes you happy. Just go away and let me be miserable. I love you and if I have to let you go for you to be happy then you are free to go."

He walked away then turned, "Were you hoping I would say yes, then you could feel okay that you let another man have what I have begged you for."

I laid in bed and cried, I loved him. What had I done?

We were off Wednesday night and Thursday night. I tried to prepare myself for the week-end, I was certain I would hear about Curry and his latest conquest. Whatever I thought I should prepare for it was not what actually happened. I went to the ER, I was prepared to see my name off the schedule from January 1st on, but my name nor any trace of it was on the December schedule. Curry sat leaning back in a chair reading a magazine in the nurses' station. I was mad! I walked up and hit the back of the chair with my fist almost causing him to lose his balance almost falling.

"What's going on Curry?"

He looked at me, feigning surprise!

"I'm not sure why you're asking me what's going on. You should be addressing Dr. Reed in ICU, he is now your mentor."

He turned back to his magazine, seeming unconcerned.

"Curry this is not what we agreed on. I only had to go to ICU if I stayed my whole time."

I started to cry, I was barely holding it together, I grabbed hold of his arm.

"Please Curry don't make me go to ICU, please I......."

"Sit down McKenna. I'll be right back."

He tried to sound harsh but I could hear the quake in his voice. He didn't physically make me sit in the chair but I knew he meant business. He left, heading straight for the doctor's lounge.

He came back shortly and indicated I was to follow him, we walked toward the break area.

"McKenna we are not good together any more. I'm trying to give you the best opportunity for the time you have left."

"But you're not. I can't learn anything from him mainly because he doesn't want to teach me. Curry I'm sure when you look at me I make you sick to your stomach, but don't throw me away again, please don't."

He stood there shaking his head.

"Curry don't you see I need you more than ever right now. If you're getting me ready to be your shining star then teach me everything I need to know to make that the best f...."

"Stop Tipton right now. You may work the remainder of your time here. If you're here to learn then present and maintain your demeanor as such. No moping around, when you come here for your shift- look at me when I'm speaking to you Dr. Tipton!"

I couldn't make myself look at him because I didn't want to see the reproach in his eyes so I had fixed my eyes down. It wasn't until he told me to look at him that I realized I was staring right at his fly! I felt my face get hot!

"Yes sir!"

I raised my eyes to his face, for one second I thought there might have been a hint of mirth but it was gone in a flash!

"As I was saying, when you come here you start your shift with a smile. No one wants to follow a bitter boss! Be positive! I don't care how bad things seem you will not and I mean <u>will not</u> shed any tears. Leaders, male or female, take it on the chin and figure out later what they did wrong and how to correct it for the future. One of the best female leaders I know is Dr. Curry. You will never see tears on her face!"

Like I said, sometimes things come out of my mouth that should really stay in it!

I snickered!

"Dr. Tipton you find something humorous in what I just said?" He barked!

"No sir, I'm just trying to remember a time I've seen her smile."

He looked away. He knew I had him on that one! The old

Curry would have smiled.

"I'm focusing on no tears. You have no problem with the smile thing. Starting today I want you to pick apart every trauma scene you are involved in. I don't need your help in doing what I do best but I do need you to look for the flaws and ways to improve whatever you are doing. According to Tate you will have a crew of about 30 professionals, they run two shifts daily, each shift has a nurse manager, seek them out and work closely with them. If they are weak-replace them. You can't be strong if you have weak incompetent people you depend on. A good ER nurse is essential in you doing your best, they anticipate your needs. No one works FOR you. You are all members of the team. You are young, but don't act inexperienced! You can't change your age but you can change indecision. Don't be indecisive, ER docs like good ER nurses make split second decisions and go on them. If you make a bad decision admit it and go on. You don't have to grovel, just admit your mistake. Do you understand everything I've just said?"

"Yes sir."

"Okay, we start today, right now with everything we've just discussed."

"I did understand you I just hope I can live up to your expectations."

"McKenna look me in the eye right now. What I'm saying now is friend to friend."

I turned my eyes to him, I didn't want him to see the one tear that had escaped! Damn it!

"You are hands down the best, and I mean the best resident I've had in the last eight years. You came here eager to learn, and you have. I would not have made this decision simply because this is the easy way out for both of us, I don't do things like that. I made this decision because it is a great opportunity for you to spread your wings and take off doing the thing you love best. You've overcome obstacles that were very difficult to get to where you are today. One of the most important aspects of being an ER doc is separating your job from your real life. It's difficult for us to see the devastation we do day after day and not be affected by it. You've already overcome a lot to get where you are today, this is the stepping off point. Never have I been prouder of a resident who is leaving this program than I am of you."

He reached over and wiped the lone tear from my eye, putting his fingertip in his mouth to lick it dry. I felt the tip of that tongue between my legs, I had to steady myself. He reached over and kissed my forehead, gently squeezing my arm.

"Make me proud kiddo."

He turned, walking off. I knew this was the absolute end of anything personal between us.

The weeks flew by! Curry did not give me a free pass- he critiqued everything I did, after I critiqued it. We spent a half hour to an hour after every shift going over everything that happened. He sought out the reasons why I made every decision. Curry was not only an outstanding ER doc he was an excellent teacher inspiring me to be a good student.

Curry had given me a lot to think about, both professionally and personally. One of the biggest mistakes I made was Jeff. I used him to cover the gaping hole left in my heart by Curry. I kept blaming Curry as the excuse for not getting involved in a serious relationship with him. The problem wasn't Curry it was me. I kept blaming him, telling him he would tire of me and leave me. Curry was not a man to commit to love and marriage unless he had thought it thru and was sure that is what he wanted. He wouldn't have left me, I would have chased him away with my insecurities and refusal to trust him in all things. Just like with little man I was so insecure I had cheated him out of the experience of getting to know our unborn son. Babies recognize Daddy's voice as well as Mommy's. Maybe he would have picked up that I needed to go to see the OB that day instead of thinking the pain was normal. I had to face my mistake, if I had trusted him my little man might be living now, but I hadn't so we both had to suffer the loss of our beautiful little boy.

After I pierced Curry's heart with my unfaithfulness I had to try and save the only relationship I had left, so I accepted Jeff's call after the third day of self flagellation and agreed to his invitation to dinner. I was nervous enough but I be damned if he didn't take me to the same restaurant Curry and I had just been to!

He asked me why I hadn't answered his calls for three days. I wanted to take the coward's way out and say I was just busy with work but I couldn't after he told me his parents were coming here for Christmas and were anxious to see me again. So I put on my big girl panties and tried to let him down easy. I also had to tell him about my big move.

"Jeff I'm not going to be able to celebrate Christmas with you and your parents because I'm making a huge career change."

"What's happening with Dr. McKenna Tipton!" He sounded excited.

"I've been offered a position in Fredericksburg, Virginia. I'll be heading up a staff of about 30 professionals operating a free-standing ER. It is a full service ER, if anyone needs admitted they'll go to the affiliated hospital. I start January 2nd. So my last day to work at University will be the 25th."

"Ken, why the sudden decision to do this? What about your contract with University? What about us?"

"Both the Dr. Currys have signed off and I've been released, they're even going to give me my stipend until July 1st.".

At this point I expected him to be upset but not angry!

"This is all Curry's doing isn't it? He didn't want you until you lost the baby and you made it clear you weren't interested in him, so this is his way of getting even! He can't have you so he's making sure he puts enough distance between us hoping this thing we have will fail. This is pretty low even for him. Casanova can't stand it when he gets rejected!"

"Jeff listen to me. This relationship was doomed to fail not because of him but because of me. I haven't been truthful to myself or you. I love Curry, I've never stopped. I thought I could push my feelings for him aside and transfer them to you and everything would be okay. But I can't. I feel like I've used you and I'm sorry."

"So when we made love you didn't really want me?"

"I did want you but for all the wrong reasons."

"As long as you were fucking Jeff Burroughs I guess I can take one for the team!"

I couldn't believe he just said that! Take one for the team? I think he saw the steam ready to come out of my ears!

"Settle McKenna, settle! I was just trying to make this easier for both of us No man wants to think he's a substitute screw!"

I started laughing!

"Jeff you are the greatest guy I know."

"Just not as great as Rod Curry!"

"It's not even that. It's just the wrong time, had I met you first I'm sure Curry would be sitting in your place right now."

"So this is it? This is the end? I won't see you again?"

"If you still want to be my friend, I'd love to see you again."

"You know there is such a thing as friends with benefits?"

"You mean fuck buddies?"

"Lord McKenna it sounds so crass when you say it like that."

"I'm not like that, I have to have that romantic attraction when I make love to a man. I do want to talk to you and be friends."

"I'd like that also but Ken I'm ready for marriage, a family, a house with a white picket fence...."

"And a dog?"

"I was going to add cat because I'm allergic to dogs."

"That's a deal breaker, I don't want a cat because when we had kids it would spite urinate. Nothing worse than stale cat pee!"

He laughed!

"Actually there is and that is being dumped by the woman you thought might be your wife."

"I'm certain your mother might think you being married to a stripper is worse."

Suddenly he stopped laughing!

"How dare you accuse me of being married to a stripper!"

He sounded outraged!

"I'm sorry, I'm sorry, I ....."

"She was an exotic dancer!"

Then he started laughing again! He reached over and grabbed me to kiss me, and honestly it was the best kiss we had shared. I put my arms around him, getting very tearful.

"Thank you, you've been the best friend ever! I do love you, just not in that way."

"My upper brain understands that but my lower one is having trouble grasping that meaning! Let's get out of here before I'm very embarrassed walking out."

That was the last I saw of Jeff. He did text me to see if I needed any help with moving but Ralph and Nan's sons had already claimed that task.

My last night to work was Christmas night. I said my good byes, gave hugs, got kisses, cried, cleaned out my locker and started to my car. I was trying to figure out how to get the door open with a box in my arms when suddenly it opened for me. Curry stood there with the silliest grin I'd ever seen him wear!

"Come on Tipton you didn't really think I'd let you leave without a proper good bye did you?"

I wanted to hug and kiss him all at the same time, this man was my lifeline and today was the last time I'd ever see him. I was breaking up inside.

"You've never missed an opportunity to make me feel miserable so why am I not surprised you're here! You probably have a pin-up of your next intern in your locker already!"

"Nah, not my type?"

"Married?"

"Married and male!"

Curry took the box from me, I pulled the seat forward for him to put the box in the back seat. He was bent over in those scrubs and all I could think about was feeling him up! I reached forward ...

"Surprise!"

Every single member of our team was standing there! Two of the guys picked me up and put me on their shoulders, depositing me in the front seat of Nan's car! We spent the next two hours at the Waffle House reminiscing over the last eighteen months, plus they gave me a coffee cup inscribed, 'I'm the boss. Make me prove it!' Their signatures were written on it. I didn't know how they got that done. I looked it over, immediately I saw Curry's was missing. I held back the tears! I was going and he didn't even take the time to sign his name to this cup of memories. We went to Nan's car and we all repeated the hugs and kisses, all except Curry. I was falling apart on the inside so I wanted to get to my car as quickly as I could. I didn't say anything on the drive to my car, the tears rolled down my cheeks. I hoped Nan would think it was all for the team I'd worked with. I still held the cup in my hand when we reached my car.

"I just have to say good-bye Ken, I'm going to miss you, you have to come visit."

"I will," I choked out, not being able to hold back any longer.

I got out and got into my car and started it. Nan waited until I was ready to leave as she drove off she motioned for me to put my window down, which I did.

"Look at the bottom of the cup Ken." She drove off.

I waited until I got to my apartment. Inside my door I turned it over, "Created by Curry" was inscribed on the bottom in his handwriting! He had created me, I am who I am because of him. I collapsed in a torrent of tears. I couldn't do this, I couldn't. I had to leave in the morning to drive to Fredericksburg to be there before the moving van arrived and I couldn't do it. I cried all day.

At 7:00 PM I called Curry. I tried not to cry but I could not not cry.

"Curry I can't do this, I can't I'm not ready. Please don't make me do this, I can't. I can't leave little man, I can't, who will take care of him? Please, please let me stay."

There was silence on the line, finally he spoke.

"Dr. Tipton you signed a contract. I have no place for you. The new resident starts in one week."

I hung up. He was done with me! I broke his heart when I went to Jeff for comfort. This was it, he was done! I laid on the floor and cried. My apartment was empty I was sleeping on the floor that night with some pillows and blankets. I dozed off, I thought I was dreaming. I felt warmth surround me, I was curled in a ball. I was my only comfort.

"Kenna, don't make this harder than it already is. I'm broken baby, I'm broken and you're not any better. '

His silent tears flooded my neck and shoulder. I turned to him, clinging to him I cried and cried. He held me.

"Curry please don't hate me for what I did. There was no passion, no love, vacant sex only vacant sex. I know you don't understand this..."

"Sh, sh baby I do. I understand, that's all there has been since I made love to you that first time. I don't want this but we have to do it, we have to."

"Lay on me Curry, let me at least feel the weight of your body on mine, give me something to remember."

He rolled on top of me, kissing my forehead and cheeks. Then he cupped my face with his fingertips and kissed me softly on my lips. I forced my tongue in his mouth, suddenly the comforting kiss was replaced by passion. We tore at each others clothes until we lay skin to skin, nothing separating us.

He pushed the blanket aside.

"I have to look at you one last time, look at your perfect body, fondle and suck on your beautiful breast."

He took my nipple in his mouth, sucking on it, finally releasing it with a hard bite sending shocks thru me.

"Taste me Curry! Do you hate me too much to taste me?"

"I want to taste and touch every part of your body if you'll let me."

"Then I want to taste your cum, I want to suck on you until you lose control."

"No more talk Dr. Tipton."

He raised my legs and put them over his shoulders. Before he lowered his mouth to me he whispered, "Let me make you come, I didn't bring a condom and I can't put you at risk of getting pregnant again."

I could only nod, I wasn't on birth control but I needed him so. I got lost in what he did to me, how he made me feel until I exploded with pleasure.

He held me and kissed me, I felt his need and it was my need too.

I prodded him until he was over me, he tried to pull away as I pulled him onto me and into my waiting lips.

"No Kenna, I can't trust myself. I won't be able to control myself."

"Curry this is our last time together, don't push me away. We need to be honest in our feelings to each other tonight. I'm not your innocent resident. I'm a woman in need of the love of her life that she has to leave behind her. Don't do this to me."

He nodded to me, his eyelids already heavy with pleasure. I pulled him to me and made him forget who he was, where he was until he cried out, almost in agonizing pleasure.

He held me tight, I couldn't bear to think of being physically parted from him. We laid in the afterglow of two people making passionate love with the dread of separation hovering over. After a while he sat up.

"Do you have anything I can use to get a drink of water?"

"There's a bottle of water in the fridge."

We were laying on the living room floor so I watched his tight buns walk all the way to the kitchen. He returned after having opened the bottle and taking a drink from it. I held out my hand.

"I thought you didn't drink after someone else?"

I couldn't help my snicker!

"Well I think it's rather a moot point after you've deposited your junk inside my mouth and I swallowed it all. Maybe you just don't want to drink after me?"

He handed me the bottle, I took a drink, recapped it and handed it back to him. He set the bottle down sedately and dived into me!

"I did deposit my junk there and that's not the only place I want to put it!"

He had me pinned to the floor, arms over my head, he laid between my legs. I felt him hard against me. He was the biggest panty wetter there ever was! If I had any on that is! I felt that gush of wetness, I raised my legs and locked them over his back sliding onto him

"Well that was the smoothest move I've ever seen you make Dr. Tipton! Who taught you that? And don't you dare say I did."

His face was two inches from mine, his other body part- not even two millimeters!

"I teached myself that."

"Oh, you did?"

"Yes I did."

"Well aren't you clever! Now what should we do about this little predicament that you teached yourself?"

I couldn't stand it! We were both breathing so hard, trying not to do what we both wanted to do so badly!

"Fuck me Curry."

"I can't McKenna, I don't have a condom."

"I just finished my period five days ago it's safe and you can pull out."

I quivered when I said 'pull out' because when he did that before I thought it was the most erotic thing I'd ever experienced.

"I think you liked that."

"Yes," I swallowed hard, my heart was beating so fast.

He nudged me, "Not that, I meant pulling out!"

I tried to pull my hands from over my head.

"Curry you are a prick sometimes!"

He laughed really hard this time.

"If that was meant as an insult, you missed. I think that's rather an endearing name coming from you."

"Curry!"

"Don't get your panties in a wad Dr. Tipton, because I am going to fuck you, fuck you so good you'll never forget me."

I got tears in my eyes, "Curry I love you, I'll never forget you. Never."

And fuck me he did! I knew why he was a legend in his own time! He would leave his mark on me, because little did I know but he 'nailed' me again!

CHAPTER SEVENTEEN

CURRY

I stayed with McKenna day and night for the next five nights. Her moods were up and down, mostly down. My life was filled with strong women, when the storms of life hit them they weathered them without their sorrow being obvious to anyone except the men in their life. My mother had weathered losing my grandfather with the help of my father. Her grief was very private, the only public expression of it was at his funeral when my father shielded her from everyone, even us kids. My grandmother did the same, she sat staring at something that obviously was not there. She and my mother smiled and thanked everyone for their thoughts and prayers on the day of the funeral, all other displays of grief were done in private. Of course my mother or grandmother never lost a child. Even though I was there for Kenna we did not have that connection, she did not believe I was there to stay, that I loved her and little man and didn't want to leave as soon as she recovered from this loss. She went to sleep in my arms every night but woke up (at least she appeared to be awake), her speech incoherent, she searched every where for something she could not find. I'm sure she was looking for our lost child. Once she was exhausted she settled down and didn't wake up again until the morning. She had no memory of the events so I couldn't discuss it with her.

My first night back at work my mother stayed with her. She wasn't very good at concealing her anger at me so it was no surprise getting a text from her expressing her displeasure at me!

It was a horrible night trauma wise, gunshot wounds to the head and gut, MVAs with no seat belt resulting in a flail chest, a domestic where the wife gave her husband a 38 caliber vasectomy! So it took a while to get back to her. I was on automatic pilot. I did what needed to be done with reaction only- no thinking. My heart was not there.

I was finally able to respond, I tried to keep it light and flirty. She got frustrated when I flirted with her. God she was so beautiful I'm sure I'm not the only guy who has ever done this, but I wanted to be the last! I wanted to marry her and have a family. I wanted her to stay on so we could work together. We were so good together, I felt like we were made for each other.

My mother said things had gone well but Kenna had disappeared inside little man's room and she did not intrude on her. I found her falling apart on the floor clutching a small blanket. It looked like it was hand stitched so it was probably a work of love done by McKenna or her sister. I've spent hours not sleeping, thinking what my son might look like. Kenna has such dark brown eyes that they looked black at times and dark, dark brown hair. Emmy looks like a little replica of Vivian except for her lips, those she got from me. He would have been a smart little tadpole with Kenna as his mother.

I thought she was beautiful the first time I saw her but her brain is what attracted me to her initially.

I picked her up and took her to bed, she turned to her side, away from me. I spooned her body, she shook with sorrow and despair.

"Oh baby if I could only make it better. He's gone McKenna and I can't bring him back."

"Why Curry why? He belonged to me, he was truly mine. I

know you can't bring him back, no one can do that."

"Sh, it will get better but I can't tell you when. I can tell you I want you to marry me and we can have children together. I know that won't bring little man back but your arms will not be empty."

"I can't do this, I can't."

"No you can't do this by yourself but we can do it together. I love you and I'm not going anywhere, we'll be together."

"Will you Curry? Will you really do that for me? I'm just tired, so exhausted sometimes to where I don't think I can even hold my head up."

"I know, I know, sh, sh go to sleep. I'm right here for you."

I went to sleep and I know she slept too but she woke up before me. When I realized she was not in bed with me I looked the apartment over. Her purse and cell was gone. I tried not to panic. I knew she wouldn't hurt herself but she was so preoccupied with her grief she might unintentionally walk out in front of a car!

I called her number. It rang several times, I kept saying to myself, "Pick up McKenna, pick up."

"Hello."

"Where are you? Are you okay?"

It was such a relief to hear her voice! She didn't seem to be crying, not even distressed.

"I'm with Jeff."

"Would it have killed you to leave a note?"

I was pissed! Here I was worried sick about her and she hanging *with Jeff!*

Like it was the most natural thing for her to be doing after I found her drowning in her grief not six hours ago!

"We're having lunch."

She wouldn't eat for me or with me, I pleaded with her to eat. Wouldn't touch a crumb. It was becoming real to me, she really didn't want a relationship with me. She might not want it but I wasn't giving up. however I am not a push over either.

"Well maybe you can work on that relationship."

I ended the call before I said something I regretted. I wasn't angry at her, but I was fighting mad at asswipe! He saw me with her, he was watching the night I took her to the hospital. I'm little man's father, even if she told him we had no relationship it was pretty obvious we had something going on, little man was proof of that!

After I had time to rethink my call to McKenna I realized I should be appreciative to Jeff for getting her out and getting her to eat. She sounded relaxed, I hadn't heard that in her voice in a long while. God I loved this woman and things could be so different between us now. She was something different, I did notice that with that first passionate kiss on New Year's Eve. She was so responsive and sensitive! I was not used to women who thought sex was anything other than a romp in the hay, a way to a physical release. Some tried to make the relationship more but certainly not for the reasons McKenna had expressed to me that morning.

Today was my afternoon with Emmy, she had decided she wanted to go roller skating and she begged me to bring McKenna along so she could show her all the routines she learned in her class on Saturday mornings. I planned on asking Kenna if we could share with Emmy about little man. I know she'll be so excited to share the news she'll go right to Vivian! Loving Kenna and having a baby together was certainly not done to just piss Vivian off but it will big time! I have to keep that little bit of information to myself. I packed my bag for work and left to pick Em up at 4:30 PM. I'll shower and dress for work at my place. I hoped McKenna would maybe think about me and miss me enough to maybe call just to say hi, but no such luck. It probably was good she didn't go skating with Emmy and me since Vivian insisted on going also. She was especially chatty considering she hadn't spoken a hundred words outside of work to me in the last month!

She did confide in me she was having some abdominal pain,

left upper quadrant specifically, asking me what I thought it could be. I really wasn't in the mood to discuss her attention getting behavior when every ounce of genuine concern for another human being was being saved for Kenna!

I had never not wanted to go to work until we lost little man. McKenna was my chief concern and I was really concerned that night because my mother thought Kenna could go solo tonight. She thought her going to lunch and resuming eating were both positive signs of some of her advancement thru the stages of grief she had yet to experience. So I relied on my mom.

I wanted so badly to reach out to her from the time I got to work until I finally did text her. I was hoping (obviously erroneously) she would miss my presence. She didn't! So at a little past midnight I text her.

"Are you okay?"

"Yes, watching Fifty Shades."

Jesus, that is not a movie you watch by yourself, unless you want to be terminally frustrated! Joining her right now would be a ball buster unless she jumped my bones as soon as I walked in the door.

"Do you want me to come home?" I loved flirting with her.

"I think it is in your best interest if you stay at work!"

My kinky McKenna was back! I laughed! God I loved her, I loved just thinking about her.

"No I think it is in **your** best interest if I stay at work!"

And I meant it, I wanted her. I couldn't look at her and not want her, she had taken me mind, body and soul.

I had suggested to Vivian that we really didn't need the number of staff members allotted us. I mentioned the fair thing to do was to maybe transfer the latest addition to our team to another team who needed extra hands. My goal was to get rid of Angel! She was a pain in my ass! Constantly following me around and really getting in my way. Of course everything has to be Vivian's idea, so she declined my suggestion.

"Roddy, I don't know why you're being so generous, the numbers show you need every staff member you have."

I made the problem so I had to learn to live with it!

I looked at McKenna's texts every chance I got through out the night, so come morning I was so hot for her body I left without saying one word to anyone. I got to her apartment as fast as I could, I let myself in and headed straight for the shower! I showered, shaved and gave a certain part my anatomy a pep talk about being patient. I should have given myself the pep talk because as soon as I crawled in behind her, her warm smooth body touching mine I lost control! She was so ready and receptive to me. We achieved a new degree of intimacy, her initiative was the impetus for something very new between us! At least I thought it was a positive step in our relationship but then she got angry at me and made me leave. She forbid me to ever go back again

God, I was falling apart bit by bit, Nan had no information to give me because she didn't communicate with her either. It was like she had shut out everyone she knew.

She came back to work a week early, with a doctor's release. I assume she went back for her six week check up early and the OB cut her loose. I'm sure asswipe put in his two cents about her returning to work.

We worked together just as we always had. Her eyes never met mine and I didn't force the issue. She very seldom went to dinner with anyone in our department.

Emmy and I spent as much time together as we could since the beginning of the school term was coming soon. She constantly asked to see McKenna, she even told me Posey told her in doggie talk he missed McKenna. She asked me for Kenna's phone number and I gave it to her, I don't know if she ever called her I was hurting too bad to ask.

Something was going on with Viv. Helen told me she had been seeing the doctor several times a week but could not get it out of her what was going on. She looked and acted like the old Vivian to me so I stayed out of her affairs.

McKenna got more and more withdrawn at work. I could do absolutely nothing to help her in any way. I knew better than to ask, she was very specific that she wanted me out of her life and I was too weak to give her a fight about it.

Her due date was approaching. I checked with Nan to see if she had reached out to her or talked to her about it. She had not. The same with her sister.

The morning of the 7th of October I stayed in bed. I looked at the pictures Nan had sent to me. She took those on the day we lost little man. Kenna had on this short dress that kind of cinched over her belly. Nan took a profile of her and that beautiful belly. God how could I have missed that! She had a glow, she was so beautiful. I looked at his ultrasound pictures. With the Level 2 ultrasound I could very clearly see him sucking his thumb. I had to let her know I loved her and shared her sorrow. I knew she wouldn't talk to me so I wrote her a note. It was too late to mail it so my only recourse was to give it to her at work.

Even though McKenna didn't talk to us she did talk to someone -on her cell phone. I had a pretty good idea who it was and it made me that much more miserable. Later on when things were at a stand still I decided I'd go stick my card in her locker door. I went to the doctor's lounge, she was in there talking on her cell. I was still able to stick the card in her lab coat pocket as it hung on her open locker door. If she found it or even read it she gave no indication to me. With McKenna life just seemed to be one big sad party and no one in our work group was invited.

We didn't have to work tonight so I met Emmy after school and took her for ice cream.

For some reason Queen Vivian invited herself along. I could be nothing but gracious to her in the presence of our daughter so I was. To be honest with myself I didn't have the energy or the stomach to spar with Viv, so things went well.

As I gave my beautiful sensitive daughter a kiss good night she patted my cheek and asked a loaded question!

"Daddy you seem so sad! Are still sad over Miss McKenna and her baby? Maybe she can get a real husband and get another baby. Don't you think that would be really nice?"

"I do darlin' but that's for McKenna to decide. I love you, good night."

"Night Daddy! I love you to the moon and back!"

"Thank you precious girl. You are the joy of my heart."

She laid down and before I even got her covers tucked she was sleeping!

"She's not the only one to love you to the moon and back."

The voice startled me, it was Vivian standing in the door in a diaphanous black nightgown. I didn't know what she was trying to pull but I walked past her choosing to totally ignore what she said.

"Good night Vivian."

I wanted to call Kenna so badly, I had reached out, what happened now had to be her decision.

I took a shower put on my boxers to go to bed. The nearer I got to my bedroom the less I wanted to go there to toss and turn. I sat on my bed, all my thoughts were on McKenna.

Who would have our son looked like? Would he and Emmy have features that made them look like brother and sister. I put my PJ bottoms on and walked to the liquor cabinet in the great room. Posey 'woofed' softly at me.

"Go to bed boy, there's nothing here but misery and sadness."

He went to his bed in the laundry room. Soon I heard his ridiculous dog snore. God he could almost shake the rafters! Who ever heard of a dog snoring anyway?

I fixed a gin and tonic, sitting on the sofa I sipped it. I thought I heard a knock on my door but had to listen a second time to realize it was just that- someone at my door. I gave a huge sigh of disgust! Since the doorman didn't call on the intercom it had to be someone in the building, God, it could only be Vivian. I wasn't even going to answer the door but she knocked again, so I went to the door, unlocked it, jerking it open while putting on my nastiest face.

My heart leaped to my throat, it was McKenna! Jesus all she had on was a pair of shorts and a tank top, before I could say anything she jumped into my arms!

"Curry make love to me, make me forget who I am and where I am."

This was exactly what I wanted! I was asking no questions.

I laid her on the bed slowly undressing her. I helped her slide her panties off, I loved the scent of her. Being able to look at her like this and inhale her scent was the only aphrodisiac I would ever need. We made love as if this was the last time we would ever be together. I made her come again and again, hearing and experiencing her passion both in what I did to her and what she did to me. I was so filled with love for her. It was early morning, we lay together in the afterglow of sweet passion. I wondered if I had perhaps started another life in her, which made me chuckle.

"What," she asked?

"What are we going to do if I got you pregnant tonight?"

She moved away from me, not looking at me.

"We're going to do nothing, absolutely nothing because I have Plan B in my purse which I intend to take tonight."

Wow! Her words were cold, even colder was the message they delivered.

"Why did you come over here tonight?"

"I came for sex, I thought we could comfort each other because you knew what today was to me."

"So I'm just a booty call?"

"Well if you want to take it that way you can. This was only comfort sex. We're through Curry. You were the itch I had to scratch, I scratched it and I'm done."

She got dressed and left. She was tearing me apart, I

couldn't deal with this any more. Vivian had at least made a clean break! McKenna wanted to torture me because I had rejected her. I had to do something. I had to be able to work with her but not look at her, listen to her, but not touch her. We were both self destructing trying to handle this thing that existed between us. I had to figure out how to do this and save both of us.

When McKenna came back to work, everyone noticed the difference in her. She had always been so approachable now she avoided everyone. It was obvious that if someone was about to say something not work related she managed to hide somewhere.

It was getting close to the last time I could take Helen, Emmy and Posey to my parents cabin in Tennessee to enjoy the fall foliage. I wanted to invite McKenna to go as a friend but I knew she wouldn't go even if Helen or Emmy invited her. Vivian again tagged along. God I wished she'd stay out of my life. Dealing with my feelings for McKenna, trying to make sure our ER team was not affected by mine or Kenna's attitudes was pressing me. I was looking forward to going to Tennessee even if Viv was going because I knew she would behave herself due to Helen's presence. It was Thanksgiving, and while I wanted to have a traditional Thanksgiving dinner I didn't want Helen to do all that work. Goodness knows Vivian wouldn't dirty her hands to do what she considered menial labor. So I made reservations at a very upscale hotel for the four of us to enjoy our Thanksgiving dinner.

There again was a battle between Emma and her mother about what was considered appropriate attire for eating dinner out. I agreed with Vivian that sneakers and 'nice' jeans (nice according to my daughter) was not ideal, however Emmy would only be seven years old once in her life and in a few short years she'd be a lady with her own distinctive style of dress. As usual Vivian won out but Emma refused to let Helen do any thing with her hair. It was that same beautiful red hair as her mother with the exception it was wavy like mine. Unfortunately Vivian could not leave well enough alone and continued to make negative remarks about Em's hairstyle. I should have intervened and said 'enough is enough ladies' but I did not so Viv took one last pot shot at Em about said hair.

"Emma your hair is such a beautiful color but hanging down every time you turn your head it looks a tangled mess."

"Mommy very beautiful women wear their hair just like this. I know Daddy thinks it looks very attractive on me (Whoa! Where did that word come from?)."

"And where would you get such an idea like that, knowing what your father thinks is beautiful?"

"Because he said it! I heard him!"

"Really dumpling I think you misunderstood him."

"No Mommy, I heard him say Miss McKenna is the most beautiful woman he has ever seen and she wears her hair just like this! Right Daddy? Right Helen, you know Miss McKenna!"

There was a prolonged silence, Vivian looked like our daughter had slapped her in the face with that comment! While I didn't mind Viv being pissed (actually rather enjoyed it) at me I didn't want my daughter's comments about another woman to be the piercing arrow that it seemed to be.

"Emma Elizabeth that will be enough! You will not sass your mother. There will be no more comments from you about hair. It is inappropriate for you to contradict your mother on anything."

Why I didn't stop there I don't know. I'm not sure how I thought my next comment could smooth troubled waters!

"There is a very common saying Petals, "Beauty is in the eye of the beholder.""

God that only cemented what Petals said about my feelings regarding McKenna! Helen was suddenly very interested in her lap, Vivian swallowed hard. I felt horrible, I had to try and fix this situation.

"Whatever I may say it is a well known truth that redheads are my gold standard of beauty. Emma your mother is certainly the most beautiful woman I've ever met, the proof of that is that I married her and together we created you! Got it Petals?"

She beamed! "Got it Daddy! You are very beautiful Mommy even though you look mad most of the time."

We could have gone without that being said all week-end! But to my utter surprise Viv's response was gracious.

"I apologize for looking angry Emmy, I just have a great many decisions to be made in the next few months."

"That's okay Mommy I love you. I love you, I love you to the moon and back. I know you don't mean to look mad."

Emma jumped up, putting her arms around Viv giving her the greatest hug ever!

I was feeling pretty good about what just happened when I received an actual pat on my back.

"Rod Curry! How are you?"

I turned, Tate Williams was smiling broadly at Vivian. Before I could respond he extended his hand to Vivian.

"Tate Williams, you must be Rod's better half! And I do mean better!"

I was waiting on Viv to correct him, but she did not.

"Tate great to see you! This is my daughter Emma Elizabeth and her mother Vivian, and our family friend Helen."

We gave each other the man hug ending with very good natured back slapping!

"What's happening in Tateville?"

"My family and I are taking some days off. I start a new position mid December."

"How long are you here for?"

"We're leaving on Sunday."

"Same here. Are you free for a round of golf tomorrow morning?"

"I'll check with my wife Desiree and give you a call. Got a card?"

"Sure," I handed him my card, "I'd like to catch up with you if we can."

"I'm sure the only thing on is shopping, shopping, shopping. That's what happens when you have three daughters."

I laughed and shook his hand. "I feel your pain brother!" Nodding my head in Em and Vivian's direction.

We chatted for a few minutes then he took his leave.

That evening after Em was in bed I took my computer to the great room, planning on watching a movie. I found one to my liking, plugged in my ear buds settling down to cut myself off from reality for an hour or two. I felt a warm hand on my leg, I looked to my side and Vivian was attached to that hand! I had no patience, this thing with McKenna was eating me up, almost like I was hollow on the inside. I moved her hand quickly, while jerking my ear buds out!

"What the hell is your problem?"

I didn't shout but it was not my normal tone of voice.

She leaned against me, putting her head on my shoulders.

"What ever happened to us Roddy?"

"What kind of question is that? You know very well what happened to us. YOU kicked me out, you broke my heart, you practically tore my infant daughter from my arms all because you weren't finished fooling around."

"I know what I did and I know now the mistake I made and I want you back."

"Why? Because you can't stand to see me find the love of my life, to be over what you did to us- not just me. US! Emmy and me."

"You *love her?*"

"Of course I love her. Why do you think I've been practically going out of my mind because I can't make this thing about the baby right! She can't get past it!"

"She wanted that baby?"

"More than she wants her own life right now."

"Did you want that baby?"

"Yes Vivian, he was my son and I wanted him."

"But why? You had only met her? Why would you want a woman who is pregnant?"

"Because I want her anyway I can have her."

"So I guess it's too late for us?"

"Vivian, it was too late for us long before McKenna ever entered the picture."

"But Rod I love you and I want you back. I want us to be a family. She's practically a child."

"Really, because there is almost the same age difference as there was between us."

"But you were so much more mature."

"Not really, but I was so in love with you and I wanted you and whatever came with you. You wanted marriage and a child, because I wanted you I wanted that too."

"Are you saying you're sorry we got married and had Emma?"

"I don't regret marriage and Emma. I regret how it ended then how it's end ruled my life for almost two years."

"If it took two years to get over me surely you still have something in your heart for me."

"It wasn't getting over you that ruled my life for two years. It was getting over the feeling of failure, the feeling of not being man enough to hold you, we had a daughter together, I planned on spending the rest of my life with you, having more children. You want to know what finally made me feel lower than a fly on shit? Do you want to know?"

"Of course I want to know."

"I find that very hard to believe! The lowest point of our break-up was when I discovered you had your tubes tied when you had the emergency appendectomy when Emma was six months old!"

"Rod that was a huge mistake in judgment. I should have discussed it with you but Mother had just been diagnosed and I knew it would be so hard taking care of her. You already had started talking about another baby and I just couldn't cope with being pregnant and having my mother so ill. You wouldn't understand."

"I understand totally, but you didn't give me the opportunity! We were husband and wife, we were one and if it wasn't good for you it wouldn't have been good for me. Up until you came to me and told me we were finished I expected you to tell me every month you were pregnant again. The entire time I was fucking you you knew, you knew that was never going to happen for me again. We talked about this, you wanted to have two babies close then you could get on with your career! That was your idea and it was acceptable for you to make that decision but God damn it to hell Vivian you could have at least let me in on your little secret!"

"I knew you didn't want me to have my tubes tied, but I was getting too old to have babies! I would never get my body back in shape if I had babies that close to menopause!"

"I understand your concern over your body but you could have looked pregnant six months after you delivered and I would still have been crazy over you. You were the most beautiful woman I'd ever met, your body was perfect but that was not all I loved about you! I don't want to discuss this any more, it's a moot point, nothing is to be accomplished by hashing and rehashing what you decided about our marriage six years ago."

"Don't you like the way I look now? Doesn't my body please you?"

"Vivian when I look at you all I see is a woman who gave me a child that I love more than I ever thought possible to love another person, she is beautiful like you, but I hope to God she does not grow up thinking whatever she wants she can have, that she learns there are consequences for her actions and she knows what it means to love someone else more than life itself."

"If you love her so much then why aren't you with her?"

"Because I treated her in a way that hurt her so badly she doesn't know if she can recover from it and doesn't want me until she knows the answer to that."

"I'm here Rod. I'm here waiting on you."

"Don't Vivian, it's over for us. Even if McKenna never comes back to me that ship has sailed. Good night."

I tossed and turned all night. I wondered what Kenna was doing. Was she missing me as acutely as I missed her. Did she miss laying beside me, feeling my desire for her, wanting my touch as much as I wanted hers. I wondered if she hadn't taken Plan B would she be carrying my child inside her right at this moment. I drifted off to sleep thinking about her telling me I had to keep my boxer's on because she didn't want to see "that thing!" I chuckled at her saying, "I don't want you to see my body Curry, my belly is fat and my ass is big." Just more to love! Funny thing I didn't see either of those things she didn't want me to see, I only saw her, her love and desire for me and her need to see my desire for her.

I was up and out by 08:00, I hit a few balls before I met Tate. We matched each other in play, both piss poor! He invited me for brunch and I accepted after I checked in with Helen. Petals and Posey were outside enjoying the great weather. Oddly Vivian was still sleeping.

"So what's the new position you're starting?"

"We're relocating from Pittsburgh to Fredericksburg, Virginia. There's a conglomerate of medical services including a hospital and a free standing ER. My wife is tired of being the wife of an OB guy. My part in every holiday, every birthday, anything special has been modified because I had to leave to do a delivery. Say, you don't know a hot shot young ER guy looking for a place to start a good career in working the ER as well as still doing the managing part. That might change in a couple of years with the choice of going strictly management or doing the ER thing."

"Sounds like a good opportunity. When do you need

someone to start."

"January 2nd. The guy there is a real asshole to put it bluntly and I've already given him notice. A pain to get along with, expects the nurses to do his work then complains continually about how "sub-par" his outcomes are."

That scenario sounded familiar!

"What's the percentage of trauma to other diagnoses?"

"About 50/50. That's why I need some guy who is good at trauma. Only about 50-60 % make it to be admitted to Mary Washington, the affiliated hospital. We have a trauma flight crew but they have to have something to work with. We're a Level 2, the other docs are all board certified, so we're looking for that certification along with top ER skills. You know as well as I do it's one thing to say, another to do! I want some one who can do and do well!"

"I see."

This had McKenna written all over it. She'd have to take her boards for that but I had no doubt she would ace them! She was self destructing at University and I wasn't far behind her. I couldn't stand the thought of her going thru six more months then having to find a place to go. If she accepted this position I'd know where she was, what she was doing and WHO she was doing it with! It was a crazy idea but she was dying slowly inside and I couldn't watch that!

So I gave my best pitch for McKenna Rose Tipton. He was interested, very interested!

"Rod, you are the GURU of emergency medicine if you vouch for this young woman then I'm willing to meet and talk with her. She can't get any better recommendation than you. How do you know her?"

"She's my resident?"

"Whoa! Wait, if she's so good why are you willing to let her go?"

"I'm not willing but I have to let her go."

I laid my heart out to Tate, we had been pretty close at one time so I knew he wouldn't judge me. He's a guy who married a nurse so he was acquainted with relationship nuances in medical circles.

"Oh, just to inform you, Vivian is my ex-wife, and there's nothing between us. Our only commonality is our daughter. Can you do a video chat with McKenna?"

"Absolutely! Here's my card. We're still in the process of getting moved but I intend on being in my office from Tuesday going forward."

"I have to talk to Giovenetti and the other Dr. Curry in order to get her released early. I want to figure out some perks for her. We had a son, born at six months due to placenta abruptio, she has not handled that well. She will probably fight me on this but I have to get her away from her current environment."

"Get her away from the environment or you?"

"It's both. You will not regret this decision Tate, and in a year or two when she starts thinking straight and finds someone else to share her life she will be grateful she made the move."

"Are you sure you want her to find someone else?"

"I don't but until she does she won't even begin the healing process."

"Wow! You either love this woman far more than you can ever express or you are more altruistic than I remember."

"It's not altruism."

He reached over and patted my shoulder, "We'll make this work Rod, somehow this will work."

Monday I called and requested a meeting with Viv and the big guy. Her secretary couldn't make it happen until Tuesday morning. I spared no details about McKenna's difficulty getting over the loss of our child, and my part in the whole mess. Giovenetti weighed in.

"Rod I don't like sweeping things under the carpet like this.

I'll okay everything but if she refuses to go we can't make her. She's done nothing to violate her contract. You however have made a mess of things! She's a brilliant young woman with a bright future and I had hoped it would be here."

"Lou it was not my intention to make a 'mess of things' as you call it. If she does well, and I know she will there's nothing to prohibit her from returning here is there?"

"No."

"That's how she'll hear it. I don't want her to leave but right now I'm as toxic to her as this environment."

"Let me know if there are any repercussions. Vivian you've been silent thru this meeting. What do you think about Rod's plan?"

"I'm backing him 100%."

"Thank you for your input because I know it is also 100% unbiased."

Lou's a great guy but needless to say sometimes he's in the dark, 100% in the dark!

Now I had to execute the last and most difficult part of my plan. The most difficult because she wouldn't want to go and I didn't want that either. I couldn't put this off so I went directly from the meeting to her apartment to personally set up a meeting in the most positive environment I could provide. She wasn't there so I left a note, I wanted her to know this was entirely professional or she would not come. God I hoped I could do this when the time actually came!

Monday and Tuesday night were normal nights, McKenna actually seemed better at work, more relaxed. Maybe this would go smoother than I thought.

I was a bundle of nerves all day Wednesday. I wanted to see her so badly, be with her, hold her, place my lips on her gracefully long neck and beg her to marry me again but I could not. It dawned on me that this could have been the first 'date' in our relationship. Jesus I'd love for this to be different. I wanted the opportunity to be with her away from the

ER, look at her from across the table, drink wine than later drink in each other! I dressed with care that evening. God the last time I went to this much detail and paid this much attention to what I was wearing was the day Viv and I got married. As anxious as I was my buddy kept rearing his anxious head! You would have thought my anxiety would have been a deal breaker for him but it was not! When she walked in the door of that restaurant I knew I was doomed! I didn't think I could do it. She looked out of this world beautiful. The dress accentuated her small waist (still would fit between my hands) and her breasts almost made me salivate- those also would fit well in my hands!

I helped her be seated and I could not resist looking down the top of her dress, I think she may have figured that out since I lingered a bit too long standing behind her chair.

Just looking at her almost took my breathe away, she looked absolutely fantastic! I noticed she wore the Jimmy Choos so I took that as a positive sign- she wanted to look good for me.

I wanted this to be a good memory for her, most of our shared memories were painful ones. Starting with the first time we made love going right to the night she walked out on me on her due date.

Memories were all I possessed of her and I am like a teenage boy whose almost every waking minute was spent thinking about sex- the sex he had just experienced or the sex he was anticipating. McKenna was my first thought in the morning and my last thought at night! A great many of my thoughts about her are of course sexual in nature, but many are about how our life together could be. I remember when Em was a baby the sheer joy I experienced caring for her. Helen was a great teacher. Watching her with Em was the ground work I needed to be a daddy! Shit I couldn't even pass Diaper 101 when she was born but I got very good at it, really cherishing the time we spent together. I remember the pride I felt when I saw her in Viv's arms for the first time. All I could think about was I helped create her, she was part of me! My Emma time is very important and I know I would have loved that little boy as much as I love and cherish my daughter.

"Would you like me to order a Long Island Iced tea for you?"

"No but I'd like some sangria with my dinner."

"Great, I see blackberry listed here. Would you like to try that?"

"That sounds very good."

"How was your Thanksgiving? Did you and Paige make a traditional dinner or just settle for some Chinese?"

"Actually Paige went with Simon to visit his parents in Washington state."

"You had to be alone on Thanksgiving or did you go to Nan's?"

I wanted to kick my own ass for not checking with her. God she didn't need to be alone so soon after little man! She continued to look at her menu as though she didn't hear me.

She cleared her throat.

"I was in California celebrating Thanksgiving with a friend and his parents."

"Oh........well great. I hoped you enjoyed the trip."

I wanted to be sick to my stomach! She had spent the holiday with her "special friend".

We were quiet, not talking at all until our orders were taken and we had received our drinks.

"Emmy, Helen and I spent the week-end at my parents cabin in Tennessee. The foliage was spectacular."

She didn't make any comment so I decided to lay the ground work for the plan for her.

"We had Thanksgiving dinner at a hotel which was serendipitous."

"Curry you've lost me! What's serendipitous about eating dinner in a hotel?"

"I ran into an old friend of mine, he's an OB guy but he's giving up his practice to take a management job."

"Please tell me you're not giving up the ER to take a management position!"

"No, no but he has a free standing ER that needs someone to take over in a management position. It sounds like a good opportunity for some one to take it over and run with it. He is ready to give that person a carte blanche opportunity."

"Oh."

God! She has no idea why we're here. I didn't think I could do this! Right now I want to get down on my knees and beg her to forgive me, to please give me another chance. I love her and not seeing her is going to be torture, even worse then seeing her sadness. I stopped talking about the reason behind our meeting. We made small talk during our dinner.

"Would you like dessert Dr. Tipton?"

"No, I'm completely satisfied. The food was delicious."

"I'd like to chat with you some more, maybe we could go into the bar and talk. It's a bit more private."

She agreed, now I really was in a pickle. I had to do this, I had to. Even though she seemed better since she returned from California she was still not the McKenna who came to me eighteen months ago. So I started again talking about my meeting with Tate, then I just blurted it out.

"McKenna I've given you a letter of recommendation. He'd like to meet with you and if you're both in agreement he'd like you to start on January 2nd."

"But Curry my contract here is not up until July."

"I've released you from your contract here. You've already far exceeded what was expected of you in this program."

"So you want me to leave in a month?"

"This is a great opportunity for you McKenna and it may not be here in June or July."

"You didn't answer me! Do. You. Want. Me. To. Leave. In. A. Month?"

"I told you this is a great opportunity for you."

I was falling apart inside, I had hurt her again, I would never be able to get her to understand I was trying to protect her.

"This is not an opportunity for me it's an opportunity for you to get rid of me! I'm a constant reminder that you fucked up!"

"Whether you're here or not I live daily with the mistake I make."

"I'm not going!"

"You have to go,"

"No I've done nothing to break my contract and I'm not going! I'll fight this!"

"McKenna it's already done! I've signed off on it, so has Giovnetti and Vivian."

"Of course this is what Vivian wants, it has her name written all over it. She's wanted me gone since that little party in the bathroom! You've ruined me now you want to send me away!"

"No baby, I don't want to send you away."

"Don't you "no baby" me, I'll fight this. I've done nothing wrong!"

I couldn't stay away from her any longer, this was hurting her, cutting her in two. I moved to the other side of the booth beside her. I took her in my arms.

"Baby you are self destructing in front of me every day, I can't let you do that. Come on I'll take you home."

She had crumbled completely, her sobs were unrelenting. I had to get her away from here so I just picked her up and took her to my car and drove her home. She was still sobbing when we reached her apartment. I laid her in bed with her clothes on, I took her shoes off, then I removed mine. I spooned her body. I feel this is the right thing to do but it is so hard. She finally quieted.

"McKenna if you feel so strongly that you want to finish

out your contract I'll withdraw my letters but you will go to ICU for the remainder of your contract. You flourished there before, and besides that asswipe needs to think he has some competition for his job. You're already far more qualified than he is."

"But Curry I can't go. I can't leave little man, I don't have a head stone yet. I want him to have one so when ever anyone looks at his little grave they will know he was loved and will be missed."

"Let me help with that McKenna, he was mine too."

"What are you going to say if they ask who you are?"

She was so so serious, I couldn't help but jerk her chain a little. "I'll tell them we're lovers and he was our love child and I want that written on his headstone."

I nudged her with my hip!

She snickered!

"Oh Curry! You are ate up!"

"No that's what I need to do to you."

We stopped suddenly and stared at each other!

"Curry I'm sorry I embarrassed you in that bar tonight."

"McKenna Rose Tipton I am so proud to be with you that nothing you could say or will ever do can embarrass me."

I wasn't expecting her response!

"What would you say if I was humping your leg! Would that embarrass you?"

"It's not what I would say that would embarrass you but it's what I would do in response to that."

CHAPTER EIGHTEEN

MCKENNA

I got up early and showered. By the time I was out of the shower Curry had gone to the 24 hour store on the corner bringing back coffee for both of us. We sat on the floor knee to knee talking, it wasn't 05:00 yet.

"Kenna once you get settled in, maybe we can have a video chat and decide what you'd like little man's headstone to say, what you'd like if you want a design carved into it, whatever else you'd like."

I choked back tears- tears for my little man, and tears for my big man I had to leave behind.

"Okay, and whatever you'd want," meaning what he wanted on the stone. I saw a quick movement of his lips as if he started to say something but stopped.

"Tell me Curry," I demanded.

He seemed so serious, as he lowered his head, "I'd like for you to hump my leg!"

He started laughing, my big man could change my mood in a second! I literally pounced on him, knocking him backward, he was a bit shocked!

"Oh, I want to do more than that! I want you to make love to me."

"McKenna Rose Tipton, I am your mentor and as much as I want to do that we can't. I told you I don't have any condoms and I won't have you using Plan B to destroy something we both want."

"It didn't happen Curry. I never even had that in my purse. I couldn't have done that either. I'm ashamed but I only said that to hurt you."

He nudged me with his hip, I was laying on top of him his legs spread wide.

"I can take that, but I can't take you laying like this. I'm ready to do my dance as it is!"

"Your dance?"

"Yes baby, my dick dance! I can hardly hold it still, it wants that pretty little pussy of yours so badly!"

"Then do it Curry! Do it!"

He flipped me, he was laying on top of me. He nuzzled my neck, kissing it softly as he whispered to me.

"Oh that I could, I can't. If that happened again to you, I'd never even know it. You'd

never tell me because you know I'd insist on marrying you and you won't let me do that. You don't trust me to love you until death would part us."

I pushed him away!

"Don't! Don't even talk like that!"

I was angry at him, he had to spoil the moment by talking about death, about how my little man had been taken from me! I started to cry. He pulled me into his lap, holding me close and shushing me.

He kissed me and suddenly I had to have him and he must have felt the same because our expression of our love came to fruition. I was angry at my refusal to see and accept his love for me and we had missed out on so much.

"How can you even stand to hold me in your arms like this, to love me like this after I've pushed you away for so long. Please forgive me, please please forgive me."

The realization of what I had done washed over me and I began to cry tears of regret and profound sorrow.

"Sh baby, just make me one promise."

"What?"

"In one year if you still feel the same about me, if you haven't found someone else, will you marry me?"

"How do I know you'll still feel the same about me?"

"I will! I'm giving you four months to settle in, then I'm going to call you and court you the way a beautiful desirable woman like you should be. I'm going to sweep you off your feet. I'm going to be the only thing you can think about!"

Little did he know that had already happened! I dreaded leaving him because I was afraid he'd find someone new, and he did.

He kissed me, helped me from his lap and took me by the hand leading me to my car. He opened the door of my beetle and held it for me. I got in, he reached in, I closed my eyes, bracing myself for the last taste of his lips on mine that I'd ever feel! Instead he kissed the side of my forehead, patted me on the shoulder.

"Make me proud kiddo."

He closed my door and walked away! I started my car, fighting back the tears I wanted to shed! It was like the day they told me my little man was gone! I couldn't do this, I couldn't! I looked thru the mirror for Curry, he'd already left! This was it, he'd already given me away! Given me away to uncertainty, to loneliness, and to a place so far away he'd never have to look at me again! Regardless of what he said he was done so I needed to move on. I squared my shoulders and set my phone on Google for the Fredricksburg address I needed. It was the hospital. I had almost 700 miles to drive, it would take me close to 12 hours maybe less if I drove hard. As much as I hated leaving Curry and little man, I had to go. He gave me no choice. I had no little man, I had no big man, I had no job, I had no apartment, and the worst was I had no hope for tomorrow. I had nothing! I had no where to go except away. So I drove, not knowing what the future held for me. I didn't even care because I had no heart left to care. The small piece I held on to was gone the second Curry walked away from me. Where do you go when you have no heart left?

The End

www.ingramcontent.com/pod-product-compliance
Lightning Source LLC
Chambersburg PA
CBHW060344030726
47497CB00003B/594